ESCAPES
CAN BE
MURDER

Connie Shelton

ESCAPES
CAN BE
MURDER

Charlie Parker Mysteries, Book 18

Connie Shelton

Secret Staircase Books

Escapes Can Be Murder
Published by Secret Staircase Books, an imprint of
Columbine Publishing Group, LLC
PO Box 416, Angel Fire, NM 87710

This book is a work of fiction. Names, characters, places and
incidents are either the product of the author's imagination or are
used fictitiously. Any resemblance to actual events or locales or
persons, living or dead, is entirely coincidental. Any slights of
people, places or organizations are unintentional.

Book layout and design by Secret Staircase Books
Cover images © Jana Jurkova, Michael Shake, Peter Wollinga,
Ayutaka

First trade paperback edition: June, 2019
First e-book edition: June, 2019

Publisher's Cataloging-in-Publication Data

Shelton, Connie
Escapes Can Be Murder / by Connie Shelton.
p. cm.
ISBN 978-1945422713 (paperback)
ISBN 978-1945422720 (e-book)

1. Charlie Parker (Fictitious character)—Fiction. 2. New
Mexico—Fiction. 3. Maine—Fiction. 4. American politics—Fiction.
5. Women sleuths—Fiction. I. Title

Charlie Parker Mystery Series : Book 18.
Shelton, Connie, Charlie Parker mysteries.

BISAC : FICTION / Mystery & Detective.

813/.54

Acknowledgements

As always, I have a huge amount of gratitude for everyone who helped shape this book into its final version. Dan Shelton, my husband, helpmate, and expert on all things helicopter—you complete me. And thank you Stephanie, my lovely daughter and business partner, for your part in keeping our business strong!

Editors Susan Slater, Stephanie Dewey and Shirley Shaw spot the plot and character flaws and help smooth the rough bits in the prose. And topping off the effort are my beta readers, who drop everything in their own lives to read and find the typos that inevitably sneak past me. Thank you for your help with this book: Christine Johnson, Marcia Koopman, Lisa Train, Sandra Anderson and Judi Shaw. You guys are the best!

Author Note:

Readers familiar with Tiguex Park in Albuquerque will undoubtedly know there is no four-story garage immediately near the park (although, in my opinion, the nearby museums could use more parking space!). Please forgive this writer a bit of artistic license in giving Charlie this vantage point at a crucial moment in the story.

Chapter 1

Forest, the likes of which I'd never seen before, stretched out below. In the pilot's seat, I felt a band of sweat forming under my bra; a trickle ran down my spine. It isn't that I haven't flown over trees before—I have. But these were thicker, leafier, and *so* multi-colored in the early-October bright light. It was distracting and a little unnerving. I glanced toward the left seat where Drake dozed, confident enough in my skills to let me find the heliport on my own. I chose to believe he wasn't just oblivious.

I checked the GPS for the millionth time. Safe Port, Maine, lay ahead somewhere. The instrument assured me it was true although, unlike the one in the car, this baby didn't tell me to change lanes or make a left turn at the next intersection; I had to keep checking. I only wished I could

actually *see* a town somewhere out there. I brought the Jet
Ranger to five hundred feet above the treetops and slowed.

Five minutes later I spotted a white spire glowing
in the middle of a red-orange pool of leafy splendor. A
church. Gradually, the solid forest began to reveal gaps—a
park, a neighborhood of two-story white-sided houses, a
market with a large parking lot. Ahead, I caught sight of
the rugged coastline. Somewhere along there would be the
regional airport where we were to check in for our job.

Normally, smaller ships like ours stay fairly close to
home. We work a two- to three-state area: New Mexico,
Arizona, sometimes Colorado. Rarely beyond. But this
time Drake had decided to attend the annual helicopter
trade show in Dallas, and for some reason it seemed like
a great idea to fly our own machine there. Chatting with
an old buddy from his Kauai days, he realized one of the
big Midwest airshows would start in three days. We headed
across country for that. And when he ran into the man
he'd worked for on his very first job in Pennsylvania, and
Bert told him they were short-handed on a New England
crew … well, that's the short version of how I came to be
searching for a tiny helipad at a small regional airport on
the coast of Maine.

My GPS told me I was within three miles of the airport
so I keyed my microphone and radioed the Fixed Based
Operator, as there was no tower at a place this small. A
male voice with a thick New England accent responded,
clearing me to land. The verbal exchange roused Drake
from his sleepy state and he immediately knew exactly
where we were. He has this irritating way of becoming
instantly alert when he wakes, unlike me who, especially in
the morning, loves the luxury of an extra fifteen minutes

in bed and at least one cup of coffee before I'm expected
to give a coherent answer to anything.

I followed the flight path given by the radio operator
and sure enough, right there between the edge of the
forest and the waves lapping at the rocky coast, I spotted
the landing strip and a green clapboard building. Three
single-engine planes tied down at the north end of the
strip provided the big clue that it was actually an airport. I
aimed the nose of the Jet Ranger into the wind and set her
gently onto the square pad at the south end.

"Nice job," my sweet hubby said with a flash of the
gorgeous smile that had won me over.

I sat there a minute, going through the shutdown
procedures, while he looked around for a sign of the
foreman who was supposed to meet us. We would be
ferrying supplies to a remote site where a larger helicopter,
a Sky Crane, was stringing wire on power poles across a
section of the county where a new factory was being built,
a business that evidently required fiber optic cable for high
speed internet. Why they'd chosen the middle of nowhere
for this facility was a mystery no one had yet explained to
me. But ours was not to question why, ours was just to lift
nets filled with crates of tools and the nuts-and-bolts type
stuff, along with food and water for the ground crew, and
the occasional rolls of cable. Or so I'd been told. If the job
foreman showed up, we would soon know.

Mainly, I hoped we would have decent lodgings with
warm blankets on the beds. I could tell already that the
temperature had begun to drop the minute I shut down the
heater in the cockpit. Drake had reached into the back seat
for his coat and handed me a jacket as well. I set the rotor
brake and slipped my arms into the cozy fleece.

When I looked up, I saw a short man with bandy legs and a barrel chest walking toward the helicopter. He wore baggy jeans, red flannel shirt, and a cap with ear flaps—the New England image was alive and well. He had red hair and a beard to match, vivid blue eyes with squint wrinkles radiating from the corners, and a smile revealing uneven teeth. He walked up to Drake and shook hands.

"Jed McAllister." He introduced himself as I walked around the nose of the aircraft.

"Drake Langston, and this is my wife, Charlie Parker." I could tell Drake immediately liked the guy.

Jed greeted me without a quiz about my name, saving me from the explanation that it's really Charlotte and the way-too-old story about my brothers tagging me with the nickname because I'd been such a tomboy as a kid. I have to admit, beyond thirty-five now, I'm much more into creature comforts.

We tied down the rotor blades, locked the doors, and retrieved our bags from the cargo compartment on the Jet Ranger's left side. Considering that we'd left New Mexico more than a week ago, packing only three days' worth of clothes, one of my first concerns would be to find a laundromat. Jed led the way through the lobby of the tiny FBO, giving a speedy introduction to the young guy behind the desk—Harry. As far as I could tell, he was the only person working at the facility, at least for the moment.

In the parking lot outside the chain link fence that separated the real world from the aviation world, Jed pointed toward a white Ford Explorer that must have been ten years old.

"That's yours for the duration," he said. "We'll do a quick tour of Safe Port so's you get your bearings, and I'll show you the inn where we booked you a room. I think you'll find it comfortable. Just don't let old Mrs. Comfrey boss you around too much. She tends to do that."

We busied ourselves stashing our things in the back of the SUV and taking seats. Jed drove, with Drake in the shotgun seat and me in back. I saw what Jed meant by the quick tour. The entire town consisted of one main drag, which followed the coastline, and a web of side streets with the type of clapboard houses I'd spotted from the air. The church, the supermarket, two gas stations, a bookshop, an auto parts store, and (yay!) a coin laundry flanked the main street, which was imaginatively called Main Street. At Safe Port's one traffic signal we turned left; at the next corner sat a large three-story building with wrap-around porches, gingerbread trim, and a sign: Wayside Inn B&B.

It exuded New England charm. The muted sage and cream paint created a calming color scheme; wicker furniture groupings and potted plants gave the porches a homey feel; pumpkins and potted chrysanthemums put bright spots of color on the steps and along the cobbled walkway. Tall trees in flaming shades of yellow, orange, and red completed the picture.

"I'll leave you here," Jed said as we pulled our bags from the car. "The missus wanted me to invite you over for dinner." He waved up the street. "One block up, two blocks over, yellow house with a skiff on a trailer parked in the driveway. Hope you don't mind lobster."

I assured him I would never, ever, *ever* mind having a lobster dinner.

"All righty, then. Drive on over when you're ready. She likes to put the meal on the table around six." With that, he started off walking in the direction he'd indicated for home.

We looked up at the front porch of the inn to see a sturdy woman wearing a flowered housedress and cardigan, her arms crossed over her ample chest. Brown over-permed frizz framed a plump face, and the deep grooves beside her mouth indicated that she probably didn't smile a whole lot. Mrs. Comfrey.

"Jed says you folks goin' workin' with him," she said by way of greeting. She turned toward the front door and we followed. "I put you in the east room. Got a private entry facing State Street, so's you can leave early, come back late, whatever it is you need to do."

We followed her down a long hall leading to the back of the house. She opened the door to a room with a pink and white color scheme, frilly curtains, and spare pillows everywhere. It was a seven-year-old girl's dream. I swallowed a comment. Drake just smiled and thanked her for the information about breakfast hours, house rules about quiet, and the offer to make breakfast sandwiches to take with us, so long as we placed our order twenty-four hours in advance.

"Tired?" he asked me the moment the door closed behind Mrs. Comfrey. His arms came around me and I let myself soak up his warmth and the nice feel of the massage he was giving my lower back muscles.

"A little. But mostly I feel like I need to stretch my legs."

"Three days almost non-stop in the aircraft will do that."

We made a plan: pull all the clothing from our bags and get to the laundry, use the time while the machine cycles ran to take a good long walk, then shower and dress in something fresh so we could make it to Jed's place before six. I couldn't get the image out of my head of lobster claws dripping with butter.

Chapter 2

Jed and Darlene McAllister proved to be excellent hosts. The lobster dinner was everything I'd dreamed of—especially when Jed informed us his brother's boat had just brought the critters in from the ocean this afternoon. I might consider giving up green chile and relocating if this was ordinary life in Maine.

Drake and Jed talked logistics for the job we were here to do. I listened, since I would be in on it, and Darlene moved quietly from kitchen to dining table, bringing more coleslaw, fresh ears of corn, and topping up the small bowls of melted butter for each of us.

Everything Jed said about the job concurred with what we'd been told—we would carry supplies and personnel out to a fairly remote site where a crew was stringing fiber optic cable through thickly wooded areas that were inaccessible to vehicles. A Sky Crane was doing the heavy lifting and there was one other support ship. We were there because the job's second aircraft had been called in for a week of maintenance and it was too expensive to keep the other machines on standby at their daily rates. We would make two runs up to the work site in the early morning, carrying men and supplies and another flight at the end of the work day to bring the men back.

"The middle part of the day is yours to do what you want," Jed said. "Explore around, have some fun. As long as you're back at the site by four o'clock each day, we're good."

Darlene had cleared the dishes by now, declining my offer to help. She came back with bowls of local blueberry ice cream just in time to hear Jed's comments. "You should get out and see the area some," she said. "Portland's not far if you get on the interstate, and Bar Harbor's real cute for a day trip. There are some tours of lighthouses, or you could pick a nice day and go sailing."

"Loads of scenic coastline here, that's for sure," Jed said. "Bet you don't see much of that where you're from."

Truer words were never spoken. We have a dozen or so navigable lakes in the entire state. I'd already seen more watercraft in the last four hours than in a lifetime in New Mexico. Maybe we *could* make the most of our week here and the flexible work schedule by soaking up the local color.

Despite our getting to bed at an astonishingly early hour, the alarm went off way too soon. We were to meet Jed and the rest of the crew at daybreak. Without the requisite twenty-four-hour notice there were no breakfast sandwiches coming from the kitchen of Mrs. Comfrey (we did at least extend the courtesy of telling her not to cook for us this morning). Breakfast would consist of a stop at the gas station's convenience store and whatever empty-calorie, high fat goodies we found. Yum.

I was munching down my fourth mini donut when we pulled into the parking lot at the airfield. The three guys who would ride out to the work site with Drake smelled of bacon and eggs. I was jealous. At least our coffee in Styrofoam cups was good and strong and I was now coherent. Tomorrow we would have to get our order in with Mrs. C. or check around to see if there was some kind of early-bird café in town.

While the workers loaded their gear, weighed and supervised by Drake, I programmed the location coordinates Jed gave me into our GPS. Drake would take the first flight. I would ride along to learn the routine; after that we could alternate flights. The estimated flight time was forty-seven minutes each way, and the money we'd make in a week would cover all our expenses since we'd left home. Not bad.

The fall foliage was no less spectacular when the sun rose over the Atlantic and revealed the many hues of the trees as we pulled pitch. The monster-big Sky Crane had taken off only minutes ahead of us, and it was an easy matter to follow it to establish our general direction. The faster machine was soon out of sight, though, and Drake followed the map on the GPS. I concentrated on learning a few landmarks—a large rock outcropping north of town, a patch of pure scarlet trees.

In precisely forty-six and a half minutes we set down. While the crew offloaded their equipment, I looked around. As with similar jobs of this type, almost nothing was kept at the work location because the job moved farther along the powerline route each day. By tomorrow the cable would be attached to the poles here and a section a mile away, or five or ten, would be ready.

Jed had told us the entire span to be covered was one-hundred-twenty miles, it was roughly half completed, and the work had to be done before first snowfall, which could happen anytime in the next few weeks. I didn't do the math; it boiled down to full days, every day, to beat the weather as nature took its course and winter approached. There had been a brief mention about us staying on, if necessary to keep the job on schedule, even after the regular contract ship came back from maintenance. I wasn't sure either Drake or I were up for that, but we kept our plans open.

The return flight went more quickly, with a tailwind and less weight on board. I flew the second trip as we delivered crates of tools and boxed lunches for the crew. When we landed back at the airport afterward, we realized it was only ten a.m. and we now had the luxury of freedom until midafternoon. We decided to find ourselves a real breakfast—those mini donuts hadn't sustained me very long.

Drake performed a couple of routine post-flight mechanical checks, while I gave the windows a once-over with glass cleaner and paper towels. When I turned to put away my supplies, I saw an older man walking toward us. His step seemed hesitant, as if he was in pain, but his eyes were squarely on our helicopter. When he noticed I was watching, he gave a little wave.

"Hi." My brain went through a bunch of quick scenarios—he thought we were giving tour flights, he was an aircraft buff, maybe a retired military man with fond memories of his own time at the controls. Those were the usual. He wore chinos and a plaid shirt buttoned to the neck, with a string tie that sported a sizeable chunk of turquoise.

"You're from Albuquerque," he said as he approached.

"We are. How did you ...?"

"Recognized your chopper here, your logo. Heard there was some helicopter work going on hereabouts, and I need one. Lucky for me you're from home."

Drake climbed down from the engine cowling. The older man walked over and shook his hand, introducing himself to both of us as Fergus McNab, a retired farmer from Hatch. The small southern New Mexico town was known nationwide for producing the best chile anywhere.

"We're on a contract right now, but maybe we could help," Drake said. "What do you need?"

"I need to find my son."

"If he's lost Search and Rescue is your better bet." I couldn't figure out why an out-of-state aircraft would be a lucky choice for him.

"Aw, no, it's nothing like that. Rory lives up here."

So, why aren't you simply driving up to his house? But I held my questions.

"It's kinda complicated," Fergus said. "Could I buy you all a cup of coffee and explain about it?"

It turned out he'd arrived by taxi—another piece of the puzzle, no doubt—so we all piled into the Explorer and drove the short distance to Maxine's Café, a home-cooking-style place. We settled at a table in the half-full restaurant.

"We were planning on ordering breakfast," I said. "Can we get you something too?"

"Just coffee for me, thanks." His gnarled hands played

with the little paper sugar packets until the waitress poured him a cup.

Drake and I ordered bacon-and-egg meals and I brought up Fergus's reason for seeking us out.

"So, you need a helicopter to help find your son, but he lives here?"

A sigh. "I guess his place is pretty remote. I've never been there. I don't drive in unfamiliar places anymore, and I sure as hell can't hike. What Rory tells me, I get the idea it's a couple miles' hike from this cabin of his down to where he can pick up the road when he needs to come to town."

"So, I gather you're in touch with him?"

"Now and again. He's got a phone but it's usually up to him to call me, and the connection can be awful. Calls get cut off, problems like that. I only know roughly where this place of his is."

"What if you need to reach him? Like now—how do you initiate contact?"

"Oh, I've got the number. Just saying, it's real hit-or-miss whether I'll get through. For what I need to tell him now … Well, I just need to see him in person." His eyes reddened.

I thought of his uncertain gait as he'd approached us. Some kind of health problem. And to go to this kind of effort and expense … it must be serious. I laid down my fork and reached across the table to pat his hand.

Drake was nodding. "We'll see if we can get you there, Fergus. After breakfast, we'll go back to the airport and sit down with our sectional maps."

The old man perked up at the positive news and decided maybe he'd like a cinnamon roll, after all.

I picked up one of my crisp slices of bacon and chewed slowly. There was a hell of a lot of forest out there and he'd provided really skimpy information. Could we possibly help this man?

Chapter 3

Aviation sectional charts are a miracle of old-fashioned technology, with details of the landscape never shown on an ordinary road map. In the air, where roads and bridges mean nothing—other than as landmarks—the important things might include a small stock pond, a farm, or a windmill. Especially in the wide open spaces of New Mexico, where a town is rarely on the horizon, these little clues and our compass headings were often all that got pilots from Point A to Point B before GPS. Even now, watching for them lets us know we're on course.

Fergus had given us the bare minimum: "Rory's cabin is about ten miles north of town here."

So we spread out the sectional on a table in the hangar and started looking. Nothing but a high rock outcrop was indicated directly north, but at sixteen degrees—northwest of town—we spotted the words 'rustic cabin' beside a small inland lake.

Fergus got excited. "He said there's a lake. He catches fish out of it all the time. And he has a patch of flat ground where he's planted a little garden."

The map was not quite that accommodating, but Google Earth helped. Old tech and new tech—a winning combination. The new tech actually showed three possible cabins in the same area. The one we'd picked from the sectional showed signs of life—beaten down earth, the garden Fergus mentioned, and enough space between the structure and the lake for us to land.

"Does Rory know you're planning to fly in there?" Drake asked.

Fergus shook his head.

"How would he feel about a helicopter suddenly showing up and hovering over his house?"

The older man's eyes widened. Only a little, but I spotted it.

"Would he be likely to come out shooting?" I could tell even Drake hadn't considered that possibility. I had the distinct feeling Rory McNab was hiding from something out here in the Maine woods.

Drake spoke up. "Fergus, I need you to get through to your son and let him know what we're doing. I don't care about his reasons for being up here, but I'm sure not taking chances with our lives or our aircraft."

Fergus nodded. He pulled out a little flip-phone and pressed a couple of buttons. Even from where I stood, I could tell the ringing sound was erratic and crackly.

Drake looked at his watch. "Look, we don't have time to do your flight yet today anyway. By the time we plan logistics, get out there, and allow you some time with Rory, we'd be due back here to fuel up and bring back the cable crew. Tomorrow's the soonest I could promise you."

Fergus nodded, looking somewhat disappointed.

"I want your word that you'll reach Rory and inform him before we head toward that cabin."

Fergus nodded again, extended his hand, and they shook on it. "I'm eighty years old, son. My handshake is my promise."

I handed Fergus one of our business cards with our cell numbers on it. "If you aren't able to reach your son tonight, it's okay. Just let us know and we'll schedule your flight later."

We watched Fergus walk out to the taxi Harry had called for him, his feet shuffling and shoulders hunched. "I feel badly that we couldn't just crank up and fly right out there," I said.

"Me, too, hon. But something's not quite making sense and there's more to the story."

"He's ill. Don't you think that's the reason this news has to be shared in person?"

"That would be my guess. But why couldn't he have told his son to come back to New Mexico for a visit? Or even to come down from the lake and meet him here in town?"

"He didn't think of it?"

One of his dark eyebrows went up. "Um, maybe."

Our afternoon flight went predictably, we grabbed dinner at a steakhouse that boasted lobster rolls on the menu—I could really get used to this—and then we settled back at the Wayside Inn for the evening. Drake watched half of a football game; I showered and settled to finish the last two chapters of the book I'd been nursing along for a week. We were both nodding off by eight and realized we would be facing another early morning.

Earlier than I'd imagined, as it turned out. My phone rang at two a.m. When I saw it was Ron's number, I came instantly awake. My brother doesn't call often, and a middle-of-night call from anyone is rarely good news.

"They've taken Gram to the hospital," he said.

"Oh no." My nerve endings tingled.

"So far, they're not telling us much." A sound, like a rough hand rubbed over scratchy whiskers, came through. "They're doing tests to see if it's a heart attack."

"I should come. I can't believe I'm not there for her."

"When I get the chance, I'll tell her we've talked. Charlie, don't worry. It'll be okay."

When someone over ninety is rushed to the hospital in the middle of the night, it's not a sure thing that everything will be okay. I foresaw a million problems, but Ron didn't have answers. He told me to sit tight and said he would call in the morning with an update. I knew there was nothing to be accomplished by rushing out the door—no flight could get me there in time to make a real difference.

By now, Drake was sitting up in bed and had switched on the lamp. He had got the gist of the situation, but I had to go through it all again. Somehow, repeating details brought some perspective. Eventually, he pulled me close and turned out the light.

"Shh, shh," he whispered. "Hold on to me. It'll be all right."

I held and I shushed, but there was no way I was going to fall asleep and trust that it would be all right.

Chapter 4

By four o'clock I gave up the pretense of sleep. We would be getting up in another hour anyway. I slid out from under Drake's protective arm and tucked the comforter around his shoulders. In the bathroom, I dressed in sweats and a thick fleece pullover and drew my hair up into a ponytail. With coat, muffler, and phone in hand, I slipped out the back door and took a deep breath. The scent of wet leaves calmed me. Wisps of fog hung over the treetops and floated past the street lamps. I set off at a brisk walk.

It was only two in the morning in Albuquerque. I hadn't heard from Ron; there was no point in calling and waking him now. I pictured him in a hospital room at Elsa's bedside, trying to make himself comfortable in whatever recliner or cot they would have provided. I envisioned her peacefully sleeping, under observation by the doctors, but in no real danger. I couldn't imagine life without my Gram.

The sidewalk blurred and I tripped on an uneven concrete edge. Stopping to wipe my eyes, I took in a deep breath and blew it out. Elsa would tell me not to 'borrow trouble.' She was right—worry never solved anything. I covered two more blocks, turned right heading uphill, circled the several blocks, and ended up with the Wayside Inn in view. A rummage through my pockets told me I'd forgotten to take a key.

I climbed the steps to the porch, pulled my scarf to cover my ears, and settled myself gently into the cushions on one of the wicker chairs. Other than the tip of my nose feeling a little like a Popsicle, I was comfortable enough from the exertion of my walk. The time alone felt soothing and I waited until the light came on in our room. A tap at the window, Drake's curious glance out the curtain, and he let me in.

"Guess I didn't realize this door locks automatically," I said.

"How long were you out there?" He flinched when my hand touched his bare shoulder.

"I didn't want to wake you up. Just needed some space."

"Nothing from Ron yet?"

I shook my head. "I'll call him once we get you out on the flight. You don't mind taking the first one?"

"I'll take them both. You're distracted, plus you may need to be in town to make some plans."

He really is the best, most understanding husband in the entire world.

* * *

The fog had thickened by the time we got to the airport, but Harry assured us it would clear within an hour after the sun rose. Drake had already obtained flight weather data and had told me the same thing. Still, with things a little off-kilter in my world, I didn't want him taking off unless he had perfect conditions. Despite Elsa's wisdom on the subject, a person can only handle just so much worry at once.

By eight-thirty, the sky was a milky white with large patches of blue. Drake and the cable crew were ready to go and I watched the aircraft become a little dot in the sky. I got on the phone with Ron, knowing he was probably not even through his first cup of coffee for the day.

"It *was* a heart attack," he told me. "Right now she's stable and she slept well for several hours. Still, nothing is certain. She is ninety-two years old."

I didn't need reminding. "I'm coming home. I can get a flight out of Portland, and although there are a couple of connections, I can be there by tonight. There's just one thing I need to do here first, but Drake can shuttle me to the Portland airport."

"You know you don't need to …"

"No. I do. I'll be there. I'll call you when my arrival time is certain." I hung up before he could say anything more, although I had a feeling he wasn't going to try to talk me out of coming. A quick visit to my favorite travel app and I'd booked my trip to Albuquerque.

Drake had barely returned from the first ferry flight when Fergus McNab showed up.

"I see I'm right on time," he said. He had a small carry-on sized suitcase with him.

"We got a late start because of the fog today," I told him. "Let's see if we can find you a comfortable place to settle while Drake does the second flight. It'll be about ninety minutes."

Fergus looked none too happy. "I called Rory. He knows I'm coming. I made out like this is a surprise for my birthday. It's next week."

"Fergus, there's something more—" My phone rang and I saw it was Drake.

"Is that Fergus McNab sitting inside with you?" he asked.

"I told him about our getting a late start this morning. He's okay with waiting."

"What about your flight out of Portland? What time is that?"

I realized we would be cutting it close by the time Drake ferried two workers out to the job site, came back for Fergus and did his flight, then came back for me.

"We've got the space," he said. "Bring him out. I'll take everyone at once."

I stowed Fergus's bag in the cargo compartment alongside three metal baskets of tools, then buckled the older man into the front seat. It was a bit of a squeeze, but I put myself in the middle back seat, between two burly linemen in hard hats. The forty-five minute run wasn't the most pleasant ride I'd ever taken—I could swear at least one of the workers wore yesterday's shirt and hadn't showered—but it was over soon enough. Once they and their gear were gone, I moved to the seat behind Drake so I had a view of Fergus. I intended to continue the earlier conversation, although it would be hampered by engine and rotor noise and the static of the intercom line.

"Fergus … are you really going out to celebrate your birthday? Yesterday you said something … it sounded like this visit to your son is pretty urgent."

"I s'pose it is. Doctors give me six months. I figure within a few weeks I won't be able to make a trip like this."

"Are you in chemo or something like that?"

"Nah. Did that once, not doing it again. I go only often enough to get my pain meds renewed. I'm eighty. What's the point in going through all that, just so's I can live an extra, what—maybe another year at best. I'd rather be done with it."

I understood. Although, with the fresh news about Elsa being in the hospital, my own urge was to do everything to save her. Maybe the decision is easier for the patient than for those around him or her.

"So, wouldn't it have been easier to get Rory to come visit you? He must be pretty young and fit if he's living in a cabin all alone up here."

His mouth worked for a moment but he decided to ignore my point-blank question. "I'm staying a week," he said, looking at Drake. "That is, if you're willing to come back and pick me up."

"I'll do that," Drake assured him. We had worked out credit card payment for the service, and as long as the fiber optic cable job didn't interfere, there was no reason not to accommodate the man. "We're getting close, according to the GPS coordinates. Let me know if you spot the lake or the cabin, okay?"

I got the feeling it was an exercise more to keep Fergus busy and me from asking more. It truly was none of our business why the customer had booked the flight. Drake has such an eagle eye for things on the ground, he certainly doesn't need anyone's help. But I watched anyway and did spot a glint of sunlight on water, at about the same time Drake pointed ahead.

He brought the helicopter down to a hundred feet or

so above treetop, circling to be sure we had the right lake and the right cabin. Sure enough, the shingle roof looked exactly as it had on the screen of my tablet yesterday.

"Rory said he would drag his red canoe down to the shore of the lake," Fergus told us. "There it is. It's his place!"

While Drake concentrated on landing in the clearing between the water's edge and the cabin, I scanned the area surrounding the simple log cabin. No road or driveway in sight. There must be a small path leading to a way out. Fergus had mentioned Rory hiking in and out. A person couldn't live modern life without some method of shopping, could he? Fish and a vegetable garden could only go so far. How had he brought in tools, furnishings … how did he get a cell signal? As appealing as a life off the grid sounded, my inner organizer had to know how everyday matters would work.

Our skids touched lightly on the rocky ground near the lake. Drake said he would keep the engine running if I would help Fergus with his bag. I hopped out and unbuckled our passenger, giving him a hand as he climbed out. The little suitcase was surprisingly light; he must have packed no more than a couple of changes of clothes and a shaving kit. Securing all the doors and compartments, I carried the bag and followed Fergus to the front door.

Behind a screen door, I glimpsed the silhouette of a slim man with hands on hips. When he realized I was walking up to the covered porch, he stepped out of sight.

"I'll get it from here," Fergus said, reaching for the bag the minute his feet touched the porch.

I stood on the split-log step and handed it up to him. "Okay, then. Thanks for flying with us. Drake will be back to pick you up next Thursday. You have our numbers if there's any change in plans."

I climbed into the front seat where Fergus had been, buckled myself in, and put on a headset.

"All set, I guess," I said to Drake. We verbally went through our little checklist about having closed the cargo doors, etcetera, and he brought up the engine RPM. I turned toward the cabin to wave goodbye, but the wooden front door was now closed and nary a curtain moved at any of the windows.

"Well, that task is done until next week," he said as we lifted away from the spot.

I let go of the questions I'd wanted to ask Fergus. Silly of me to think I needed details about someone else's personal life. He was a man with sad news to deliver to his son. I had to leave it at that. My bigger concerns lay at home where someone very close to me was hovering at life's edge.

I'd left the B&B this morning without packing a bag, since I'd had no idea what news Ron's phone call would bring. A glance at my watch told me there was no time to go back for clothes and toiletries, and they didn't matter anyway. Drake pointed the nose in the direction of Portland where I would be delivered in fine style for my commercial flight to Albuquerque, and he would refuel and go back to Safe Port in time to fly out and pick up his crew.

Twenty-four hours ago, I could not have predicted any of this. Twenty-four hours from now, what will fate have delivered?

Chapter 5

By my calculation I'd been awake nearly two days straight by the time my feet hit the sidewalk outside the Albuquerque terminal at eleven p.m. and Ron's vehicle pulled up. I wanted to rush to Elsa's bedside, but one look at me and Ron vetoed that idea.

"She's asleep, under enough medication she won't even know you're there. And, frankly, you look like a bag lady and don't smell all that great."

"Gee, thanks." But I knew he was right, and what are brothers for anyway?

I walked into a too-empty house. Freckles had been staying at Ron's for the last two weeks, and not much lingered of the familiar doggie scent of her fur, her paws, her food. I missed her and, depending on how much time I ended up at the hospital in coming days, I would soon bring her home. Being dog-less was the main thing I hated about travel on our helicopter jobs.

A shower and comfy bed beckoned. I must have slept well—next thing I knew it was seven o'clock and a sunbeam brightened the bedroom. I pulled on fresh jeans and sweater, grabbed my purse and hoped my Jeep would start without a hitch, having sat in the driveway so long.

Next door, Elsa's house looked forlorn. To my practiced eye, the living room drapes should be open, a sprinkler would be spritzing the lawn, and those fallen leaves would not be lying on the front porch. I walked over and picked up the newspaper and checked her mailbox, gathering the few things that would be a giveaway to the fact no one was home.

Later, I should go over and be sure everything was all right inside. I could tidy the kitchen, put fresh linens on her bed, make sure nothing in the fridge was too far gone. The idea that she might not ever come back here was unfathomable. I tamped down that thought as I tossed her mail and paper on the passenger seat beside me. I would hold tightly to the idea that she would be sitting up in bed, ready for the morning news and a coffee together, when I arrived at the hospital.

Toward that end, I pulled through the drive-thru at McDonald's and got myself a muffin sandwich, orange juice, and two coffees to go. I wolfed down the food, realizing I couldn't remember my last meal—it had been somewhere in Maine, more than a day ago. A parking spot at the Heart Hospital was relatively easy to find this early in the morning. I carried my cardboard tray of coffees and rode the elevator, following Ron's directions to Elsa's room.

A nurse wearing a bright, flowered scrub top, vivid green pants, and a name tag—Corrine— caught me at the doorway.

"If that second coffee is supposed to be for our patient, I'm gonna have to put a veto on it. No caffeine for our Miss Elsa yet."

"Can I drink my own in there?"

She nodded and I picked up one of the cups, handing over the tray and the other cup.

"Darn it," came Elsa's voice from the single bed in the room. "I'll bet you had doctored it just the way I like—two sugars and one creamer."

I couldn't help but laugh. She might look tiny and frail in that industrial-looking bed with all the monitors and wires around her, but her spunky attitude was alive and well. I set my cup on the bedside stand and gave her a fierce hug.

"You're home," she said. The few words and little movement seemed to have taken all her energy. Her arms dropped back to her sides and her head sank against the pillow. Her color didn't look great, only a pale shadow of her real self.

"I came right back when Ron called. So, what's all this about? What do the doctors say?" I settled into the chair at her bedside and took a sip of my coffee.

She sighed. "Well, they think I had a heart attack. Silly. I just didn't feel too great last night and Ron called 9-1-1. I would have been fine."

Except it was obvious she wouldn't have, and she'd lost track of a whole day; she'd been out of it for a while.

"I brought your mail and the paper," I said, reaching into my bag and setting everything on her nightstand. "Since that nurse isn't going to let you go hiking or anything right away, you might have time for some reading."

She barely acknowledged the items. Her eyelids seemed heavy. About the time I thought she would drift off to sleep, Corrine bustled in.

"Time for vitals," she said cheerily, boosted by the coffee I'd given her.

"Can we talk a minute when you're done?" I tilted my head toward the doorway. She nodded.

"Gram, I'll be around, and Ron will come by in a while too. You let me know if you need anything, okay?" She nodded, but her eyes were on the nurse as she whipped out a digital thermometer.

I picked up my purse and walked out to the hall to finish my coffee and toss the cup in a receptacle near the nurses' station. When Corrine appeared, I approached her and asked for the truth about Elsa's condition.

"Are you a relative?"

"She's my grandmother." It was only a tiny shade away from the truth. "She raised me."

She glanced through the pages of the written chart. "I don't see a next-of-kin here … but the man who came last night …"

"That's my brother, Ron Parker. I'm Charlie—Charlotte. He would have given all that information. He's got her healthcare power of attorney. We have her insurance paperwork, we can get whatever—"

"Fine. I do see his name here."

"Is Elsa going to be okay?"

"At her age, nothing is certain. By 'okay' if you mean will she leave the hospital, most likely. The doctor will probably order her to a cardiac rehab center to get her strength back. Is she normally fairly active?"

I thought of the garden in Elsa's back yard and the size of the house and property she maintains nearly on her own. "For her age, very active."

"That works in her favor. We'll try to get her back

to her normal activity level so she can return home. Of course, until she passes certain tests for her daily needs, she may need care in a nursing home."

I felt mildly reassured, but not entirely. The bit about the nursing home would not go over well with our patient. I was standing outside Elsa's door, watching her sleep, when Ron walked up. I filled him in on what I'd just learned.

"Let's grab some breakfast downstairs," he suggested.

I didn't admit I'd already eaten. My coffee was gone and I could at least get a refill. Avoiding the heavy subject of Elsa's future and how that might impact us, I asked about Victoria and the boys. All fine. He asked about Drake and our trip.

"Fine there, too. Everything was going well. Did I tell you we met a chile farmer from Hatch who lives here now? His name is Fergus McNab." We were in line at the cafeteria now. "His son is living in some remote cabin up there and the old man had us fly him up to it."

Ron had loaded a plate with bacon and eggs; I refrained from remarking that he could end up in the room next to Elsa's if he wasn't careful. I could hardly throw stones in this situation, since I'd done pretty much the same thing earlier.

"So, the father has something terminal," I continued as we took our seats, "and he was up there to inform his son. Guess it's been the week for bad news."

Ron had taken a sip of his coffee, his gaze faraway and thoughtful. "Did you say Fergus McNab?"

"Um, yeah." I had succumbed to the lure of raspberry Danish near the cash register.

"He came to me once with a case."

"Really? I don't remember that."

He forked up a mass of scrambled egg. "It was a long

time ago, right after we opened RJP. We were still fixing up the office and you might have gone out for more paint, for all I know."

"What kind of case?"

"Whew, let me think … His son had done something wrong and his trial didn't go the way they'd hoped. The father wanted me to help get him off. I said private investigators couldn't get around the court system. If he thought there was new evidence, we might work on that aspect."

"But we didn't. I don't recall any of this."

"No, the case had already been decided. The boy was guilty."

"Fergus McNab." I mulled over this news. "Was the son's name Rory?"

Ron shrugged and picked up his coffee cup. "I don't remember. Honestly, I'm surprised I recalled this much. The man's name is a little unusual, and when you said he was a chile farmer … that's what triggered the memory at all."

I thought of Fergus and his quiet, sincere manner. He didn't seem the type to be manipulating the court system. I wondered if there was more, if he was now manipulating Drake and me.

Chapter 6

I couldn't let go of the McNab story, even while I sat at Elsa's bedside. She roused briefly and recognized me. We talked for about two minutes before she became drowsy again. The doctor came around and I got very much the same story from him that the nurse had given. If Elsa didn't have another incident in the next few days, and if her strength warranted, she would be able to go to rehab, then decisions would be made about where she would live. He refused to commit to any particular outcome.

"She's an elderly woman living alone. You might want to consider the practicalities of her being back in her own home," he said, glancing through the window at her sleeping form in the bed.

I left the hospital in a dreary mood. Ron and I would need to have a serious talk soon, but he'd already told me he was on a case with a deadline and needed most of the day to finish the work. Running my Jeep through a carwash brightened the outlook a bit, literally, but I knew I wouldn't manage to concentrate if I tried to settle into my normal accounting routine at the office. Fergus McNab's story kept coming back to me. I was only a few blocks from the main library, so I headed in that direction.

The newspaper archives were a place I wasn't unfamiliar with, and once I got the reference librarian to set me up with a viewing machine, I was a happy little clam. Ron had said Fergus came to him about ten years ago. I went back in time to the month we were setting up our offices, then began scrolling backward from there. It didn't take long to spot the story.

The first major headline "Prominent Attorney Accused of Jury Tampering" had appeared about six months prior to his visit. It was a front-page, below-the-fold story describing a case in which Albuquerque attorney Rory McNab was being investigated by the State Attorney General's office after allegations of jury tampering. McNab had been senior partner in his own law firm and was representing a long-time Albuquerque family whose number one son had gotten in trouble when he dabbled a bit with controlled substances. Allegedly.

The article was long on background about the well-known family and their history in the city, with a fair number of column inches devoted to Rory McNab's previous high-profile cases. Short on details about the actual jury tampering charges.

The second piece I found covered Rory's own trial; again the media had skimmed over the actual wrongdoing in favor of hyping the burgeoning career of lead prosecutor Herman Quinto and his announcement that he would run for the state legislature in order to pass laws preventing this sort of 'terrible malfeasance of the law.' I'd heard Quinto's name for years now. He seemed the sort of politician who took every opportunity to step in front of a camera.

My neck and shoulders were getting sore from sitting in one place and scrolling through pages, but I didn't want to make another trip back to the library. I kept going until I spotted one more thing. Three days after his trial began Rory McNab was found guilty on all ten counts of jury tampering. Each carried a maximum prison term of nine years.

Whoa. I backed up and read it again. If that was so, why wasn't Rory behind bars right now? There was a lot more to this story, and I suspected it might account for his clandestine lifestyle and the secretive way he'd greeted his own father at the cabin. A niggling uneasiness began in my spine. I knew the whereabouts of a felon. Shouldn't I be reporting this to someone?

I stood up and stretched to work the tension out of my shoulders. After briefly pacing back and forth in the archive room, I sat again. I needed to know more before barreling out to wreak havoc on Fergus McNab's life. The man had obviously been through a lot more than he'd told us.

A glance at the time told me I should be getting back to the hospital. Ron hadn't been able to stay with Elsa this morning, and I felt as though one of us ought to be there. I printed the three articles on Rory McNab, then gathered my purse and left the library.

Elsa was propped up in bed when I walked into her room, a bit more awake than she'd been this morning but far from her lively self. When I asked how she was feeling, she raised a veined hand dismissively. "I want to go home."

I put a smile in place and ignored the huge question we would all be facing soon. I am terrible at bedside manner. No caregiver role should ever be entrusted to me because I'm always at a loss for what to do. "How about some water?" I held up the plastic cup with a bent straw in it.

She turned away from it. A tap came at the door. I looked up to see a bouquet of flowers atop a narrow body and legs. The arrangement was so big it concealed the young orderly's face completely.

"Mrs. Higgins, look what you've got!" The perky voice and masses of color instantly brightened the room. Why hadn't I thought of bringing flowers? See what I mean about being inept at these things?

Elsa smiled for the first time since I'd been here. "Well, look at this. Who sent them?"

I picked the tiny envelope from its plastic prong holder amidst the blossoms. "Let's see."

"I don't have my glasses. Read it for me," Elsa said.

"Thinking of you and hoping you are 100% well very soon," I read. "It's from Ron and Victoria."

"Ah, so sweet of them."

Of *her*. Thank goodness for Victoria. She made at least one contingent of the Parker family look good.

"I'm bored with this—lying around in bed isn't my style," Elsa said, once the newness of the flowers had worn off. I didn't point out that she didn't look strong enough to put her feet on the floor, much less head for home. "Tell me about your latest case," she said in a thin voice.

I went through Drake's and my recent trip across country, embellishing a few things for entertainment value, such as the small town in Iowa where we'd landed behind a small rural café just because it had the appeal of a '50s-style diner. I hadn't yet got to the part about the lobster dinner at the McAllister's house before she nodded off to sleep again.

Elsa—so many special times together, so many times she'd been there for me when I didn't deserve it. A pink carnation in the bouquet on the table reminded me of being fifteen, sullen and rude because I didn't get a date for a school dance, fiercely jealous when my friend Stacy had stopped by to show me her corsage. Elsa smoothed over the moment by pulling a sheet of chocolate chip cookies from the oven and serving them to us girls with tea instead of milk. There had to be a thousand of those instances during my teens and twenties, my oblivious years.

A stargazer lily took me back to my wedding day; Elsa barely knew Drake, yet accepted him completely into the family. There was the time of the house fire, when we'd moved in with her for a few weeks. Never a complaint or tense moment from her—those were all mine. How could I have been such a little shit at times, when all she ever did was love me unconditionally?

I reached for the tissue box on the nightstand, helping myself to a wad of them. "You'd just better get well," I whispered softly. "*Please.*"

I watched her sleep for a while, until a nurse peeked in at the door. "Sleep is the best thing for her right now. She's gaining her strength back."

"Thanks." I began to feel a little antsy to be doing something. I walked down the hall and stopped near the waiting area. Checking the time difference, I figured I should be able to catch Drake between flights right now, so I called him.

"Hey, how's she doing?" he asked.

I gave an update on Elsa and then on what I'd learned

about the McNabs. "I feel strange about this, knowing where Rory is, not reporting it."

"Well, you don't know the whole story," he said. "If my experience with reporters is any indicator, you don't know a *fraction* of the story."

He was right. I'd been abducted once and what came out in the news was a far cry from what had happened.

"Charlie, think about it. Maybe the sentence was far less than the maximum, maybe it was overturned on appeal, maybe he served time and got out on good behavior."

I stared at a piece of art on the wall, a smear of pastel colors that didn't resemble any actual thing. "You're right—any of the above could be true."

"A felony conviction would have killed his legal career, so maybe the guy just opted for a quiet life away from society."

Maybe. His words made a lot of sense.

"Sweetie, you love to find a mystery under every rock. Of course you would want to decipher this one too." He paused. "I miss you."

I felt myself getting emotional again so I walked to a door marked Stairs. In the quiet of the stairwell, I told him I missed him, too, and choked back tears as we said goodbye. Deep exhale. It had been a way-emotional day. Maybe if I went to the office for a while.

I left the hospital parking lot and made my way west on Lomas, then wound through the side streets until I came to our renovated Victorian. Its gray and white façade calmed me and I pulled down the long drive to my customary parking spot at the back. I'd no sooner opened the back door than I heard the skitter of toenails on hardwood. Freckles, our brown and white spaniel, came racing into the kitchen and skidded the final ten feet, sliding into my legs. I knelt and hugged her tightly.

"I figured you'd be in sometime today," Ron said from the doorway.

"Thanks for bringing her. Can't believe how much I've missed this little mutt."

"I can. She missed you guys, too, although I have to say the boys did a good job of winning her over with treats. And now Victoria's dropping hints about us visiting the shelter … All your fault."

He talks gruff, but he's really a softie about animals and kids.

"Sally made fresh coffee right before she left for the day," he said, pulling his favorite mug from the sink. "Want some?"

"I think I'm coffee'd out at the moment. Just thought I'd check in, but I want to get back to Gram after a while. Be sure to thank Victoria for the flowers she sent. They are beautiful and she loved them."

"What makes you think I didn't order them?"

I shot him a look.

"Okay, you're right. Oh, hey—you got my curiosity up about the man you met in Maine, that McNab guy, so I looked up his son's case online. Interesting twist." He'd turned back toward the hall, and I traipsed along as he headed up the stairs toward his office.

"What twist?"

He tilted his head toward his doorway in a come-check-it-out gesture. I diverted across the hall long enough to drop my purse on my desk and take a look at the staggering pile of junk mail that had accumulated during my two-week absence. I ignored it and stepped into Ron's office. His desk was covered with an equally impressive mass of paperwork, but his was all there by his own hand.

"What twist?" I repeated. I was feeling like an oldster for not having gone to the internet first.

"Want to read the articles or shall I give the condensed version?"

"Condensed." If it was worth learning more, I could always Google it myself.

"Okay, so, Rory McNab was a hotshot attorney—"

"I got as far as his conviction on ten counts and nine years in prison for each."

"Okay … well, after that, it gets interesting. The sentencing hearing was delayed twice, first by the court calendar, then by a motion from McNab's defense attorney. All this time, he was out on his own recognizance and, other than having been ordered to surrender his passport, he was pretty much free to come and go for a few months. The sentencing hearing was set for November first, and this time it looked as if it really would happen. With most likely less than a month of freedom left, Rory decided to take in a ball game with his dad and an uncle. He went to Phoenix and never returned."

"What?"

"Simply did not show up for his sentencing hearing. His attorney was backpedaling as fast as she could, but didn't have an explanation. The judge sentenced Rory to the full ninety years, after saying he'd been prepared to go with a much more lenient two-to-ten until the defendant pulled this little stunt."

Holy cow. I did some quick head-math. Rory is nearly fifty now, would have been about forty when all this happened … I could see where the full ninety years would have been a death sentence.

"What happened? I mean, he disappeared—no doubt

law enforcement was all over this, trying to find him."

"Right. They were. And, of course, Fergus McNab and his brother were questioned by the cops and hounded by the press. The brother was so clueless that he was almost immediately dropped as a suspect."

"But Fergus knew more." I was trying to put it together in my head and not coming up with much.

"Mr. McNab's story was that he'd driven to Arizona to spend a little time with his brother, Rory's uncle, and when they were able to get three tickets to a big Cardinals game Rory flew to Phoenix to join them. Guys' weekend out, that sort of thing. On the Monday after the game, Fergus drove his son to the airport and they had breakfast there while waiting for Rory's flight. The old man swore the last time he saw his son was as he passed through airport security and waved goodbye, saying, 'I'll see you in Albuquerque'."

"And …"

"Fergus says he then went out to the parking garage but his car was stolen. He searched everywhere, got the airport security people to help, finally had to report it and rent a car to get home."

"Surely, the police checked airport security video?"

"Surely. But that's where the public information hits a dead end. Three days after this story was big news something bigger came along, an earthquake in Central America, and since both New Mexico and Arizona citizens were trapped by it, the media leapt on that and the McNab story began a slow decline into oblivion—at least news-wise."

The question came back to me again: Was Fergus McNab a sad man with a sad story, or had he manipulated things right from the start?

Chapter 7

I spent the afternoon at my desk, tidying, opening mail and just doing general office stuff. By three o'clock there was hardly any evidence that I had been gone a couple of weeks. I rounded up Freckles and we went out to the car. Decided to stop at a florist shop on my way to the hospital. One glance through the enormous bouquets in the fridge told me that there was no way I could compete with Victoria's wonderful spray of flowers. So I opted for something very simple.

Two roses in a cut glass vase—one red, one pink. I chose a card with a garden flower motif that I knew Gram would love and just wrote a simple greeting—*I love you*.

By the time I arrived in the hallway outside her door, the food cart was two doors down from hers. The smell of institutional food pervaded. Gram's bed was propped up

and she had a tray in front of her with green gelatin, some
sort of pudding, probably vanilla, and a glass of juice. She
didn't look as if she was any more enthused about it than
I would have been.

She brightened when she saw the roses and teared up
when she read the card. When she got weepy, I did too
and gave her a big hug. Finally, I suggested that maybe I
could help her with her dinner. I unwrapped her flatware
and handed her the spoon so she could work on the meal.

We chatted while she finished her Jell-O and worked
on the pudding, but obviously that was not a favorite thing.
I promised her I would talk to the nurses about getting
her something a little more substantial tomorrow, and
that seemed to brighten her mood. After about ten more
minutes of chitchat I could tell she was getting tired. I gave
her another hug and helped crank her bed downward so
she could rest.

Freckles had waited patiently in the parking garage, and
she was so happy to see me when I came out I couldn't
resist stopping at McDonald's to get us both cheeseburgers.
She wolfed hers down in three bites. I took a little bit more
time with mine. Information Ron had given me earlier
about Fergus McNab had stuck in my mind. I was eager to
get home, get on the internet and find out more for myself.

In a follow-up article after Rory's disappearance,
Albuquerque police had worked with a detective at the
Phoenix Police Department named Chet Foster, a man in
his late sixties, I guessed from the brief video clip. He had
short grizzled hair, a neat shave, and wore jeans and a sport
coat. The reporter questioning him dished out queries in
an aggressive way. Foster met her with straightforward
answers and not a hint of backing down.

I jotted down Chet Foster's name, along with that of Herman Quinto, the prosecutor in Albuquerque. What the heck, I might as well try to reach them and find out what had gone on after the story quit being top slot in the news. It only took a minute to find the phone number of the central Phoenix Police Department, and I placed the call. Within minutes, I learned that Foster had retired four years ago. A minor setback but not enough to stop me.

A search of phone numbers gave me a listing for a Chester Foster in Mesa, Arizona. I dialed and had him on the line almost immediately. As soon as I mentioned the McNab case, Foster assumed I was a reporter and nearly hung up on me, but I stopped him quickly, explaining that I work for a private investigation firm in Albuquerque and was doing a follow-up on the original case. Even that didn't seem to elicit a response from him. But when I dropped the fact that I had recently seen Fergus McNab, he perked up again.

"I don't know what I can tell you, Ms. Parker. At the time we had such limited resources we really couldn't keep tracking Rory McNab forever. He wasn't a violent criminal, after all. And I tell ya in a city like this we get half a dozen murder cases a day. Sorry, just don't have the resources to track down some hotshot lawyer. One that doesn't even live in our own state."

"I understand that he somehow escaped from the Phoenix airport, and it was suspected he drove away in his father's car."

"Yeah, that's what we thought at the time. It didn't take long to find the car. It had been abandoned on the outskirts of Tucson, and we found it just a few days after. Of course, both Rory's and Fergus's prints were in the car; they had both driven it in recent days. The prints on the steering wheel were blurred, so it was assumed the car thief wore gloves."

"What about airport security? Didn't cameras show Fergus leaving?"

"I personally sat there watching those videos for days. We saw Rory McNab and his father moving through the airport, having breakfast at one of the restaurants. After they ate they both went into the men's room. Fergus came out. Never did see Rory come out."

"So. Fergus clearly lied about seeing his son off at the security gate then?"

"Yeah, we pretty much knew that right from the start. Didn't take but one check of the airline manifest to see that Rory was a no-show on the plane."

"So, what about the parking garage? There are security cameras out there, too, aren't there?"

"There are. Apparently, the McNab car was parked in a blind spot. By coincidence or by design—we never knew. We saw the vehicle leave the garage but couldn't identify who was at the wheel."

I asked a couple more things, but that seemed to be the extent of what Chet Foster could tell me. I understood. Cops see a lot of cases and this one couldn't have been one of the more important ones to a Phoenix detective. I thanked him for the information and hung up.

An autumn chill had settled on the house and I went into the bedroom to rummage for a sweater. Freckles was begging to go outside so I followed her and walked over to Elsa's to be sure everything was okay at her house. As always, she had a lamp on the timer in the living room so at least the place didn't look abandoned. I checked her thermostat setting, as the evenings were getting cooler.

Discovered she had it set at seventy-eight and turned it down several notches. No problem with any freezing pipes here, but there was no reason to run up her gas bill either.

Back through the break in the hedge, I checked a couple of things in our backyard. All looked well. Freckles did her business and we were soon back inside where I heated water in the kettle for a warming cup of chai. Mug in hand, I went back to the computer and re-read the story Ron had showed me earlier.

It kept bugging me that Herman Quinto was the prosecutor on the case. Quinto was a familiar name, as he had since become a state senator and this year was running for Congress. I made a note to contact him and ask about the prosecution of Rory McNab, wondering if he would even remember a case from so far back in his career.

If I couldn't reach Quinto, I could always call Tyler Carson, a guy I know in the current prosecutor's office. I debated that idea for a good eight minutes while I finished my chai, but still I hesitated. Tyler wouldn't know the case from all those years ago and would have to be brought up to speed. And there was something that kept me from making the call. Some hesitation over Rory's situation? I didn't think so. More likely, my hesitation was because I really didn't want to bring more trouble on Fergus McNabb in his present condition. I hate these moral dilemmas.

The poor dog was sitting near the living room window, pining for Drake. If I had come home, he should too. She didn't understand that it would be a few more days. I picked her up for a cuddle on the couch. An episode of *Grace & Frankie* helped take my mind off the cares of the day here at home, and the half hour gave enough of a break before we both decided it was time to hit the sack.

Chapter 8

The next couple of days passed in much the same way—me spending time at the hospital with Elsa, and Ron handling duties at the office. Elsa was starting to become a little cranky with the situation. She was feeling better but the doctor wouldn't clear her to be home. Ron and I needed to talk about what would happen when she was released. Would she actually get to go home or would the doctor insist that she go into nursing care? Each time the words nursing home came up in conversation, Elsa became grumpier than ever.

Victoria decided it by inviting me to dinner. She would make a nice roast and the three of us would talk about the future over the meal. I went straight to their house, a small bungalow in an older section of town, just off of Lomas Boulevard and arrived about five o'clock. The aroma of roasted beef filled the air. Victoria was working on a salad and assigned me the task of opening cans of green beans. I could handle that.

"You can't really blame her," Victoria said. "Elsa has been an independent lady for so many years now. She'll not want to leave her home."

"I know, I know. I can't disagree with any of that but, gosh, it's so hard. How are we going to explain it to her? She's not happy about this idea at all."

"No one would be, Charlie. We just have to face the fact. None of us wants to hear those words—nursing home. But it might be the reality of it. We just don't know yet."

She handed me knives and forks and some plates, which I carried to the dining table and set places for the three of us. The boys were with their mother this week.

I have to admit that we feasted on succulent roast beef, potatoes, carrots, and green beans for a full ten minutes before any of us brought up the main subject again. "So, Ron, what do you think if she refuses to go? There's always the option of home care, but is there money for that? We don't know yet whether she has a good insurance policy."

"Well, little sis," he said, "I'm putting you in charge of that. When you go back home tonight go through her papers and see if you can find anything about such a policy. Maybe that will end up being our answer."

And so that's what I did. It felt horribly like prying, looking through Elsa's papers, but what choice did I have? Midway through the search my phone rang and I saw it was Drake.

"Hey, hon, guess what? I finished the job a little early and I'm going to be able to head home day after tomorrow."

"Did you get Fergus? I hope he and his son had a good visit."

"I got him, and yeah, sounds like everything went okay."

"That's great news! I still have my hands full here with Elsa's situation, but I really would love coming home in the evenings to you, and Freckles misses you like crazy." At the sound of her name, the dog started dancing around me in a frenzy of excitement.

Drake laughed, hearing the dog's happy yips over the line.

"See? We're both excited about your homecoming."

"Don't fix my welcome home drink just yet. It will take me several days to get across country. I'll give you a call each night and let you know when I get to the airport."

Knowing Drake would be coming home soon brightened my outlook.

The next day I stepped into Elsa's room, happy to see her sitting up in bed with a magazine in front of her. She tossed it onto the nightstand and eased her thin legs over the edge of the bed. "Charlie, I'm so glad you're here. I've been wanting out of this bed all morning."

"If the doctor says it's okay, I don't see why we couldn't take a little walk down the hall."

"Well it darn well better be okay," Elsa said. "They've been bugging me to get up and moving so I'm going to do it."

The monitors had been reduced to a couple of small devices that sat on a wheeled dolly, so after helping Elsa into her robe I tied the sash for her, took her arm, and steered the little rig with my other hand.

"So, tell me what's new," Elsa said. "I'm bored with this place. I'm used to being around you and keeping up with your exciting life." She was probably thinking about this past summer when there was quite a ruckus involving a family across the street. Sweet old Elsa had been my neighborhood spy for a few weeks.

I laughed, not sure what new excitement she thought I'd be involved with, but certain I provided more action than she'd seen here. I told her about the man we had met in Maine but didn't go into details about his son or the legal case. I still wasn't sure what to do with the information I'd gathered. Meanwhile, she still seemed a bit peevish.

As Elsa and I turned around, three doors down from her room, I said, "I'll talk it over with your doctor and see what he says about releasing you. For now, they said you will probably go to a rehab center until you're really back on your feet again."

"Well, I'm going to be back on my feet before anybody knows it. And there will be no putting me away in some old folks' home."

I chuckled as I helped her take off her robe and settled her back into bed. With that kind of determination, I totally believed her. There's no way one hospital and a dozen doctors were going to keep this ninety-two-year-old down.

I tucked the covers around her shoulders and said goodnight. Ron called as I was getting into my car, saying he'd promised to pick up his three sons and take them out for pizza. I could join them if I wanted to. With nothing else to fill the empty evening hours, I did.

By Saturday morning when I got the call from Drake that he had landed at Double Eagle, the small airport on the west side, things at home were nearly back to normal. I drove out to meet him, expecting that we would clean up the aircraft and then have a nice lunch out somewhere before settling in and enjoying an evening together in our own bedroom.

I had parked my Jeep, clipping a leash to Freckles' collar and taking her with me to greet Drake after the long separation. We walked through the FBO and out on the tarmac toward our blue and white Jet Ranger. It took a moment for me to realize two people were getting out, but it only took a second longer to figure out who the second one was. Fergus McNab.

Chapter 9

Fergus looked like a badly faded image of himself when I helped him down from the aircraft. And *that* faded image surely was a faded version of his prior self before all this had happened. I sent a puzzled look toward Drake with a shoulder shrug, and he sent one back to me. Fergus excused himself to visit the men's room and I asked Drake what the heck.

"He wanted to ride along, I couldn't convince him that the ride would take quite a lot longer by helicopter than his commercial flight, but it seemed like he wanted my company so I agreed to bring him," Drake told me.

"So you guys had a couple of days together … did he say anything about his son's case?"

"A little. I suppose he'd better tell you about that himself. I offered him a ride from the airport—hope that's okay with you."

"Well of course it's not a problem." I glanced toward the car. "As long as he doesn't mind riding with the dog."

"I'm sure he won't," Drake said. "He's pretty tired, so the quicker we can get him home the better."

By the time Drake had pulled baggage from the cargo compartment I spotted Fergus inside the FBO's office. We were on the road five minutes later, heading for Albuquerque's southeast heights. Fergus gave directions and we ended up at a small trailer park of about three dozen single-wide homes. Most were neatly maintained, some with gardens and little picket fences, but Fergus's place was definitely in need of some TLC. The poor man obviously had not been able to tend to his yard over the summer months. The small patch of grass was much overgrown and some lanky, straggly cosmos had long since finished blooming.

A sixty-something woman from the trailer next door watched as we got out of my car, giving us the wary eye, but she seemed less worried once she spotted Fergus with us. While Drake pulled the small leather suitcase from the back, Fergus fumbled in his pocket for keys. I lowered the side windows so Freckles could wait out here. Drake carried the suitcase and I took Fergus's arm to help him up the steps. It wasn't an easy journey.

"Well, we might as well get this out," said Fergus. "I know you're dying to ask me about Rory. Drake told me that you heard about my boy's case."

"I didn't start out to pry—truly I didn't," I said. "Someone mentioned it to me and I found the news items. That's all."

"If you have a mind to go telling someone his whereabouts, I'll tell you here and now, I'll warn Rory and he'll be gone before they can get to him."

"Fergus, honestly, I have no intention of reporting him, but I guess I need to know more of the story. If Rory is innocent why did he run?"

Fergus spun around faster than I would have believed he could. "Because of that bastard Quinto. The man had my kid in his sights for years and then he figured out a way to bring him down."

"What do you mean, had him in his sights?"

"Miss, have you ever been close to a news story? Those nosy reporters never get nothing right. They don't get an answer that'll sell papers, they make something up."

I actually had been close to several news stories and couldn't really disagree with him. "So tell me then, what was different? What really happened that was not reported?"

Fergus sighed. "I'm a tired, sick old man but come on—let's sit down. If y'all want something to drink look in the fridge or grab a glass and turn on the tap. Sorry, I'm just too tired to wait on ya."

I declined but Drake went and looked in the fridge. He came back with a couple of beers, pulled the top on one, and handed it to Fergus before we all sat down and he pulled the top on the second one for himself. The couch where I sat was actually fairly comfortable and I suspected it had been decent quality furniture. I imagined a time when Fergus was married and his wife took good care of things, including him. But since she had passed and Rory had been away, finances must have dropped off and home maintenance lagged. I looked toward our host to see what he would say next.

He took a long swig of the beer, sighed again, and looked me in the eye. "Well, the first thing I'll tell ya is, Rory's innocent."

I tried not to roll my eyes or give off other signs of

disbelief, but really—isn't that what any parent would say?

"That goddamn trial was a sham. Came down to the prosecutor and that judge being in cahoots all along, and I swear to you if anybody tampered with anyone on that jury it was one of those two."

"Do you have evidence of that?" I asked.

"There ain't no evidence. If there was I'd of had my boy out of there right away, but those slimeballs, they turned everything on him. They turned everybody against him, especially the jury. And that judge—the whole verdict was rigged right from the start. I tell you, it was *rigged*, right from the start."

He was becoming so agitated that I worried the questions were going to do more harm than good. I turned my tone gentle as I talked to him again. "Can anyone do anything at this point—something we might do to help you, or to help Rory?"

His eyes flared with fire. "Aw, Charlie, it ain't your problem but I'll tell ya, now that I know I don't have much time left, I'm real tempted to go after that prosecutor and the judge myself."

I fully believed him. At this moment he looked like a man who would do *anything* for his son. I reached over to where he sat in his recliner chair and placed a hand on his forearm. Even as my mouth opened to speak I had a feeling I might regret what I was about to say.

"How about if Ron and I look into the matter and see if we can come up with some new evidence in Rory's case? Something might come out that would exonerate him."

I imagined that I heard a little sputter from Drake's corner of the room but my eyes were on Fergus to see what his reaction would be. I didn't have any sense of deception or hidden agenda from him. If anything, the tremble in his lower lip indicated pure relief. Surely if he knew his son to be guilty, the last thing he would want was a private investigation firm digging back into the case.

"Charlie, that would be wonderful. I got a little life insurance policy. It's yours if you'll put in the time to get my boy back home." He coughed deeply. "Trust me, it won't take long to get you paid from it."

"Let's not worry about the money right now," I said.

I pulled a small notepad from my purse, determined to get some answers. I started by telling Fergus what I had read in the papers and came right out and asked him if he had helped Rory to escape. At first I could tell he wanted to deny it—obviously he had been denying it for years now—but after a moment he merely nodded his head. "Yeah, I helped him."

"Once Rory had gotten safely away what did you do next?"

"First I tried to talk some sense to his defense attorney but the woman was loaded with cases and told me she had done all she could do for Rory. Personally, I think the embarrassment of losing such a public trial, with all the details in the papers, had humiliated her. She brushed me off, and after a couple of weeks wouldn't even take my phone calls anymore."

"What did you do next? Did you try going to the prosecutor's office? Or higher up in the court system?"

"What would be the point? That was the bunch who turned on Rory in the first place. They weren't doing nothing to help get him off. Plus I was afraid the more I brought up his name the harder they would start trying to look for him. You gotta understand, I was taking a lot of heat for this myself cause they knew—they suspected—that I'd helped him."

"So, you tell me Fergus. What can I do to help?

"Start with Herman Quinto and then take a look at Judge Blackman. That man's crookeder than a snake and dirty all the way through. In fact, if I could, I'd …"

"I have to tell you Fergus, going after Quinto won't be easy. He's a state senator now, and with the election for Congress this year he's got a lot of powerful friends."

I wished I hadn't been quite so frank. Fergus drooped in his chair like a balloon I'd let the air out of. I wanted to pose a dozen more inquiries, find out the names of other people I could talk to, perhaps witnesses who had been sympathetic to Rory at the time. But Fergus was clearly wrung out and I couldn't grill him any further. I would see what Ron and I might dig up, and maybe after a few days' rest Fergus could help us out again.

I turned to Drake and suggested he help the older man unpack his bag and get into bed; in the meantime I would go next door to see if the neighbor woman was a friendly sort who might lend Fergus a hand.

"I told him going on this long trip was a dumb idea," said the lady who introduced herself as Betty Wilkerson. She led me into a living room stuffed full of too-large furniture, complete with a variety of crochet-square afghans, throw pillows trimmed in lace, a collection of tiny elephant figurines in a glass-fronted cabinet, and two fluffy cats who glared at me with yellow eyes.

I went into the quick explanation of how we met Fergus and why we happened to be bringing him home, but didn't indicate that I had any idea why he'd gone to Maine.

"He seems exhausted at the moment," I told Betty. "I don't know if a few days' rest will help …"

"A little—maybe," she said. "I suppose he told you

how sick he is."

"Not the details. He just said he doesn't have long to live. So sad—he seems like a kindly man."

"Yeah, *now* he does. He can be quite a pistol. Don't know if he told you, he's refused all medical treatment. Did a round of chemo a year or so ago and thought he'd got the all-clear, but when this came back he said he's not going that route again. He humors the doctor just enough to be sure he gets pain medication. He's a stubborn old coot and he had a firecracker temper until this illness hit him." She paused, reflecting. "It's just so sad about his son. I know Fergus would give anything to have Rory around now, to spend time with him before he … before he goes."

I wasn't sure how much to reveal so I hedged. "Yeah, he told us a little …"

A wall phone in Betty's kitchen rang and she dashed for it. After listening for a few seconds her gaze slid over to me. Her head nodded. "She is?" A full-on frank stare at me. "Okay, if you say so."

I felt the pressure of her scrutiny—hers, plus the two cats. I hoped a nonchalant pose wouldn't reveal how unnerving was the spotlight of their stares.

"That was Fergus. He says you're a private investigator and you're gonna get Rory off."

"Uh, well …" I hadn't exactly promised that outcome.

"I just gotta say … Fergus has been a good neighbor. Before he got sick he helped me out lots of times. Mary Ann was the moon and stars to him and it nearly killed him to lose her, but that Rory—he's everything that man has left. Fergus would never ask his son to come back to New Mexico and risk going to prison, but I can tell you—it would mean so much for them to have some time together.

Please?"

And so, it looked as though I had a new case to work on.

Chapter 10

I didn't actually need to run it past my brother whether or not we would take Fergus's case. We're partners and if I push for it, I can pretty much do what I want. Still, it didn't bolster my confidence when I met Drake at the Jeep and he gave me one of those looks, the kind that says 'What have you got yourself into?' Obviously, he'd heard the other half of the call between Fergus and his neighbor and he was up to speed.

"Hey—you *said* you wished you could help." One of his dimples shows more than the other when he's teasing me.

"Okay, yeah ... be careful what I wish for, right?" I drummed my fingers on the steering wheel as we waited for a slow traffic light to change. But, joking aside, I really did feel for the family.

Now I just had to figure out where to start. I'd read the news articles with a focus on what had happened to Rory McNab and how he'd escaped his prison sentence. Those were the basic facts—I assumed they'd got that much right—but what lay beneath it all? If Fergus was right and Herman Quinto had a personal grudge against Rory—why?

Since it was on the way home, we popped by the hospital to check on Elsa. She seemed perkier, especially when Drake teased her, but I had to admit she was still a faded version of her prior self. I suppose the body at that age just doesn't bounce back from something this serious. Still, the nurse gave a positive report. We coaxed her to eat more of her half-finished dinner before heading out. From the car, Drake phoned ahead to Pedro's to order our favorite green chile chicken enchiladas to take home. I could tell he was feeling the fatigue of his long flight and we were both eager to settle at home together for the first time in weeks.

A good dinner, a hot shower together, and Drake was ready to tuck under the covers. We cuddled until his breathing became slow and deep, the utter relaxation he needed. I, on the other hand, had a mind whirring with questions and they all revolved around Fergus and Rory McNab. I slid gently out from under Drake's arm and rolled to the edge of the bed, then made my way silently to the kitchen.

Armed with a cup of good tea, I carried my computer to the couch and nestled against the cushions. I had bookmarked the sites where I'd read the articles on Rory's trial. A reread didn't reveal anything new, but I found myself paying more attention to little details. One photo, showing

Rory and his defense attorney descending the courthouse steps, caught my attention. Rory appeared to be a cross between pudgy, spoiled rich kid and slick successful lawyer, an image I felt sure he had groomed on purpose. Three other people were walking beside them. Fergus was in the background, noticeable because he wore jeans and a plaid shirt, while the others were in business suits.

A female with dark hair walked two steps behind Rory's attorney—I recognized her as a legal secretary with the firm where Drake and I had gone to update our wills last year. She had obviously changed jobs at some point in the subsequent years. Her name didn't immediately come to mind, but I could surely find it.

I went back through the articles, making a list of names. The defense attorney was Helen Bannerly, an attractive blonde with straight posture, pictured wearing a cobalt blue suit. There was Herman Quinto, of course, in another photo. His salt-and-pepper perfectly styled hair marked him as a sure success in politics. He was shown with a satisfied grin as he was quoted saying that justice had been served when the verdict came in. Beside him was an entourage of three others from the prosecutor's office. I wondered whether they still worked on that side of the courtroom or if they would have moved on to other careers, as Quinto had. One piece listed several of the witnesses and I jotted down their names. It would be a start.

I also planned to go back to the original trial, the one in which Rory had represented a small-time drug dealer and was later accused of tampering with the jury—the case which had led to Rory himself being on trial. At the time, he'd been head of a small firm—just himself and a partner, Christopher Brown. Since Brown was not included in the indictments against Rory, he had obviously distanced himself the minute things began to turn ugly. I would look him up and see where his career stood today.

Among the crowd of reporters surrounding the victorious Quinto I spotted a woman who looked vaguely familiar, but that wasn't what caught my attention. She was staring at Quinto and the look on her face was one of pure hatred. Now, what was that about?

Suddenly, I had a lot of possibilities, and one lead can always segue into another. I saved the photo images and sent them to myself in an email. It might not hurt to have these with me on my phone when I began talking with the people from the case. One thing I've learned from Ron's investigative repertoire is to start with the easiest clues first. You never know what will come from a simple interview or where it will go. My plan was to begin tomorrow with a quick visit to our lawyer where I would chat up the secretary whose photo I had recognized and see what I might learn from her. In my experience, secretaries often know far more than their self-centered bosses.

With a written list at hand, photos of the central players, and the clock showing nearly midnight, I shut down the computer, rinsed my tea mug, and yawned my way to the bedroom.

Drake was up at daylight, wanting to get to the airport to perform some minor maintenance and clean up the helicopter in time for a job scheduled for tomorrow. I took enough time to toast an English muffin for myself, feed the dog, and go next door to Gram's to water her neglected houseplants. I could now give a positive report when I stopped by to visit her later in the day.

Freckles gladly hopped up to the back seat of my Jeep

and we headed toward the office. In another hour the law offices a block over would be open and I would begin the first of my inquiries on behalf of Rory McNab. I used the time to start the coffee and check messages on the office line, since our part-time receptionist, Sally Bertrand, had left word that she had to take her kids for vaccinations or some such thing and wouldn't be in until mid-morning. It's all I can do to keep up with appointments for myself and one dog—thank goodness I never added kids to the mix.

Armed with a steaming mug and accompanied by the brown and white blur who raced up the stairs ahead of me, I settled at my desk to take care of some billing for clients whose cases Ron had worked while I was out of town. Time passed in a happy blur as I watched the Receivables column grow. At some point Ron stuck his head in to say good morning. Sounds downstairs indicated Sally had arrived, and a glance at the time showed it was well after ten. Time flies when you're making money.

My empty mug in hand, I stepped across the hall and, for once, caught Ron *not* talking on the phone. I briefed him quickly on my visit with Fergus McNab and the fact that I'd landed us a new case.

"This is the one we talked about the other day, right?" he asked. His attention darted between a litter of notes on his desk and his computer screen.

"Right. Rory McNabb, hotshot lawyer accused of jury tampering, Herman Quinto was the prosecutor at the time."

"Yeah, yeah. So what's the plan?"

"I've got a list of people to interview, mostly the legal teams from both sides during Rory's trial."

"Lawyers and politicians. Fun." He made a smirky

little move with his mouth. And this is the guy who thinks nothing of tracking cheating spouses. I didn't see much difference—a rat is a rat.

"I'm starting with the easiest. A legal secretary in Rory's defense lawyer's firm just happens to now work for the firm where Drake and I did our wills. She was friendly then— I'm hoping she'll be up for having a coffee or something."

"Good luck. Oh, I stopped by to see Elsa this morning. There's a good chance they'll release her to the rehab center by the end of the week."

"That's great news!"

"They want a family member to help her settle in, and if she's released to go home, you do realize you're the logical person to be there with her."

Yikes. "Can you …?"

"I'm up to my eyeballs in background checks right now, Charlie. Intel just hired a slew of new developers and they all have to be vetted before the end of the month. I might spare a little research time if there's some way I can help with the new case, but I just can't break away for anything more, at least not for a couple weeks."

I realized the truth of it, not to mention Ron would not be the best at elder-sitting if Elsa was home alone. She needed a woman companion, so it would be me or Victoria unless we came up with some hired help.

With all that hovering at the back of my mind, I got Freckles into her crate with the lure of a treat, grabbed my purse, and headed out the door.

Chapter 11

The law offices of Sanchez and Bean are only a block west of our own and one street over. I should have walked, but I made the excuse that you never know when you'll need quick transportation in this business. I got in my Jeep and arrived approximately two minutes later.

John Sanchez is a lawyer who probably began practicing about the time my dad worked at Sandia Labs—he's been in the circle of our family acquaintance that long. Ron and I joke that he'll surely retire one day, either that or they'll just prop his cold, stiff body in his chair and let him stay on forever. His walk may have slowed but his mind hasn't, and as long as he's sharp on the subjects we need him for, we'll keep going there. Fortunately, he's kept a string of younger associates and paralegals to do the heavy lifting.

His secretary was the one I remembered from our

visit last year and who I spotted in the photo from Rory McNab's case. Her dark hair had grown longer, falling in graceful curls below her shoulders. Model-perfect makeup, an expensive suit in brick red, and matching pumps—she made me feel like a street urchin in my jeans and hoodie. She greeted me with a quizzical look.

"I know, I don't have an appointment …" I confessed. "I was hoping to pop in and get another copy of my will?"

She'd been friendlier when we came according to protocol and spent our billable hour with her boss. I noticed her purse had been on the credenza behind her and she reluctantly slipped it into a drawer. I'd interrupted her attempt at an early lunch, but she put on her professional smile.

"Certainly. If I recall, it's Parker … Charlotte."

"Wow, excellent memory." I sent a high-beam smile her way, being a complete toady.

She indicated the chair in front of her desk and excused herself. She disappeared into a room down the hall and I heard a metal file drawer open. In precisely two minutes, she was back with a manila folder in hand. Meanwhile, I'd removed my hoodie to reveal a decent angora sweater and wiped a smudge of dust from one of my boots. I wondered if my morning swipe of lip gloss had worn off already (probably), but this was about the best I could do to make myself appear more businesslike in quick order.

"I'll run a copy of it for you," she said. "Let's just make sure this is the document you need." She handed some stapled pages over to me.

I glanced over the first page, then flipped to the end where I had signed and dated it. "This is the one."

Away she went and I heard a copier whirring, one that apparently ran a lot more efficiently than ours. The pages were done, collated, and stapled before I had the chance to do more than notice the nameplate on her desk. Kate Letterman.

"Thanks, Kate, I really appreciate this." I pretended to study her face a moment. "You used to work for Helen Bannerly, didn't you?"

"Um, yes. That's been a while back." She gave a glance toward Sanchez's closed door.

"I'm working an old case from about ten years ago …" I handed her one of my RJP Investigations business cards.

Another nervous glance.

"Oh, I'm sorry. You were on your way out and I interrupted. Could I buy you lunch and chat a bit? Or we could set an appointment later this afternoon?"

She searched for a reasonably polite way to refuse. "I was just going to grab a sandwich and bring it back—"

"Perfect. Munchies? I was heading there myself." It was a good guess that she would choose the most popular sandwich shop within two miles. "We can ride over together and have plenty of time for what I need."

Yes, I know. I was being pushy and obnoxious. If she'd been a bit older and more confident that she wouldn't piss off a valued client of the firm, she would have told me to buzz off, but she wasn't and she didn't, and I bulldozed my way into her car for the ten-minute ride.

"We're looking into the old case against Rory McNab," I said, realizing small talk wouldn't work well at this point. "Helen Bannerly defended him and you worked for her during that time, right?"

She nodded, concentrating on the oncoming traffic at the intersection where we'd stopped. "You could talk to Helen—she's now with Wickman and Harding—but you do realize anything she and Mr. McNab talked about at the time falls under attorney-client privilege."

I mentally filed the name of the new firm. I'd been under the impression that, back in the day, Ms. Bannerly was on the fast track for senior partner at the old firm. Maybe that went away when she lost the McNab case.

"A lot of people seemed to think Rory was innocent," I said. "And Helen Bannerly was a good lawyer. What went wrong?"

We'd arrived at the popular restaurant and Kate stalled by parking and locking the car. "A *lot* of people?—meaning his father?"

We walked inside, precluded from saying much while we studied the menu and placed orders at the counter. I shoved my credit card forth to cover the food. Kate added a dessert at the last moment. No dummy, she might as well get something for the effort of putting up with me. We stepped aside to wait until our number was called.

"Okay, yes, his father," I admitted. "Fergus is elderly now and terminally ill. He'd like to see his son exonerated."

A flicker of sympathy crossed her face. "Any parent would. Especially when the golden son had such great plans. Rory would have run for state Senate the following year. It's a big dream to give up." She said Rory's name with a softness that told me there had been some feelings, at least on her part.

Our order came up, packed into two white bags, as we'd requested. Kate still wasn't going to give me her full lunch hour. We carried them to the car and I got right to the questions again as she started her engine.

"So, what do you think? Was Rory really guilty, as Herman Quinto tried to make it seem?"

"I sat through the trial," Kate said. "Helen wanted her secretary handy in case we needed some last-minute documents or something. Plus, I was able to act as a buffer between the lawyer and the family. Fergus McNab became quite angry at what he perceived were Helen's deficiencies in the defense."

"Was he right?"

She bristled a little. "*I* didn't think so."

"Back to my original question … Was Rory guilty?" We were nearing her office, and I didn't have much time for more details.

Her eyes grew soft and she shook her head slightly. "I don't know. At the time, I thought the verdict was pretty harsh."

"And his sentence? That seemed extreme, didn't it?"

She'd parked next to my Jeep, a clear sign it was time for me to get out. "I really can't comment on the case, Ms. Parker. Sorry."

"Can I get a copy of the trial transcript?"

"Normally, the attorney would keep one, but since Helen Bannerly is no longer with the same firm, it's unlikely she would have it. It's better to request a copy in writing from the court."

I could see that dragging on a while, but I would do it when I got back to my computer.

"Depending on the case, some courts seal the records and others only keep them seven years."

"Kate—I get the feeling you cared for Rory McNab. Can you tell me anything that would lead me in the right direction to get him off?"

"Again, I'm sorry but I can't comment on it." She picked up her lunch sack, locked the car with a beep of the key fob, and strode toward the building, heels clicking on the sidewalk.

Can't, or *won't*? I muttered a few impatient phrases as

I got into my own vehicle. I've seen lawyers remain close-mouthed about old cases, but I could usually work my way into a secretary's confidence. I must be losing my touch.

Kate disappeared into the building. I had a perfectly good sandwich for lunch, and it was a lovely autumn day. I buzzed back over to the office, where I got Freckles and her leash, and we walked the few blocks to a tiny neighborhood park.

No one was around so I let her off the leash for a good run, but she'd already sniffed out the chicken salad from my enticing white bag and wasn't going anywhere more than five feet away from me. I planted myself on the ground at the base of a sycamore that hadn't begun to shed its leaves yet, sitting cross-legged in the shade and delving into the lunch bag. Freckles got a potato chip and immediately wanted another. I savored my chicken salad on whole wheat and pondered what to do next for the McNabs.

A visit to Helen Bannerly was a must, although I held little hope that she would simply open up and tell me much about Rory McNab and why she lost his case ten years ago. Would she even remember him, considering the time gap? But then there had been the hoopla about his disappearance. Surely she had been questioned about that. Yeah, she would remember.

I tossed a stick a couple of times for the dog but she was far more interested in snagging the final crust from my sandwich. It's a bad habit to start with a dog, creating a routine that involves a treat every time I put something into my own mouth—don't do it.

Great advice, but I did it anyway. We were soon back in the car and I was driving up Menaul Boulevard to the offices of Wickman and Harding. I lucked into a shady parking spot when a big white Suburban backed out.

It occurred to me that Helen could easily be in court today or on vacation to Barbados or something, so I pulled one of my tried-and-true tricks by calling the office and asking to speak with her. The receptionist put me through to Helen's secretary, who asked if I had an appointment but, although I admitted I didn't, agreed to put me through when I kind of made it sound as if I worked in the governor's office.

Of course, my real motive in calling ahead was to be sure Ms. Bannerly was in the office and was not in the middle of an appointment with someone else. I left windows open for Freckles, reviewed my face in the mirror and added a touch of lip gloss, picked up my purse and headed toward the building's elevator. I walked into Suite 302 in time to spot Helen Bannerly at the desk of a secretary, so I breezed past the receptionist (as gatekeeper, she was not a very good one since she barely protested) and walked directly up to my quarry.

"What was this person's name?" Bannerly was quizzing her secretary and the poor woman seemed a bit flustered.

"She said it so fast I didn't catch—"

I inserted myself. "That would be me." Before either of them could question how I'd appeared so quickly, and that I was dressed nothing like a high-echelon government employee would be, I tilted my head toward the door with Helen Bannerly's name on it. "Could we …?"

Whether she had the innate politeness that tends to make us non-confrontational or simple curiosity, the lawyer led the way and I tagged along, closing the door behind us. Now I had to decide how to play this—stick with the illusion that I was connected to the governor's office or 'fess up about my real reasons.

Chapter 12

As I took a chair, I compared the Helen Bannerly sitting behind the desk with the images from ten years ago in the newspapers. Same blonde page hairstyle, although a few silver threads had woven their way into the gold. She'd arrived at a comfortable weight for someone in her fifties, although the thought flitted that perhaps she'd been under a great deal of stress during Rory's trial, accounting for her rail-thinness back then. Blue was still the color of choice for her business suit and I saw the reason why—it complimented her eyes beautifully.

"All right," she said, focusing those eyes on me. "What's this about? I don't believe I've ever received a personal visit from someone in the governor's office."

I let the moment for confession slide right on by. "We're looking into the Rory McNab case." Hey, that much was the truth. "You were his defense attorney."

She sat back in her chair, her mind clearly looking for some clue as to why this was coming back now. All she gave me was a vague nod of agreement to my statement.

"You weren't assigned as a public defender; your firm took the case because you believed Rory was innocent of the charges?"

"The head of the firm wanted us to take it," she said. "The story was getting a lot of press and he thought it would make a name for us. I was on track for senior partner and pushed to be assigned the case. If it made a name for the firm, it would make me golden."

I noticed she hadn't exactly answered my question about Rory's innocence. "You must have had good reason to believe you could win—witnesses to rebut the charges or at least to stand up for his reputation and character?"

"To tell you the truth, Ms. ..."

"Parker."

"Ms. Parker, I really have little memory of the specifics of the case now. It's been years. I moved on."

She didn't say as much, but I wondered if the 'move' was because her previous position went away after losing such a public case.

"I handle an average of twenty clients at a time now, complex corporate mergers, real estate deals ... I deal with each as it comes up; once finalized, I move on. I can't bring up details of a case from last summer, much less from ten years ago."

Including the most public trial, and its aftermath, that you've ever been involved in? My skepticism rose a good twelve notches.

"Surely you remember going up against Herman Quinto. The man spends a lot of time in the spotlight, especially now that he's running for national office."

Some emotion flashed across her face, gone in an instant. The blue eyes blinked and she looked down at her impeccably neat desk top. She sighed. "Look, I'm tired of being asked about that old case. It was only one of hundreds. It meant very little then and it means nothing now."

"Do you have the files? I'm sure we would like to review those."

"Nothing. Anything I might have had at the time was left behind when I left the firm, and they have a policy of destroying case files after five years. You have to understand; it would require a warehouse to keep everything, especially on closed cases."

That much was probably very true. I'd seen lawyers arrive at court with three or four cartons of files. Simple math would tell me they must have thousands of such boxes in their offices.

A ping came from the cell phone she'd laid beside her desk blotter.

"You'll have to excuse me. My next appointment is here." She stood, making it clear she meant *now*.

I didn't see anyone in the waiting area and suspected the well-timed reminder message was standard office procedure to get rid of anyone who overstayed her welcome—in this case, me. Which was fine; I'd gotten all I would from her—precisely nothing.

Out in the car, I did a quick online search for Rory's former partner, Christopher Brown, and came up with a complete resume, including the fact that he now headed a twenty-person firm in Santa Fe. I called the handy number on their website, but the gatekeeper told me Mr. Brown was not taking any new clients.

"This is a personal matter and I only need fifteen

minutes of his time," I pleaded.

"He has a short opening at one-thirty."

I would have to break every existing land speed record to make it, so that was out.

"He's in court the rest of the week." The tone of voice implied something weighty.

I made an appointment for Monday morning, knowing full well I wouldn't wait around for that one. There had to be a better way. I ended the call with my devious little mind full of all kinds of ideas.

My poor little doggie was tired of guarding the vehicle and waiting for me to run all these silly errands, so my first priority was to take her home. It would give me the chance to pick up a few things Gram had requested. She was feeling feisty enough to want her own pajamas, robe, and toiletries. With careful planning and precision timing, my afternoon might unfold the way I wanted.

Freckles raced around the back yard with complete abandon. While she sniffed the chrysanthemums that were still in full bloom, I popped next door to gather Elsa's wish list. Packing everything into a small tote bag, I locked up and went back home to give the dog an early supper and see her settled comfortably in her crate. While Freckles munched, I checked in with Drake. He'd finished the oil change on the helicopter and was polishing the windows in anticipation of tomorrow's job for the Fish and Game Department.

One more stop, checking on Gram at the hospital. She was napping, so I set the tote bag where she would see it and stepped out to speak with the nurses.

"Looks like Friday," the nurse said, consulting Elsa's chart. "She'll go to Sunrise Rehab where they'll work with her and assess her independence level. If she passes the tests for dressing, feeding, bathing and toileting on her own, she can go home." She gave me a bright smile. "Of course, you realize a lot of patients her age still require some help with those things. It would be best if she can go home with someone else, stay with a family member, have someone stay at her home with her …"

All the things Ron and I had talked about. Unfortunately, we still hadn't reached any conclusions. I thanked the nurse and told myself I would get back with my brother on this question soon. Meanwhile, I had come up with an almost-surefire way to chat with Rory's former partner.

I had the hour-long drive to Santa Fe to ponder it all, but my mind kept skipping ahead to Fergus and Rory McNab, hoping I wasn't too late to get some answers before Fergus was no longer around to welcome his son home. Fortunately, the afternoon traffic was in my favor—southbound was insane; my northbound direction, only partially crazy. I'd determined my best bet was to exit I-25 at St. Francis. Christopher Brown's office was on St. Michael's Drive, roughly in the area where the hospital and a lot of medical offices are. I wondered if that spoke to the types of cases the firm handled.

The sun was low in the west now, and most of the various office parking lots held only a few cars. It seemed the time of day when patient and client appointments were finished; a few staff remained and most of those were headed for the exits, going to cozy homes, warm dinners, and helping kids with homework. Or so I imagined.

The address I'd found on the website came up on the right and I whipped into the parking lot on threat of being run down by an aggressive driver who clearly didn't like someone address-searching on such a busy street. The building looked like dark brown adobe, a color within the Santa Fe building codes. Every window on the second floor was brightly lit. Would Brown's be like those big-city law firms where they pride themselves on working half the night? I didn't want to summon up the patience for that kind of waiting game, but I backed into a parking slot so I could watch.

Ten minutes later, meeting adjourned, lights began going out and people emerged one-by-one from the front entry. I realized I might not recognize Brown in the dim evening light, so I left the Jeep and walked to the double doors. I had a good idea what he looked like, provided his photo on the firm's website was even close to current. Dark hair, trimmed short, goatee (although facial hair has a way of changing on a moment's notice), green eyes, high cheekbones, a nose that was a little too rounded to qualify as handsome. I stood just inside the doorway, watching until I saw him come down the stairs.

"Christopher Brown?"

He turned toward me with an open gaze.

"I need to ask about Rory McNab." I introduced myself and told him I'd been hired by Fergus. "Could we talk for a few minutes? I'll buy you a drink, if you were heading somewhere."

"Just home. I'll pass on the drink. Rory, huh? Wow, that's a name from the past." He shifted a heavy briefcase from one hand to the other as two middle-aged women walked past. "Look, the lobby isn't the most comfortable ... Want to come up to my office?"

I followed him up the stairs, through a reception area and past a grouping of cubicles to a spacious office with windows that offered a surprising view of the city. I hadn't realized this spot sat a bit higher than most. The room had a recently occupied feel—coffee mug on the desk, two thirds full of milky-looking brew, wastebasket half full, a faint warmth from the computer terminal at the corner of the large pine desk.

"So—Rory. What questions could you possibly have about him?" He plopped the briefcase on the floor beside his credenza and took a seat behind the desk. I sat across from him, although he hadn't specifically invited me to.

"His father, Fergus McNab, is dying."

"Oh, sorry to hear it. I remember Fergus. Kind of a crusty old guy. Must be in his eighties now?"

I nodded. "I gather he and Rory were always close."

Christopher waggled one hand in a 'maybe' type of motion. "Fergus was very proud of Rory, of his success, especially when he started talking about running for the state Senate."

"But …?"

"I'm not sure the admiration went both ways. Sorry, I shouldn't be saying that. Rory just didn't want to grow up to be a farmer. He had his sights set on fancier, more glamorous things for his own life. It wasn't that he was ashamed of Fergus, not exactly. He just didn't want to *become* him."

"And yet Fergus put everything out there when Rory got in trouble, even going so far as to help him escape."

A sharp look from Brown. "That was never proven. I mean, the police questioned everyone connected with Rory. Fergus got the lion's share of the interrogation, but they never arrested the old man."

Not sure how much I should say, I changed the subject.

"What about the case against Rory, the jury tampering—was he guilty? Ten counts seems rather extreme."

"It was. Come on, anybody who watches *Law and Order* could tell you one juror can throw a case. Why would Rory take the risk of messing around with ten of them?"

"It doesn't seem logical. Maybe it was the nature of the case—I read somewhere that he'd defended a man accused of dealing drugs."

"Ah, yes … what was that kid's name … Baca. Damian Baca. I say 'kid' but he was legally an adult. Nineteen, I think. He came from a good family, one both Rory and I knew. Neither of us believed he was guilty and the evidence was skimpy. Everything was going our way and the jury found in Damian's favor. His grandmother was so thankful she even kissed Rory on the cheek after the verdict was read."

"So, what went wrong?"

"Herman Quinto. As a prosecutor he had the reputation for getting things done, cleaning up the streets, so to speak. He was on a winning streak with cases where he was putting drug dealers away for hard time. He couldn't believe he lost the Baca case and he vowed to get back at Rory."

"So he made up these jury-tampering charges? Wouldn't there have to be some basis?"

"It roared up on us like a freight train. Suddenly, there were deputies from the U.S. Marshals' office raiding our place and seizing files. Rory was served with a warrant. Both of us were sputtering like idiots. We had no idea where these charges had come from."

"But how—?"

"Somebody got to them. That's all I can figure." He noticed the dirty coffee mug and turned to set it behind him on the credenza. "Jurors who'd been amenable to our case suddenly testified that they'd been approached by members of the Baca family who hinted that Damian's lawyer sent them. The Bacas denied it, but Quinto made the argument that of course they would deny it. Guilty people deny incriminating evidence all the time. He came up with a couple of handwritten notes of a threatening nature, even had some recorded phone calls, evidence Rory swore he'd never seen before."

"Did he *prove* those came from Rory …?"

"It was very shaky. We were stunned when the verdict came in, even more so at the sentencing."

"And you weren't dragged into it?"

"Luckily not. It was Rory's case, and he seemed to be the one Quinto was after."

"Any idea why?"

"I've thought about that a lot over the years. I told you Rory was planning to run for state Senate—it's the same seat Herman Quinto holds now. I think, when it came to a squeaky clean reputation versus a tarnished one, Quinto realized he needed to get Rory out of the picture or at least smear him so badly he'd never get elected."

During the drive home, my inborn skepticism kicked in. I wanted to believe Chris Brown—he'd seemed a genuine sort of guy—but I also had to remind myself that everything he'd said could also be used to cover his own ass. As Rory's business partner at the time, he would have tried to throw some distance between them. And, if that was the case, it had worked. Rory had spent ten years on the run, while Chris now headed a very successful law firm, by the look of it.

Plus, everyone involved was a lawyer or a politician—seriously, how much could I trust anything *any* of them said? Both Helen Bannerly and Kate Letterman had been hesitant to talk to me, and I didn't see either of them as the shy type.

I arrived at home to find Drake in the kitchen, working his magic with a couple of steaks and baked potatoes. When he handed me a glass of my favorite merlot, the happiness picture was complete. We finished our sumptuous meal, watched an action movie, and called an early bedtime. He would need to be airborne at daylight to head for the high country and count elk with his Fish and Game client. I snuggled in next to him, but my mind was a little too charged up to let me sleep right away—I'd learned something important today but couldn't figure out what it was.

Chapter 13

Drake made himself a hearty breakfast of oatmeal, toast, a green smoothie and, to balance out all that healthy stuff, two sausage patties. I think my terrible eating habits are rubbing off on him. I poured myself a cup of coffee and emptied the rest of the carafe into a thermos for him to carry along. He was out the door at five.

I felt a temptation to wander back to bed. The sun wouldn't peek over the Sandias for almost another two hours. I nixed the idea when I remembered the scattered dreams I'd had all night: a curious mix of visits to Rory McNab's remote cabin in Maine, the hallways of a nursing home where I was walking away from a crying Elsa, and a midnight raid on Helen Bannerly's law office where I was breaking into her files to find the information I knew she was hiding from me. Of the mishmash sent to me from dreamland, only the last one held any appeal.

I brewed another pot of coffee and brought out the news stories and photos I'd printed from Rory's trial. I found it hard to believe Helen Bannerly didn't recall details or keep records from what had probably been her highest profile case. Corporate mergers, if they made the spotlight, featured the moguls. Lawyers kept themselves very much to the background. She certainly wasn't one of Albuquerque's hotshot attorneys who regularly made the nightly news with an A-List of celebrity clients. Maybe if Fergus or Rory contacted her, perhaps they would have the right client-attorney credentials to get her to open up.

Or, it could simply be that she'd vowed never to discuss the most public humiliation of her career. The more I thought about it, the more that theory seemed plausible. I set the articles aside and was debating between oatmeal or a blueberry muffin—I'll admit it, the muffin was winning—when my phone rang. My eyes went immediately to the time; it wasn't quite six o'clock yet. An early morning call didn't bode well—especially with an elderly loved one in the hospital, a husband on a flight, and a client on the run from the law—my gut reacted accordingly. I didn't recognize the number and picked up the phone, almost wishing it would be a telemarketer.

"Miss Charlie?"

I recognized Fergus's voice. "Fergus, what's happened?" I couldn't help it. I was all set for bad news.

"Happened? Well, nothing new. I just wanted to check in with you before I head to my doctor's appointment in a little while."

His slight bewilderment told me he had no clue how early it was and that normally I would have still been sound asleep at this hour.

"You said you'd let me know what you found out about getting Rory's case dismissed. What's happening with it?"

Oh boy. "Fergus, I don't have any influence with the court. You know I can't get Rory's case dismissed. It's too late for that. But I have been asking around." I told him about my visits to Helen Bannerly and Christopher Brown.

"I liked his lady lawyer, that Helen," Fergus said. "She really took an interest in our case and said she'd get Rory out of that mess. Said the charges were stupid. Well, maybe that's not the word she used; it was something like that."

"Did she say what basis she was using to prove the charges were false?"

"Well, I don't know about any basis stuff. But she said the witnesses had been coached and several changed their stories. The ones she'd interviewed ahead of time, a couple of them didn't show. Every time she asked the really good questions, the judge would overrule her. Afterward, when they gave the verdict, she was fuming about the judge. She didn't like the man right from the get-go but at the end, she was real angry because she hadn't been able to get the case moved to a different … whatever you call it, get a different judge to hear it."

"What did Rory say about it, about the judge's integrity?"

I'd been skimming back through the articles while he talked and came up with the name of Judge Aldo Blackman. This was another familiar one in Albuquerque but I couldn't think specifically of what the connections were—politics, I was fairly sure, which made sense that there might be a link with Herman Quinto and with Rory's ambitions for the Senate. Could this whole thing be as simple as a judge and prosecutor wanting to get a young upstart out of the way in an upcoming election term?

"Fergus, did you, by any chance, receive a copy of the trial transcript at the time?"

"No. Rory suggested we get it, and I thought his lawyer was going to follow up on that but then she kind of disappeared on us. Went to work at a new place and then wouldn't ever call me back."

"What about the witnesses against Rory? Do you have their names?" I wasn't sure if I would be risking a witness-tampering charge of my own by contacting them, but it didn't seem likely this many years after the fact. And maybe I could learn something.

I heard papers rustling in the background and felt somewhat relieved to know Fergus wasn't relying only on his memory.

"Well, let's see … there was a lady named Emelia Sanchez and an older man called Fernando, but I didn't write down whether that was his first name or last."

Hm, big help.

"And there was a woman—I remember her because her husband was out in the seats near me and I got to talking with him. They'd been farmers too, and we talked about the weather and crops and such."

"And her name …?"

"Oh, it was Billie Jones."

"Any others?"

More rustling of papers, followed by a crash that sounded distinctly like a heavy ceramic object hitting the floor.

"Oh, shoot—there goes my coffee," he muttered. "Naw, I guess that's all the witness names I wrote down."

I thanked him for the information and let his distraction with the spilled coffee become the excuse to get off the phone. For now anyway, I had enough research to keep me busy. I wondered what were the odds I'd find any of the players from ten years ago, much less those involved in Damian Baca's case two years prior. There was only one way to find out. I brought my laptop to the kitchen table and pushed the file of newspaper article reprints aside.

I love those movies where the heroine sits at her computer, keys in one search word, and has the entire history of her quarry laid out on the screen, including a blinking dot showing where the person is right this minute. Let me just say, it doesn't actually go that way. By the time I had addresses and phone numbers for Billie Jones and Emelia Sanchez two hours had slipped by, and I still wasn't a hundred percent sure I had the right people—Jones and Sanchez are not exactly rare names in this part of the world.

Heading for the shower, I contemplated how this whole thing would be far simpler with Ron's help. He spends all day tracking down people's histories, doing employment background checks. Of course, he has a few advantages such as willingly given contact info and a social security number. I'd like to see him do any better with the skimpy memories of an eighty-year-old from an event years in the past. Not that it mattered. I let those thoughts wash down the drain with the suds from my shampoo. Today and the information I'd just located were all I had to go by. I dressed in my customary jeans and T-shirt after doing a minimal blow-dry and ponytail with the hair. I wasn't out to win any glamour contest today, just needed to smell and look respectable enough to get a couple of senior women to talk to me.

Freckles looked decidedly mistreated when I sent her to her crate for the day. "Sorry, kid. It's going to be too warm for you to wait in the car this time." She felt better when I handed a biscuit through the door and gave a pat to the top of her fluffy brown and white head.

According to the addresses I'd found—when online sources fail, try the old-fashioned printed phone book—Billie Jones lived closer. It had been a few years since I'd cruised this semi-rural area in the south valley, but it's a part of the city which has avoided the rampant suburban sprawl of the northeast heights and the west side. The street names and familiar sights came back to me as I drove through, looking for Bernal Road somewhere off the busier Atrisco. And there it was—a small ranch-style home sat on about a half acre of land, encircled by a chain-link fence three feet tall. I pulled to the side of the road and parked directly in front of the gate.

Right away, little signs pointed to the possibility that no one was home and hadn't been here for a while. Unmown lawn, a layer of sand on the sidewalk and front porch, no car in the drive. When I walked up to the door I noticed open drapes and no furniture inside. With no idea why, I pressed the doorbell button anyway.

"She's moved away," said a raised voice.

A dark-haired woman about my age, pushing a stroller with oversized wheels, had paused by the front gate.

"I'm looking for Billie Jones—is this her house?" I stepped off the porch and walked toward her.

"She's moved away," came the patiently repeated reply. "I'm the neighbor just to the west."

"Do you know where they went?" I remembered this was the couple Fergus had said were farmers; maybe they'd moved back.

"After Mr. Jones passed, their son from Deming came up and helped her get moved. She's in one of the assisted living places."

She didn't seem inclined to go on without something

more from me. Fair enough. "I'm looking into a legal matter on behalf of an elderly Hatch farmer, someone they'd met a few years ago. Do you know which assisted living place she's in?"

The neighbor pondered this a few seconds but apparently decided she didn't want to make the judgment call on any legal matter. "It's the Sunrise Home, off Central, near the hospitals." The baby started to fuss and the woman excused herself, saying it was nap time.

How convenient was this? The place had to be associated with Sunrise Rehab where Elsa was about to be sent. Was it possible I could kill two birds with one stone, so to speak, visiting with Billie Jones and getting an inside peek at the lifestyle there?

I hopped back in my Jeep and was on the freeway five minutes later.

Chapter 14

The assisted living facility looked like a place I wouldn't mind moving to myself, if and when the time came. Two-storied buildings of pale tan stucco, red tile roofs over tiny balconies, neatly tended lawn all around, with mature shade trees and flowerbeds filled with autumn blooms at their peak. A high fence of wrought iron surrounded the property but there was nothing prison-like about it. Vehicles could freely come and go through the open gates, and apparently residents could also own cars, as evidenced by the numbered parking slots versus those marked as Visitor Parking.

I pulled into one of the latter, shut off my engine, and picked up the flower arrangement I'd bought on a whim from a florist one block away. It seemed more prudent to show up bearing a gift than a notepad and a quiz. We would get to that part later—once I'd worked out how I would get an elderly woman to open her door to a stranger.

With no one in evidence at the reception desk, I bypassed it and took a look at the tenant directory made of white plastic letters on a black background under glass. B. Jones was listed for apartment 112, so I went by instinct and located it at the far end of a hallway on the ground floor. Many of the residents had decorated their doors with wreaths or cutely painted Welcome signs. Billie's door had none of that. I pressed the button and heard a fairly loud buzzer inside.

The door opened and a tiny, gray-haired woman stared through thick eyeglass lenses at the bouquet in my hands.

"Billie Jones?"

She nodded in a wobble-necked sort of way. Unsure of what to say first, I held out the flowers. She backed away and raised both palms.

"Who sent those? I hate flower arrangements. Reminds me of a funeral."

Okay, awkward. I apologized and set the flowers on the floor in front of a neighbor's door. "I'm so sorry. I wasn't thinking."

She started to close the door and I had to act fast. "I'm Charlie Parker and I just wanted to talk to you for a couple of minutes. Really. It has nothing to do with the flowers, and that was a bad idea on my part. I'm working for Fergus McNab."

Clearly, she didn't remember him, so I went into the quick explanation about Rory's trial. It took reminders about the dates and the names of the key players before a spark of recognition dawned.

"Oh, yes, what an aggravation, being called back as a witness against that young man."

"Could we talk inside for a minute?" Two people who'd passed me in the hall had blatantly craned their necks in my direction.

Billie backed into the apartment and showed me to a flowered sofa in a tiny living room. She perched at the edge of a chair, facing me.

"The original case, where Rory McNab was defending the drug dealer, Damian Baca—" I paused for her to catch up with me. "Were you visited by someone who told you to make sure Baca was found guilty?"

She toyed with the edging on the arm of the chair, running a nail along the seam repeatedly. "I don't remember that."

"What about later, when they came after the lawyer Rory McNab for jury tampering, you were a witness that time. Did anyone tell you what to say?"

"I don't like answering this." Her voice became shaky and I could tell she was so rattled that, even if she remembered, she wasn't going to say.

"Okay. I understand. It's scary being involved in court cases, isn't it?"

A nod.

I stood to go. "Let me leave my card with you. If you begin to remember anything about those times, especially whether any of the lawyers or someone else contacted you about how you were going to vote or what you would say on the stand ... would you call me? It's really important to an old man who's dying, and to his son. They may never see each other again if we don't figure this out."

Yes, that was rotten of me to play the dying-old-man card with a recent widow. A tear slid from the corner of her eye as I laid my business card on the coffee table. I gave what I hoped was a reassuring pat on the shoulder and let myself out. Heading for the elevator, I noticed the flower arrangement was gone from the neighbor's entryway. At least I had brightened someone's day.

Since I was near the hospital, I popped in to check on Elsa. She looked much more cheerful, sitting on the edge of the bed in her own jammies and robe. An orderly was in the process of helping her up.

"We were just about to take a little walk," the young man said.

I offered to take over, and Elsa requested a stop at the bathroom on the way. "Can you manage by yourself?" I asked. She seemed steady enough on her feet so I let her go in alone. This was one of those tests they wanted her to master before going home. It seemed like a good omen that she could do this. As soon as she came out, we walked the length of the corridor and back. It was a snail's pace, to be sure, but she barely leaned on my arm for support. Test two, passed.

Back in her room she was obviously tired so I helped her settle into bed while I filled her in on our new case. Taking an interest in outside events: another positive step. I watched until her eyelids began to droop, then gave her a kiss on the cheek and tiptoed out.

Emelia Sanchez's address was in the north valley, just off Twelfth Street. I wasn't familiar with the area, but the street grid was easy to negotiate once I got away from the tangle of freeway exits that seemed constantly under construction.

I found myself in a neighborhood of older single-story bungalows that probably dated back to the 1950s, little cinderblock and stucco places that must have been starter homes where the baby boomer generation was born. Mature trees were shedding golden leaves on the small squares of lawn. Pumpkins sat on more than one front porch, and cut-outs of skeletons in windows attested to the fact that some younger families had once again taken up residence.

The address I sought had showy flowerbeds along both sides of the short driveway and rose bushes in front of the porch. The woman who was aiming a hose at the flowerbed to the east looked up when I pulled to a stop. As I got out of the Jeep she shaded her eyes with one hand, trying to figure out who her visitor was.

"We already attend church," she said, eyeing the folder in my hand. She wore khaki slacks and a T-shirt with a light jacket tied around her middle. Strands of white ran through her straight dark hair, and her cocoa skin showed a sprinkle of freckles across her nose and cheeks.

"I'm not here about that, I assure you." I complimented her gardening skills, wishing I could get my own roses to look as good this late in the year. "I'm looking into an old legal case—Rory McNab, the lawyer who was accused of jury tampering. Do you remember it?"

"Of course. How could I forget? First being on the jury where he was the defense lawyer, then getting called back. They had me worried I was in big trouble."

"Why is that?"

"Well, they tell you the lawyer was going to prison for a long time … it made me really nervous."

"Could I go back to the original trial and ask what you remember?"

"Sure, as long as you don't mind tagging around the yard with me. I got all these beds to water and it's supposed to get pretty warm by noon."

We moved to the western edge of the flowerbed and

she laid the bubbler attachment at a high spot so the water would flow to all the plants.

"The case where Rory McNab was the attorney defending Damian Baca—you were a juror on that one, right?"

She nodded and moved the hose a couple of feet farther along.

"Did anyone approach you and ask you to vote a certain way, to find Baca not guilty?"

"Yes. I'm telling you the very same thing I said in court as a witness two years later. A man came up to me in the parking lot near the courthouse after the second day of testimony. We'd been hearing all this stuff about how Damian Baca was a drug dealer, he was corrupting little kids, he was working for some bad people. But, you know, I didn't see real evidence of how bad they made it sound. It seemed like he was dealing some pot to the winos that hung around down on First Street near the railroad tracks. They didn't really bring in any young kids or teens to say he'd sold anything to them."

"What did the man in the parking lot say?" We'd passed through a side gate and Emelia dragged the hose to a bed at the side of the house filled with pyracantha loaded with orange berries.

"He said he wanted to let me know that Damian wasn't guilty and he sure hoped the jury would agree."

"Did he say he worked for Mr. McNab's law firm?"

"No … not really, but he left that impression."

"Did you ever see him later—say, at the trial of Rory McNab?"

"Not then, no. The thing is—and I didn't say it back then—I spotted him at different places. He was out in the parking lot the next day, too, but he didn't come up to me then. Just hung around. He made eye contact with me, though. That same night I ran to the market for something and he was there. Stared at me when I came out. That scared me—I ran to my car and got in real fast and drove away."

"Did you find out who he was, his name?"

She shook her head. "I'll never forget what he looked like. Hispanic, probably about thirty, hard eyes, a scar near his upper lip. But I never learned his name. After the Baca trial I never saw him again."

"What about the other jurors—did any of them mention him?"

"Not at the time. But I noticed several of them who had been ready to vote guilty, they changed their minds. In the end everyone talked about it and decided the charges weren't that serious and the evidence wasn't … what do you say—conclusive. We unanimously voted that Baca was not guilty."

"How many of those jurors were called back to testify later, when Mr. McNab was on trial for tampering and getting people to vote his way?"

She'd begun to gather a pile of clippings near the corner of the house and dump them into a huge plastic bin. Now she paused and gazed skyward for a moment.

"Let's see … there was a businessman from the northeast heights. He was always impatient to get out of there. He'd been ready to convict Damien Baca from the start, and he was one of the last holdouts to change his mind. I think he went along just to get it over with, not really because he cared either way about the verdict. Anyway, apparently he wasn't one who was approached about changing his vote—or at least that's what he said.

Then there was an older lady, real unsure of herself, and she didn't seem to give straight answers. I remembered from the first time that she was a real nervous type."

"Do you remember either of their names?"

"The lady was Billie—I remember that because I had a friend with that name and their personalities were so different. The man ... he owned some kind of an import store. Had a weird name, Karkakian or some such thing. Most of us just went by Juror Number One or Two or whatever. We really didn't have to exchange names but some of us did. That Karkakian guy threw his name out there to let us know how important he was and when it was all over he invited us to come check out his store. Selling all the time, I swear he was."

I chuckled along with her.

"Do you think the lady, Billie, had she been approached by the same man who talked to you?"

"She never said but I kind of got the impression she did. She parked in the same lot where I did because we walked out there together after court. He easily could have found her."

Not that I would gain anything by going back to Billie Jones anyway, but it was interesting to note.

"I guess you heard that Rory McNab disappeared before he was actually sentenced or went to prison," I ventured.

Emelia paused in mid-stride. "That's right—now that you mention it. I'd forgotten. Is that what you're here about?"

"Indirectly. His father is dying and wants to see his son exonerated. If there's anything you can tell me that would help prove Rory McNab was not the one involved in contacting you ..."

"I wish I could say for sure," she said, eyeing me honestly. "My impression was that the man who came up to me somehow knew Damian Baca. They might have even been related … Don't quote me on that—it's just a guess. But whether Baca's attorney had anything to do with it, I really don't know."

Chapter 15

I left after thanking Emelia profusely and decided to head toward Old Town for a green chile fix at Pedro's. Drake would be away overnight, so I might as well feed myself sumptuously at lunch and be done with meals for the day.

Ron called while I was en route, checking on my progress with the case, and he agreed to meet me there. I arrived first and secured our normal corner table, giving a quick wave to a busy Concha behind the bar and noting another regular who appeared to already be working on a tequila shot. Manny is a grizzled old guy whose history I know nothing about, other than the fact that he's frequently to be found here at Pedro's at nearly any hour of the day. He drives a battered old pickup truck, but he must live nearby. Surely Pedro wouldn't fill him with tequila shooters and allow him to drive afterward. I picture him ambling happily home for a long siesta after his liquid lunch.

A basket of chips appeared magically on the table and I'd just taken my first dip into Concha's fiery salsa when Ron walked in. Pedro used hand signals to ask whether we wanted margaritas. In the evening I would definitely give that a thumbs-up, but with half the day still ahead I'd better keep my wits about me so I settled for iced tea.

Ron parked his Stetson on the rack near the door and took the corner seat so he could watch the room.

"I told Concha we'd want our usual," I said, once the first shock of the salsa subsided. Must be the season's new crop and a powerful one, at that.

While Ron made a good-sized dent in the supply of chips, I told him about my two interviews of the morning. "I thought I'd look up the other juror Emelia mentioned, the import store guy. He sounds like the kind of person who wouldn't be shy about talking."

"I can see what I might learn about Damian Baca," Ron said. "My brain is in background-search mode anyway right now."

Across the room, Manny stirred. "Damian Baca—pah!" he said with a disdainful look on his face.

I must admit to being startled; it was the first time in ages I'd heard Manny utter three words in a row. I turned to face him.

"What do you mean? Do you know him?"

He shifted on his barstool and scratched at the five-day whiskers on his chin. "My niece's kid. Punk hotshot. Always into something."

"I heard he was in trouble with the law about ten years ago," I said. "Is that a pattern with him?" For all we knew Damian could very well have gone to prison by now. At least we'd know where to find him.

Manny shrugged. "Maybe. But now he's got friends high up."

"What does—?" I stopped, realizing Manny had turned back to his drink. He drained it in one gulp and fished around in his pocket for cash.

I started to get up, thinking I would get more information, but Ron laid a hand on my arm. He was right—if we wanted to question Baca, maybe it wasn't smart to alert the family. Besides, our chicken enchiladas arrived just then and I'm not one to let a good, steaming plate of food get cold. We always knew where to find Manny another day if we needed more information.

"So, our next step will be to learn a little more about this Damian character," Ron said, after Manny walked out the door and sauntered down the street. "I'll work on that. See if I can ferret out who these 'high-up' friends of his might be."

"If you come across a Hispanic man with hard eyes and a scar on his upper lip, check him out too. He'd be in his forties now."

Ron gave me a look. Other than the scar, it could describe hundreds of men in this city.

"Just saying. If a man of that description is connected with Damian now, he very well could be the one who intimidated Emelia and probably Billie too. It would be worth tracking him down."

"I want to look more closely at the judge," Ron said. "Aldo Blackman is a familiar name and it seems he's risen socially and politically a lot faster than most judges ever do."

He wiped his hands on his napkin and pulled out his phone, doing a quick search. When he showed me the picture, I recognized the judge. Handsome in a Bill Clinton sort of way, with salt-and-pepper hair expensively styled, a well-cut suit, and a suitably coiffed woman of about his own age on his arm. The caption said 'Judge and Mrs. Blackman at the art museum's annual fundraiser soirée.' Ron scrolled through his search results and found two additional society events the judge had recently attended.

"Wouldn't it be convenient if one of these buddy-buddy shots had Damian Baca in it? We could certainly prove a connection that way," I mused as I scanned the other faces in the pictures. No Damian and no man with a scar on his lip.

We finished our enchiladas, split the check, and each headed in our own direction. Ron's mission was Damian Baca; mine was to figure out whether Fergus's assertion that the judge was crooked had any merit. My job seemed like the tougher of the two.

Since I was only a few minutes from home, I made that my destination. Poor, abandoned Freckles could have a run outside and I could make calls and do some online research from the comfort of my living room sofa. And if I felt a nap coming on after the heavy lunch, well, so be it.

It had turned into such a glorious autumn day that I opted to carry my work project out to the gazebo in the back yard where I knew, from past experience, our router signal reached fairly well. Watching Freckles and accomplishing something felt very productive. After a couple minutes of simply enjoying the view, I started my online search for Judge Aldo Blackman and his activities.

Initial results were much the same as Ron had turned up—social occasions and fundraisers were big at this time of year. I noted the types of places Blackman had been photographed publicly—cancer research, heart disease research, and a children's home were most prominent.

There was also the theater scene and finale to the season at the Santa Fe Opera. The man got around, I had to admit, and it gave me an idea, in case I wanted to manage a face-to-face meeting.

Meanwhile, a similar search on Damian Baca's name brought a different sort of results. Where I had half expected to see that he'd eventually been imprisoned for some sort of drug charges, it turned out he'd become gainfully employed at one of the casinos on the edge of Albuquerque. Somehow, he had even managed to get promoted to pit manager. Once again, I found myself enlarging the photos and looking for the man with the hard eyes and scar on his lip. Nothing showed up connecting such a man with Baca. Crowds at the judge's various social occasions yielded the same—no visible connections.

I stretched and yawned. It was still early in the investigation, and the answers to these things never simply drop themselves into my lap. Still, I couldn't help but feel some impatience—Fergus McNab's time was short. I decided to soothe my edginess with a brownie.

In the kitchen I put the kettle on to heat and found one lone teabag of English Teatime to go along with the last brownie from a package that was probably, technically, outdated. These things have so much preservatives in them it must surely be edible. I opened the cellophane and took a nibble, gave myself a little lecture on eating more healthfully and a promise to start tomorrow. Mug and brownie went back out with me to my comfy spot on the wicker loveseat.

The quick rush of caffeine gave me an idea and I picked up my phone. Judge Aldo Blackman's office number was included on the website for the judicial district, and a quick call put me through to his clerk.

"Hi, my name's Charlotte from the organizing committee, and we just wanted to check and see if the judge received his tickets? We're so hoping he's planning to attend."

"Is that for the theater gala Friday night?"

"Yes, exactly!"

"He'll be there. I'm afraid Mrs. Blackman has other commitments though."

"Oh, that's too bad. I'll just put him down as a party of one?"

"He may bring someone else. Better keep it at two."

I *so* badly wanted to ask who the other might be, but I had greater concerns. I thanked the woman and hung up, wondering how I would manage to snag myself a ticket.

What I discovered with one phone call was that, for the right amount of money, any group wanting your donation will manage to fit you in. I choked only slightly at the price, but I was in the door.

Now I had only one problem—what on earth would I wear?

Chapter 16

The air had turned cool, my brownie was gone, and Freckles had become bored with sniffing the garden plants so we went inside. I rinsed my tea mug and debated about making another cup, but my phone rang just then. Ron.

"Hey, I found out something interesting on Damian Baca," he said.

"He's pit manager now at Sandia Casino." I couldn't help myself. It's rare I get a jump on my brother.

"Okay, you found that, but did you also come across the fact that before he started this meteoric rise in career, he got busted for trafficking and did some time?"

"Score one for you. So, how did he manage to get a casino job? I thought a prison record nixed that possibility."

"In some places, I'm sure it does. You want the full story

or shall I leave you to keep up with your own research?" A bit of testiness in his voice.

"Sorry. Go ahead."

"Apparently, he laid low for a couple of years while Rory was under investigation and being tried for the jury tampering. Damian headed south and hooked up with a bunch down in El Paso. With easy access to the border, he had a tidy little business dealing pot and cocaine. Kept his Albuquerque connections and moved a lot of product. About three years into it, fate stepped in and he got pulled over on a traffic stop five miles from the state line, on the Texas side. An alert trooper hauled him out of the car and a passing Border Patrol officer initiated a search; they hit the jackpot."

"And I'm guessing Texas was not nearly as lenient with him as New Mexico had been."

"Nope. Damian's luck held, though. He had just under the legal amount for a harsher sentence, so he only had to serve three years. It was apparently a productive three years for him, as he met some guys who knew some guys … Anyway, he was better connected when he came out, so he came back to New Mexico and managed to bypass the usual hiring process. Someone granted him a menial job at the casino—sweeping floors or something."

"That's a far cry from his position today."

"Employment records get updated, the old background stuff magically disappears from the file when you know the right person … A year later, Damian's in the training program as a card dealer, two years after that, he's managed to work his way up the corporate ladder. Now he shows up for work every night in a tux and you'd never know he was a small-time cocaine dealer only a few years ago."

A flash came to me—Rory's silhouette standing in the doorway of his cabin deep in the Maine woods, isolated from everyone he once knew and unable to be at his father's deathbed. Meanwhile, the guy he'd sworn was innocent, wasn't. The real criminal had parlayed his know-how and connections into a lucrative job while he most likely continued to operate just the other side of the law.

I'd had a vision of a quiet evening with a good book but Ron's information sparked another idea. While Freckles scarfed down her bowl of kibble I went into the bedroom and perused my closet. A pair of form-fitting black jeans and a glittery blue top that left me with bare shoulders should work. I coaxed a few curls into my shoulder-length hair and added some extra mascara. It should be enough to help me fit in with the casino crowd, but not to the point where anyone would think I was a hooker.

I wanted to see Damian Baca in person and in his own surroundings, although I still hadn't worked out what I would say to him, if anything. Maybe I could learn a lot simply by watching. Leaving lights on in the house and Freckles to guard the place, I grabbed an angora pashmina Victoria had given me last Christmas, and headed out.

Traffic wasn't too horrible on the interstate—the afternoon rush was largely over. North on I-25, I aimed for the Tramway exit. My, how things had changed. I remembered when this Indian casino began in a large temporary building that looked like a giant tent, featuring nothing more worldly than bingo. Now, it had moved to the east side of the interstate, with the majestic Sandia mountains as a backdrop, and included a huge four-star hotel, golf course, world-class spa, outdoor amphitheater with big-name entertainment, and a buffet that would knock your socks off. You really can't convince me that the players are the winners at these places.

Midweek wasn't one of the hotter nights for casino play so I managed to grab a parking spot fairly near the main entrance. The bing-bing chatter of slot machines led me to the casino door and I steeled myself for the clamor, which tends to grate on my nerves.

A smile, a jaunty walk, a drink offered by a roving waitress, and my disguise as a patron was complete. I strolled the floor, past a dozen or more rows of slots and poker machines, not to mention the blackjack tables and roulette wheels, with dozens of people desperately putting money toward all of them, hoping a fortune would come their way. A couple of craps tables drew boisterous groups and I stood among one of these mini-crowds, scanning the action elsewhere until I spotted Damian Baca.

As portrayed in his photo on the casino's website, he wore a tux, a diamond stickpin in the lapel, and his dark hair slicked back from a low forehead. What saved him from looking like a punk mobster was the open smile with which he greeted the gamblers. He did, however, keep an eagle eye on the dealers. Of course, little black half-globe fixtures on the ceiling concealed security cameras, which no doubt had their eyes on every person in the place.

An enthusiastic player at the craps table bumped into me, sloshing the sticky sweetness of my Coke down my arm. With a giggled apology, she offered me a tissue but I opted to go into the ladies room for some water and paper towels. Freshened up, I made my way to a slot machine situated where I had a clear view of the pit and the podium that appeared to be Baca's work station.

While I pretended to hit buttons on the machine, I

saw him sign a dealer out and a new one in, pass some paperwork to another employee, and step over to one of the blackjack tables to settle some kind of dispute that cropped up between a dealer and a player. All the while, his eyes scanned the tables the way a hawk in a treetop would watch for a mouse in the grass below.

Each time I saw the gaze coming my way, I refocused intently on my machine. When the eyes went elsewhere I watched for signs of anyone from the past who might be in present-day contact. An hour with no hits and I was, frankly, bored. I don't know what I had expected, but if Damian was still up to his old tricks there was no sign of it happening here.

Maybe I'd been going at this all wrong, from the start. I left the casino noise behind and went home to shower off the smoke and desperation that clung to my skin. As hot water sluiced off me, I thought about other approaches to establishing Rory McNab's innocence.

What if Fergus had been right in his assertions that the judge was crooked? For what reason would Blackman have sided with Damian Baca against a respected officer of the court? Or, was Rory McNab not quite as respectable as his father wanted me to believe? It was late before I tucked myself into bed, much later still before my brain slowed down enough to let me sleep.

Chapter 17

Come daylight, I'd reached the conclusion that I needed to go back to the source, Rory McNab. For all this effort, I still had only his father's word that the son was completely innocent and had been railroaded somehow by the system. I also only had the sketchy details Fergus remembered or wanted me to know.

The old man had a taste for sweets, so I popped in at a favorite coffee place and got him a fully loaded caramel latte and a huge cinnamon roll, while I virtuously decided to limit myself to a regular coffee with fake sweetener. Taste-wise a mistake but it kept me from drinking much of it.

I tapped at the door of Fergus's trailer and got no response. Betty Wilkerson was out front, getting her mail from the box and I sent an inquisitive look her way.

"He should be there," she said. "Knock a little harder. He plays the TV pretty loud."

I didn't hear a TV set, but I gave a firmer knock anyway. Within a few seconds I heard a grumpy "Hold your horses" from inside. He appeared in faded plaid pajamas and a robe hanging open at the front.

"Hey, Fergus, just thought I'd check in." I ignored the food spill on the front of the pajama top. "Betty said you might have a few minutes?"

I held out the coffee cup and he sniffed at the lid. "Caramel?"

I nodded and he let me inside. The trailer was heated to a stifling level—it had to be at least eighty in there. I shed my coat immediately and followed him to the sofa. A cereal bowl with residual milk and corn flakes around the edges sat on the coffee table.

"I've been reading everything I can find on Rory's case," I told him, "and I've followed up on where the major players are now, but I have to admit that I haven't had much luck finding any kind of evidence that would exonerate Rory."

Fergus had settled in his recliner and was savoring the sweet coffee.

"It would be very helpful if I could speak with your son," I said.

"I can't give out his number," he immediately protested.

"You told me you talk with him somewhat regularly— can you place the call and convince him to talk to me?" I had come up with some things to ask during my mostly sleepless night. "I'll try to keep the call short."

He dithered, using an untidy newspaper as something to fuss with while he stalled. I gave him a steady gaze that dared him to come up with an argument. Finally, he set the now neatly folded paper down and walked to the kitchen. From one of the drawers he pulled a small black flip phone.

"Let me see now," he mumbled as he fiddled with it. "Is this the right one ...?"

He held it to his ear, muttered a mild curse, and tossed it back in the drawer. Another little phone came out, a red one. Some more fiddling, and it began to ring. He had the volume turned up so loud I could hear it across the room, even though he held it to his ear.

"Dad? What is it?" came a male voice.

"The lady's here," Fergus said. "That investigator I told you about. She wants to talk to you."

A lengthy silence. "You didn't give this number ..."

"Nope. She's right here. I'm going to hand the phone over. If that's okay with you, son."

There must have been a word or two of assent. The heater fan came on, masking other sounds, but he brought the phone to me.

"Don't even think of tracing this number," came Rory's voice. "I'll dump it in the lake and have another one by this afternoon."

"I won't do that. I'm just trying to help."

"I'm paying by the minute here, so get on with it."

I wondered where he was finding the money to live on. It didn't appear that Fergus had enough resources to spare. And the cabin was so remote it didn't look convenient for Rory to be holding a job in the nearest little burg called Grandy.

"Well?"

"Um, yeah. I've been looking into the various people who were involved ten years ago, including your defense attorney and your former partner. I just haven't found anyone yet with any idea who wanted to see you go to prison. So I figure you'd have a better feel for that. Surely you've relived the scene over and over—what comes to your mind? Why would someone come after you?"

"Listen to my dad. He's right in what he thinks. We've hashed this over a million times, and I think the answer lies somewhere between an inadequate defense and a corrupt judge."

"I've sent for the trial transcript but they say it may take a while because the case was so long ago. Unless you have a copy …?"

"I don't."

"And we don't have a lot of time to wait around." I tried not to glance at Fergus as I said it, but we all knew what I meant. "Rory, can you think of anybody connected with the Damian Baca trial—or your own—who might have been scared of you, someone you pissed off in some way?"

"Who would want to retaliate against me, in other words?"

"Exactly. Think about it for a few days if you want. Give me a call." I recited my number.

"I've thought about it for years, sweetheart. Trust me, I've been over every word of every meeting, deposition, and court day. What I've told Dad is all I've come up with."

"Still, if a new idea comes along, will you let me or your dad know about it? We all just want the best outcome for this."

I received a gruff reply, not exactly a warm or grateful response for someone who wanted to save your ass from prison. Then the connection went dead.

I handed the phone to Fergus, who stashed it back in

his top-secret kitchen drawer. It wasn't as if I couldn't find it again the moment he wasn't looking, and I'd bet a dollar that Rory's was the only number on his contact list. But for now I didn't see much point; Rory wasn't in a helpful mood.

Asking Fergus didn't net anything new so I left him to make preparations for his day while I decided what to do with mine. Before showing up tonight at a social occasion where I could observe Judge Blackman in person, I thought it might be a good idea to get some other perspectives.

Who knows things about a person, things that don't make the news or the Wikipedia profile? I drove away from the trailer park, mulling that question in my mind. The ready answer seemed to be coworkers and neighbors. I'd already prowled around for Blackman's personal information. His home address wasn't easily found but I came up with it. I also knew where he worked, and it was a big, wide-open public building that any citizen could visit. I set a course for downtown.

Chapter 18

It was nearing ten o'clock by the time I located a place to park, entered the courthouse, and passed through the security station. Perfect timing, it turned out. I hovered outside Judge Blackman's courtroom less than five minutes—not long enough to be questioned about my presence—when the double doors swung open and people began to stream out. I blended into the crowd, many of whom got as far as the corridor before pausing to look around and decide what to do with the twenty-minute break they'd been given.

One man was among the ones with a purposeful stride and a destination in mind. I recognized Mike Farmer because we'd been in school together, and the alumni newsletter had contained more than one mention of his various promotions at the Albuquerque *Journal,* to his current position on the courthouse beat. We ran into each other now and then around town, and he'd once confessed to having a crush on me in the sixth grade.

"Hey, Mike. I didn't know you were covering this case."

"Charlie—wow. I didn't see you in there," he said with a nod toward the now-closed door.

"I missed the morning session." I fell into step beside him. "So, how's the case going?"

"No real fireworks. My luck, it'll get two lines on the City Beat page. Pity—sometimes Blackman's court gets some juicy stuff."

"You got a minute?" I asked. "I'll buy you a coffee."

"Sure." He pointed toward the stairs, where the scents of food drifted up from the courthouse cafeteria. We opted for the quickest version, plain black coffee, and settled at a tiny table against the wall.

"You've covered the courts for a lot of years now, haven't you? I wonder if you remember a case about ten years ago, the one where a local lawyer got convicted of jury tampering." I doctored my cup with sugar from the little white packets at the table.

"The guy who disappeared?" His interest perked immediately.

Uh-oh. This might have been a bad idea, bringing a reporter in, especially one who might tend to land on the side of law and order. I gave a noncommittal nod.

"The judge who heard the case was Blackman, and I heard a rumor that he was secretly after the defendant, that he *wanted* the man convicted."

Mike shrugged. "Don't know where you got that. I remember the situation pretty well. I was just getting my start and had been sent to cover the crime beat, so I sat in on the trial of that drug guy—Damian something-or-other.

The other case came about when his lawyer was accused of convincing certain jury members to vote not-guilty."

I merely nodded. "Judge Blackman heard both cases?"

"Yeah, as I recall. Of course, the real nasty bugger in the room was Herman Quinto. It was no secret that he was planning to run for state Senate and the younger guy … McNab. That's it. McNab was this dashing handsome guy who'd come on strong with a big PR campaign and it was looking like he might actually win it."

"Quinto couldn't let that happen."

"There was scuttlebutt—Quinto had friends in Santa Fe and even bigger friends in Washington. If he could grab the state Senate seat that year, serve a couple of terms and pass some flashy legislation, the powers-that-be would see to it that he had funding for the national race, enough money so no one else would have a prayer of catching up."

"So, getting this Rory McNab out of the way was pretty important all around. I bet Quinto was livid when he didn't actually do the prison time."

"Not that I could tell. He accomplished his goal either way—McNab's reputation and political career were shot the moment the gavel came down with the verdict—guilty."

True enough. So, why did Rory go to such lengths to move as far away as he possibly could? He could have followed the appeals process if he thought his lawyer hadn't adequately defended him, could have used an investigator to dig up the truth from the jurors or some dirt on the judge, unless … There had to be more.

Mike glanced at his watch. "Look, it's almost time to get back." He stood up and drained the rest of his coffee in one long swig. "You coming?"

"I'll be along in a minute." I'd nearly forgotten my plan to watch Blackman in action this morning, so I stopped in

the ladies room on the way. I couldn't very well quiz Mike
Farmer during the proceedings, and I really didn't want
him to infer anything if I sat with him. This way, I could
take a seat near the back and duck out at my convenience.

It wasn't exactly a standing-room-only crowd and I
found a place on a back row that gave me a clear view to
the judge's bench. I discovered it didn't much matter that
I'd missed the morning's statements—quickly enough I
realized it was a case of a punk-looking young man accused
of drug trafficking, caught bringing a carload that he'd
likely obtained in Mexico or somewhere near the border.

Shades of Damian Baca, all over again. I briefly
wondered how many times a day, a week, or a year this
scenario played out somewhere in this state. Attempts
to curb the problem seemed extremely frustrating, and I
could see boredom on the faces of nearly everyone, from
the attorneys to the jurors. The only person in the room
who *didn't* seem bored was the judge. His attention kept
meandering toward the court reporter, a pretty woman
with long dark hair. She kept her hands on the keys of
her stenotype machine, but I occasionally caught a shared
glance between them. Interesting.

Chapter 19

Witnesses came and went. Apparently the prosecution had presented most of its case during the earlier sessions, essentially the testimony of the officers who had caught the suspect and confiscated the bags of cocaine from his vehicle. The defense, predictably, trotted out the poor, misunderstood lad's grandmother, his priest, and an older sister whose demeanor said she was tired of little brother being a problem. But she said all the right words. The judge told the prosecutor to wrap up his closing arguments, as the court had something else on the agenda this afternoon. The defense would give its wrap-up Monday morning.

Beside me, a young woman grumbled. I'd noticed her when I took my seat—college age, neatly dressed in jeans, a button-down white shirt, a trendy blazer, and short-topped boots. From the way she appeared to be studying the proceedings and making notes, I assumed she was a student in law or journalism. At her muttered comment, I turned a questioning glance her way. She flipped her notepad over and wrote across the cardboard backing: **He always does that**.

I raised both palms in a hands-up, *what?* gesture. She mouthed one word—Later.

Hm, interesting. I started to pay closer attention, trying to figure out what she'd been talking about. When court recessed thirty minutes later, I decided to stick with my new acquaintance and see what she had to say. We walked side by side down the corridor and past the security station.

"I swear, my professor was right. You really can learn a lot about how a case will go by watching the judge," she finally said, once we were in an open part of the lobby, clear of most others who'd been in the courtroom.

"Judge Blackman?" I prompted.

"He's one of the easiest to read. That move of having the prosecution close one day and the defense another day—I've noticed he always does that when he wants the defendant to get off. The jury will go into deliberations with the case against the guy, in their minds, as yesterday's news, while all the glowing things the defense attorney says will be fresh in their heads. In a way, it's the way the system works to favor a defendant anyway—innocent until proven guilty—but Blackman uses it, I mean actually *uses* it."

"But don't the proceedings just flow according to ... I don't know ... how it's done?"

"Okay, so today he says his schedule has something else on for this afternoon. What could be on a judge's schedule that's more important than the case he's hearing right now? You know what it is? Golf. He plays golf at

Tanoan and he never lets a case get in the way. And how do I know that? My dad often gets stuck playing right behind Blackman and his foursome. Dad says they act like they own the course. He played with them once, said the judge cheated like crazy, and—"

"But—back to the judge's calendar here today—how can he just … rearrange things?"

"He's the judge. He can do anything he wants."

Apparently. I thanked her. "I'm Charlie, by the way."

"Cat. Cat Brennaman." We shook hands. "Nice talking with you. Gotta go—I've got a class in thirty minutes."

"Sure. Thanks for the quick lesson on court procedure."
And more information than you ever dreamed you were giving me. I left the downtown area, grabbed a quick burger at a drive-up lane, and headed to the far northeast heights and Tanoan Country Club. I figured a little time hanging around could probably net even more info on this judge with the bendable ethics. If I could take that angle and figure out how Blackman's role might have played a part in Rory McNab's conviction, we might be on the way toward getting a new lawyer to take the case and appeal it.

The club was a bustling place this afternoon. I'd been here a few times and had a general idea of the layout. The large two-story building housed the main clubhouse and restaurant above, exercise rooms, locker rooms, and golf pro shop at ground level. The pool facilities lay to the west of the building, where during the summer months moms and kids would fill the lounge chairs and exchange whatever sort of country club gossip was going around. I couldn't quite fathom what that would be—it's definitely not my thing.

I found a parking spot close enough to the entrance that

I could watch the comings and goings, and was rewarded within fifteen minutes when I spotted Judge Blackman getting out of a silver SUV under the entry portico. His silver hair matched it almost exactly. He stood by while a valet pulled a huge set of golf clubs from the back and carried them to a waiting cart. Blackman handed the young man something, and the valet got into the SUV and drove it to a separate section of the lot.

Meanwhile, the judge hopped onto his golf cart and zoomed down a path, which I recalled led toward the pro shop. I could catch up with him later. I saw where the SUV ended up—a good way, I've discovered, to keep tabs on my suspect's comings and goings. Once the valet had locked up and headed at a jaunty pace back to his station, I strolled over to take a closer look at the vehicle.

When you might end up tailing a vehicle that looks like a bunch of others in the city, it's a good idea to note anything unusual about it. I memorized the tag number. Also, I noted a resident sticker in a corner of the front windshield from an upscale neighborhood called Sandia Heights. Planted in the foothills of the mountain, it's an area that was hot property forty years ago and has since settled into mature homes of gentility, the kind of place where successful people live to get above the fray of the city traffic.

With those two bits of information tucked away in my knowledge arsenal I followed the same route Blackman had taken down the sidewalk and found myself where the golfers gathered outside the pro shop. In my jeans I didn't exactly blend in, so I tried for an 'I'm busily on my way somewhere' attitude as I wove through the crowd.

People who had completed their rounds were reliving

the highlights, describing their brilliant strokes, and they were not the least bit interested in me. A voice over a speaker called the Blackman party. I pressed back against the building to watch as the judge and three other men hopped into two carts, laughing and joking as they apparently bet on how this would go.

Interestingly, the man approaching the passenger side of Blackman's cart was none other than Herman Quinto.

I slid my phone from my back pocket and aimed it surreptitiously in their direction, snapping off a few quick shots. For what purpose, I wasn't yet certain. It was probably no secret that a prominent Albuquerque judge and a Santa Fe legislator were social buddies.

Quinto had apparently forgotten something, hopping out of the cart to rush toward the pro shop. Blackman's jovial expression went dark. When the senator returned, staring at the screen of a cell phone, the judge spoke up a little too loudly.

"Hey, none of that on the course!" He probably meant it teasingly, but it didn't come across that way.

Quinto froze in his tracks. I sensed a showdown in the making. Would a state senator outrank a senior judge? Especially in what was seemingly only a matter of etiquette? Several other people were staring, alerted by the tone of Blackman's voice.

Quinto stepped over to the cart and leaned in close, saying something low. My little camera was snapping away. Blackman adopted conciliatory body language, although I couldn't hear his words. It appeared to be along the lines of, *Hey, just reminding you …*

As the voice on the speaker called their group to the first tee box, Quinto called out to one of the others.

"Dan! Come ride over here."

The passenger in the other cart gave a startled look but got out and switched places with Quinto. The senator pointedly stared at his cell phone as he walked over and took his seat in the other cart. Both drivers roared away from the pro shop, cresting a low hill and disappearing from my sight. Okay, that was interesting.

"May I help you?" The voice near my elbow startled me. It belonged to a young man in the Tanoan Club uniform. "Are you waiting for your golfing party?" This said with an obvious glance at my inappropriate attire.

"Oh! No, actually." I batted my eyes and put on a fake British accent. "Just gathering a few bits of information for my employer. Mr. McCartney is visiting Albuquerque next month and wanted to know of a nice, fairly private place to play some golf."

I received a blank look in return. Probably should have used the name of a younger rock star to impress this one.

"I believe I've learned what I needed to know," I said with as bright a smile as I could muster. "Thank you."

My phone rang just then, saving me from further conversation. I walked toward the front of the building as I took the call.

It was the hospital.

"Mrs. Higgins is ready to be transferred this afternoon," said the polite female voice. "We have it on our records that you wished to go with her over to Sunrise and help her get settled into her new room."

Was that today? I couldn't believe in my zeal to pursue our new case I'd completely forgotten one of the most important people in my life.

Chapter 20

I practically dashed through the parking lot and was in my Jeep before the hospital woman had hung up. She assured me Ron was there and would drive Elsa to her new residence. But knowing my brother, he would simply drop her bag on the nearest table and make sure a health care provider was there to get her settled. He would find it very awkward to actually tuck our grandmotherly neighbor into bed.

By the time I arrived at Sunrise Rehab, what I'd envisioned was pretty much what had happened. I found Elsa in the competent care of a middle-aged woman who introduced herself as Delilah. Ron was holding the tote bag from the hospital with Elsa's few toiletries and nightgowns; he was looking around the room with his investigator eye.

He looked more like the handrail inspector than a family member.

Delilah and I took over, showing our patient the way to her private bathroom and introducing her to the layout of the room and the facility. I put her clothes in a drawer and her toiletries in the bathroom. Some of the flowers from the hospital were still fresh enough to display. Ron brought them in and we set those in view on the dresser, along with the dozens of get-well cards from her church friends. By the time Elsa and her escort returned from the nurses' station, we had the place looking a tiny bit homey.

"This is nice," Elsa exclaimed, looking at the cards and flowers.

I showed her where I'd stashed her personal things.

"But I'll only be here until Monday," she said. "No sense spreading out."

My smile must have looked a little uneasy; she picked up on my hesitation. Fortunately, Delilah was used to this scenario and she took over.

"Mrs. Higgins, we just want you to be comfortable here, no matter whether your stay is a day or a month or more."

"More than a month! No way!"

I was afraid we'd have a wrestling match on our hands, but the caregiver had neatly steered Elsa toward the bed while giving her assurances. By the time of the little outburst, our patient was already sitting.

"Well, the doctor's going to be here later and he can give you some more information on that," Delilah said, deftly removing Elsa's slippers and lifting her feet to tuck them under the covers. "Meanwhile, you must be tired from the move. How about a little nap before dinner?"

"Maybe a short one. But you make sure I'm awake

when that doctor comes. I'll want to have a talk with him."

"Yes, ma'am. I will absolutely do that."

I stepped forward and took Elsa's chilly hands in mine. "Tuck in now. If I don't make it back by bedtime, I'll be here tomorrow." I pulled the sheet and blanket up to her shoulders and landed a tender little kiss on her forehead.

"Back by bedtime?" Ron asked once we were out in the hallway, well away from Elsa's room. "I thought you were going to that fundraiser thing."

"Oh shit—I'd forgotten that."

"It's all right," Delilah piped up. "Their first day is always a little stressful and doc likes to see that they sleep through the night so they cope well with their new routine in the morning. He'll give her a little something and she'll never know you weren't here. In fact, she might very well have a dream and believe that you were right at her side."

That only made me feel a tiny bit better.

Ron and I parted outside the facility and he assured me I should go ahead with my plans. If there was a need, he and Victoria were only ten minutes away. Truthfully, I was curious to look through the photos I'd taken this afternoon and to make some notes about the interviews at the courthouse before I forgot names and data.

I arrived home in time to take Freckles for a quick walk to the park before sundown, and when we got back Drake's truck was in the driveway.

"Hey, how was the Fish and Game job?" I asked, unclipping the leash from a wildly ecstatic dog.

"Good. But long. I really need a shower."

When I moved into his embrace and got a whiff of his flight suit, which smelled of jet fuel and sweat, I had to agree.

"I got us tickets to a dinner. All the champagne you

want and, for the price, probably a decent cut of beef."

"I'm exhausted, baby. But let's talk about it in the shower," he said with a leer.

It turned out he wasn't too exhausted for a proper greeting for the wife he hadn't seen in three days, and the shower session ended up in a tangle of covers on our king-size bed. After that, however, he really was exhausted. He sat back with a completely relaxed grin on his face.

"You go ahead to the dinner," he said. "I'll be happy with a microwaved frozen thing, really."

"I don't want to go—"

"It's up to you, but you said it might be important to your new case. And I don't mind. I will be deep in dreamland within an hour anyway."

That much was true.

I assured him I wouldn't stay late. Since I wasn't dressing to be belle of the ball, I settled on a pair of dressy black slacks and top, a silver pendant with a sizeable chunk of turquoise in it, and a Southwestern print silk jacket. If it turned out all the other ladies were in floor-length gowns, well, too bad.

The drive to the Marriott ballroom took me through a clog of freeway traffic but I used the time to review what I'd learned and observed today. Judge Blackman's subtle glances toward the court reporter, his flashy arrival at the country club and condescending manner toward the employees there, the argument with Quinto—all were interesting glimpses of the man, but I couldn't think of any way I could tie them meaningfully to the McNab case. Tonight, I would have to be extra diligent in keeping my eyes and ears open.

The fundraiser was set up along the same lines as others I'd attended in the past, although I'm saying right here that

I'm not normally involved in this part of Albuquerque's social scene. I walked in, feeling properly invisible.

One of the large ballrooms had been set up with dozens of round tables, each seating eight or ten. Probably because the theater group was involved, the decorations and backdrop behind the podium were very over-the-top, with set pieces from some of the more famous shows they'd presented. I recognized the chandelier from *Phantom of the Opera*, and a yellow brick road pathway had been created leading to the side room with the auction items.

According to the program I received, there would be a live auction after dinner with famous memorabilia, said to include two of Bernadette Peters' gowns from famous roles and the ruby slippers Stephanie Mills had worn in the Broadway *Wizard of Oz*. How an Albuquerque group had managed to snag those, I couldn't begin to guess. Previews of the auction items were offered to Platinum Level donors.

A woman who saw me studying the program spoke over my shoulder. "That means they've pledged in advance to bid at least twenty-five thousand during the auction."

She raised an eyebrow and I did the same, and we giggled. "Well, that wouldn't be me," I admitted.

"Me either." She glanced around. "I'm here by myself. Lisa Browning. If you don't have a dinner partner, join me if you want. I'm at table 15. A red shawl is draped over the chair I chose. Meanwhile, I'm heading for the silent auction room next door to see what's interesting. Sometimes you can get something useful at not too exorbitant a price."

"Thanks. I might join you in a minute." I scanned the room, not necessarily looking for a better dinner offer, just checking it out to see who was here.

Familiar faces were all over the place and the only ones

I knew personally were my college fiancé—who, thankfully, I never married—and his wife, my former best friend. I'd got Stacy out of a potentially nasty pickle a few years ago and thought she had seen Brad's true colors. But here they were, still together. I watched as they chose a table near the front of the room, far from table 15, which helped cement my plan to sit with Lisa Browning. I spotted her red shawl and walked over to hang my jacket over the chair next to hers. It's not that I avoid offensive people—private investigation work puts me there. But I prefer not to eat at the same table.

That solved, I decided to follow Lisa's lead and check out the auction items. A good part of the crowd seemed to be heading for those rooms. That's when I spotted Judge Blackman moving toward the yellow brick road. Standing inches taller than most of the other men, and with that silvery hair, he was fairly easy to keep track of. He paused frequently to bestow his oily smile and shake hands. A younger woman stood at his side, definitely not the lady who'd been pictured with him and named as his wife. I studied the body language for a moment and caught little possessive gestures—his reach beyond her shoulder where he lightly touched her hair, her smile as she pretended to pick a piece of lint from his cuff. For a moment I thought she might be the same dark-haired court reporter he'd been eyeing this morning, but this was a different woman.

Another face from the news appeared—Herman Quinto. It was interesting to watch the way his little entourage came into the room first, creating a subtle stir and riff of whispered conversation, drawing attention before the man himself walked through the doors. With his wide, professionally enhanced smile and two-hundred-dollar haircut, he quickly pulled the attention of the crowd.

After all, the congressional election was less than a month away; we'd seen this face on television and billboards all over the state.

Blackman paused near the doorway to the Platinum Room where he had been headed—making me wonder how much a public servant actually could afford to donate to his favorite causes. His attention, too, had been drawn toward the ripple of attraction at the main entry. Standing midway between them, I felt like a tennis-watcher as I tried to observe both men's interactions at the same time.

Whatever earlier tension there had been between them at the golf course, it was gone now. Quinto waved familiarly across the room at the judge, who returned the greeting with a large smile, before each of them turned his attention back to those closer at hand.

Blackman reached into his pocket and produced some small item, which he showed to the watchdog at the door of the Platinum Room. My curiosity was piqued—it must be the magic key to the kingdom of riches. Again, I wondered how much a district court judge made—surely not enough to blow twenty-five grand on some bit of fluff at a charity auction. Keeping my eyes on my own goals, to learn as much as I could about the judge and the senator, I grabbed a glass of champagne from the tray of a passing waiter and trailed along behind Blackman.

He had already disappeared through a filmy curtain made of flashy green and gold Mylar strips, and I debated whether there was a way to follow. I pulled a small envelope from my little evening bag.

"I have a message for Judge Blackman," I said to the keeper at the door, who only shook his head.

Apparently whatever had gained entry for the judge was better; my fake message wasn't going to cut it. A woman behind me showed a silver-colored token and the man immediately let her pass.

"You'll have to wait for the judge out here," he said.

Properly rebuffed, I retreated to the nearest bar in the corner to pout. Herman Quinto had made his way around a quarter of the perimeter of the large ballroom and had nearly reached my corner. As if choreographed by the theater's best, Blackman emerged from the special auction room two steps ahead of the Quinto entourage, and I had a front-row seat.

"That was a good round today, Herman," said the judge, initiating the handshake. He dismissed his pretty little companion with the suggestion she go powder her nose.

"It was. I love it when I whip your ass."

They laughed—Quinto probably a bit more loudly—and the judge gave him a little shoulder punch.

"A little too crowded though," Quinto said, "Later, after the shindig, we need to talk. Our, uh, friend has been in touch again."

"Not here. Tomorrow." Blackman muttered the words through nearly closed lips and shifted his gaze away, as if not looking at Quinto meant he wasn't actually having a conversation with the man. Unfortunately, his attention landed on me.

Chapter 21

I took too large a gulp of the fizzy champagne and started to choke. Herman Quinto backed away as if afraid I might spew on his expensive suit. Judge Blackman moved in beside me to take my glass and then pat me on the back.

"Are you okay, hon?"

I'm not very tolerant of people calling me hon or sweetie or other endearments they haven't earned the right to use. Normally, I would have shot him a dismissive look and walked away but I was still in the midst of a coughing fit and it wouldn't have been a graceful exit. By the time the coughs subsided my eyes were watering and I'd drawn some attention.

Not one to miss a chance to appear benevolent, the judge took my elbow, asked the bartender for a glass of plain water, and led me to a chair.

"Really, it's fine. I'm absolutely okay."

One swig of the water and I'd recovered my fortitude. I'd also caught the fact that he'd sneaked a peek down the front of my blouse. Geez, did the man ever stop?

"Oh, gosh, there's my date," I said, slipping from beneath the warm hand he'd set on my shoulder. "Thanks so much for the water."

I set the glass down and escaped, heading for the room where I'd seen Lisa go to check out the less-expensive auction items. Beside the doorway stood a man in a plain dark suit, his hands clasped in front of him. He seemed vaguely familiar.

"Little problem over there?" he asked, nodding toward the corner I'd just evacuated.

His low, gravelly voice gave it away. He was a cop I'd met a couple of times when my investigative path crossed that of detective Kent Taylor and his squad. This was one of his men, who must have taken a moonlighting job as security for the gala.

"Nothing I couldn't handle. Thanks." I spotted Lisa in the room, studying some kind of book, and made my way toward her.

Medina—that was the cop's name. He'd seemed like one of the good guys. Nice to know he'd been alert enough to notice the judge's unwanted attention to me.

"So, what looks good in the auction?" I asked Lisa, briefly startling her.

"This is a first edition Virginia Woolf. And so far the bids aren't outrageous."

I noticed she had entered her name at the bottom of the list that included three other bidders.

"I'll keep checking on it. They drag these out to the last

minute, so it means I'll have to stay for the whole thing if I have any hope of getting in the final bid."

Her phrasing made me realize my energy was fading quickly and I really didn't want to stay for the entire evening either. I circled the tables of auction items, raising a bid now and then when it looked like an avid bidder would surely come along and add more to the offer—my little bit for charity. I'd just jotted my name and a five-hundred dollar bid for a weekend vacation at a mountain resort when I sensed scrutiny.

"Charlie, huh? Pretty name." It was Judge Blackman. Again.

I gave a weak smile and stepped away. He seemed ready to follow me when someone approached and stood between us. I looked over my shoulder in time to see that it was one of Herman Quinto's assistants, a young man. He handed something to Blackman who slipped it in his pocket without looking at it. The item appeared to be about the size of a wallet or a small leather-bound notebook. I quickly turned away, made a show of checking out some other auction items, making my way steadily toward the door.

The earlier exchange between Blackman and Quinto kept replaying in my head. Whatever Blackman meant by *not now*, it seemed the senator had sent it over anyway.

I caught up with Lisa at the end of the auction tables and we walked together back to the ballroom and dining tables.

"You seem to have gotten Judge Blackman's attention," she said.

"Not on purpose, I assure you."

She laughed. "And not the first, I can attest."

"What do you mean?"

"Let's just say the man has a reputation." Her mouth stretched in a tight, straight line now.

Suddenly, I knew why Lisa looked so familiar. She was the woman in the photo, the one looking at the prosecutor with the hateful look on her face. It had been a few years and she'd updated her hair and makeup, but I felt sure she was the one.

I had to know more.

The noise level in the ballroom was ridiculous, plus it was no place for a private conversation. I followed my new acquaintance through the crowd, debating how best to handle this. By the time we reached our table, I knew I needed more time and a little peace and quiet.

I dug in my bag and came up with a business card. "Lisa, I need to talk more about what you just said. Can we plan a time—maybe tomorrow morning?"

She studied my card for a minute. "Is this about some things that happened ten years ago?"

I met her gaze steadily. "Yeah. It is. I want to help."

"I'll tell you what I know."

Other diners at our table were greeting us now, and there was no chance to get in another quiet word. A master of ceremonies welcomed everyone through a microphone that occasionally squealed. He laughed and told us to enjoy our meals and promised he would be back later.

Frankly, my head was beginning to pound and I didn't care about the rest of the gala. I munched my way through the salad at my place—crisp greens and spinach, topped with blueberries, walnuts, and some little crunchy things that were surprisingly tasty. Even so, the food didn't perk me up. It had been a long day and any further spying on the judge risked getting more of his candid flirtation. I needed to get out of there.

As waiters cleared the salad plates, I turned to Lisa. "Sorry, I've got a splitting headache and am just not up for this much socializing. But I'm intrigued by what you said earlier. Could we meet up somewhere tomorrow?"

She gave a sympathetic smile and wished me luck with the headache as she passed me a card on which she'd written her cell number. We promised to touch base in the morning and make a plan.

Once I'd decided to bail on the party, I couldn't get out of there fast enough. Before the entrees arrived I gathered my things, gave a small wave to the other tablemates and ducked out. My luck held; I didn't encounter anyone on the way to the parking lot and was home twenty minutes later.

I had envisioned climbing right into bed with Drake and snuggling in for a restful eight hours, but that didn't happen. My mind was on full overdrive with what I'd gleaned this evening, starting with the little black packet Quinto's aide had passed to Blackman and ending with Lisa's statements about the judge. I had no real proof that any of this pertained in any way to Rory McNab's case— other than Lisa's reference to *ten years ago*. Her question had been so specific on the timeline, added to the fact that it was her picture in the news photo from back then. A connection existed. If I could only figure out what it was.

Eventually, I told myself it was useless to let my mind run in this endless loop. I would call Lisa in the morning and learn whatever I could. Meanwhile, I listened to a few minutes of a playlist that was guaranteed to plant some song in my head, something irritating enough to block thoughts and pictures of the major players in this stupid case.

Chapter 22

In the light of day, and not duded up in our fancy clothes, I saw Lisa Browning was another average girl about my age. We'd both turned up at the Iron Skillet Café wearing jeans and T-shirts, trainers and fleece hoodies. My hair was up in a ponytail; her short bob was tucked behind her ears. She ordered a spinach omelet and I opted for something called pineapple upside down pancakes, which promised to be 'yummy' according to the menu.

Small talk about the auction occupied the minutes until the server brought coffee and while we did our respective routines with sugar and cream. A couple of sips of the excellent brew and then I picked up the folder containing my scanty research on the McNab case.

When I pulled out the news photo showing the scowling woman staring at Herman Quinto, Lisa laughed.

"Oh my gosh. Twenty-two years old and so full of righteous indignation I was." She placed her palm over the photo of herself and gently pushed it back across the table.

"This *is* you, then. I thought you looked really familiar last night. But it wasn't until you said something about 'ten years ago' that it kind of clicked."

She nodded but didn't say anything as our food arrived and we went through the drill where the server asked who had what dish, did we need anything else, an offer to top off our coffees, yada-yada. We distracted ourselves for a couple of minutes by cutting in and taking bites. The pancakes were, as advertised, yummy.

"So, what's your part in this, Charlie? I'm curious why it's all coming back now." Lisa picked up a triangle of her wheat toast.

I gave a shortened version of how I had met Fergus McNab and his adamancy about his son's innocence. I left out the parts about how and where Rory got away. "I'm now trying to locate the major players in the original case to find out if there's a way to prove Rory didn't really try to influence that jury. I mean, it just seems so 'out there' to imagine an attorney doing that. Bottom line is, the father would like to have his son nearby during his final weeks."

"Sad about the father's desperation. As I recall, he helped his son escape, didn't he?"

"That's what the police suspected, but other things took precedence and the all-out manhunt was abandoned."

"So, Rory McNab must have been ready with an alternate identity and everything. Otherwise, it would have been simple enough for them to track his credit cards and such."

I'd had the same thought, but Fergus had not shared those details with me. "In my conversations with Rory's father, he's still sticking with the assertion that the judge did something to throw the case. I can't figure out how, or why. Can you give me any ideas on that?"

Lisa set down her knife and fork, swallowed hard, and reached for her coffee mug. "I can only tell you what I was doing there on the courthouse steps that day and why I had my bitch-face aimed at Herman Quinto."

I stabbed at a wedge of pancake while she collected her thoughts.

"Charlie, you've already figured out that Aldo Blackman is a womanizer. You saw him in action last night—showing up with that *kid* in her twenties, and then he starts hitting on you right in front of everyone. He's gotta be close to seventy himself."

I remembered the picture I'd seen of Blackman and his wife, a woman his own age. My heart went out to her.

"Ten years ago, I was that kid, the silly little grad student at twenty-two who thought the attention of an older, powerful man somehow made me special. God, I was so naïve. Until I heard little hints, rumors, eavesdropped on conversations in the ladies' room. The man was all over everybody! Any woman within arm's reach was in danger of a grope or a pinch."

"But nobody spoke up?"

"Most of us were connected with the law—legal students, court clerks, paralegals. A couple were lawyers, one a senior partner. The younger ones, like me, couldn't say anything—who would believe us? This was—is—the most prominent judge in Albuquerque, one of the biggest in the state. The women lawyers were terrified that their cases would be sent to Blackman's court and if they didn't put out for him he'd rule against them."

I felt all the air go out of my lungs. "Helen Bannerly?"

Lisa nodded. "I think so. She didn't join with us, but yeah, I'm pretty sure."

"Join with you?"

"I began to approach the women I'd heard talking about him. We decided that if enough of us came forward someone would have to listen. We could file a sexual harassment suit and bring his behavior to light. Ideally, he would be disciplined and maybe do jail time." Her hands shook when she picked up her coffee mug. She set it down again. "We needed evidence, not just our word, and actual proof was hard to come by—he never sent emails or handwritten notes. But several of us began recording phone calls and after a few months we felt ready to move. We took everything we had to the D.A.'s office."

"The prosecutor was Herman Quinto ..." I got a sinking feeling.

"Yes." Tears welled in her eyes. She took a deep breath, dabbed the corners of her eyes with her napkin, and set her face in calm lines once again. "Had we known what buddies the two men are ... Well. It was all over before it began. Quinto belittled our claims, tried to shift blame. We were all pretty girls who flirted outrageously and asked for the attention ... you've heard it a hundred times."

"But you had evidence—"

"Which sounded ridiculous when they played it back during my deposition. The really damning recordings seemed to have disappeared, and what was left was silly stuff that played right into the prosecutor's assertions. We were faced with dropping our case or going to court and being made to look like absolute fools."

Anger began to rise inside me, and I felt myself seething at the injustice of it. If I'd looked in a mirror, I was certain my expression must have been very much like

Lisa's in that old photo. "How have you coped with this? It would be eating me up."

"It did. For a long time. The women used to meet, afterward, for support and consolation. Two moved out of state for fresh starts. Most found other jobs away from the law and the local court system. We lost some good lawyers in this city. I dropped my law school studies and switched to psychology. They say everyone who goes into psychology does it to deal with their own messed up situation. Well, I sure did."

"Did it work?"

"Eventually. I met a very kind man who introduced me to Eastern philosophy. He quoted the Buddha, who once said, 'Holding on to anger is like picking up a hot coal with the idea of throwing it at someone else. You're the one getting burned.' Whew! That did it for me. Took some work but I was finally able to drop the anger and get on with my life."

By some magic, hearing her words helped quell the fire that had suddenly built in me. Being churned up over this wasn't going to help anyone. But it didn't mean I could let go—all the wrong this man was doing, all the lives he was messing with. What I needed to do was to find better evidence.

Chapter 23

I picked up the breakfast tab—as part of the investigation, it was deductible—thanked Lisa profusely for her candor, and headed to the office where I'd left the rest of my notes on the McNab case. My head felt full of ideas and new information and I needed to put it all in some sort of order and formulate a plan for what to do next.

The Victorian was dim and quiet when I arrived. Saturday isn't normally one of our office days; Sally is home with her family and Ron tries to get extra time with his boys unless he has a slew of work piling up. So, I had the rare chance to do some quiet thinking as I entered through the kitchen door and made my way toward the stairs. A pile of envelopes lay on the floor beneath the mail slot. I picked them up and headed up to my office.

Lisa Browning's words had struck a number of chords

with me, not the least of which was the connection with Rory's defense attorney, Helen Bannerly. It suddenly made sense why the woman hadn't done more to present a strong defense for her client and why she'd thrown up a wall when I asked about the case. Career-wise, she had stuck with the law, but her new firm's focus was on corporate work, something that would rarely require her to appear in a courtroom.

So, I knew something had been going on between Helen Bannerly and Judge Blackman. Herman Quinto had refused to pursue Blackman when a group of women wanted charges brought for sexual harassment. How did that add up to a conspiracy against Rory McNab?

My logical choice would be to talk to Rory again and come right out with the question. But I'd pretty much done that, and he'd not responded with anything useful. Or, he just plain didn't know. Perhaps if I produced something in the way of actual evidence, something that would convince Rory to open up, maybe we would get somewhere.

Of course, there was always the possibility that Rory truly did not know how he'd ended up in the sights of these men.

I caught myself chewing my lower lip while I went through the mail, sorting it into stacks for Ron and me, tossing the junk. I delivered Ron's mail to his desk, set mine aside and pulled out a yellow legal pad. Sometimes writing things down solidifies the idea, so I came up with this list:

What Evidence?

Taped conversations with judge's victims—nothing in writing

What happened to those recordings?

Wait—small black packet (notebook?) passed from Quinto to Blackman last night

Judge continues womanizing ways—would a current lover speak up? Find them.

Judge's wife out of town this weekend

This last bit I'd overheard as Blackman greeted another man at the party, a guy who'd commented on the older man's good fortune with 'knockout' assistants. I tapped my pen against the notepad, trying to think what else to add.

Talk to Helen Bannerly again, this time with more knowledge and evidence—What evidence?

My thoughts seemed to run in a loop and everything led back to the fact that I needed something more concrete than speculation. And the best way around that …

I knew where I was going with this, even before I dared fully form the idea in my head. It was a stupid idea, completely iffy, and possibly dangerous. My cup of tea exactly.

Before I could talk myself out of it, I grabbed my purse and phone, locked the office and headed to my Jeep. If traffic wasn't horrible, I could be in Sandia Heights in fifteen minutes. I have to admit I hit the gas pedal a little harder than necessary—okay, a lot harder.

The prospect of finding that small black packet was exciting, and this was the time to do it. Evidence had once existed against the judge and it had disappeared. If I could get hold of that little journal or whatever it was, I might find the clues to unlock this whole thing. Unless he was a big believer in banks, he probably had a safe somewhere in his house. If he did prefer the safe deposit box method, he would go Monday morning, since he couldn't have done so between Friday night and now.

Today was my window. In fact, it was this morning. One of the remarks I'd overheard between the judge and one of his cronies was a little wager on a golf game planned for today. If he hadn't left already for an early tee time, I could simply watch until he did. With the wife gone, unless they had full-time staff, the house would be mine for several hours.

I felt my pulse rate pick up. With luck, the recordings Lisa had mentioned might also turn up. I was so intent on imagining the possibilities that I nearly missed the exit at Tramway Road. I made a too-quick move but recovered control and forced myself to slow down. Nothing could be gained by maiming myself in the process.

Sandia Heights is a neighborhood of winding trail-like roads clinging to the foothills of the big mountain that dominates Albuquerque's terrain. The homes, mostly built in the '60s and '70s, are a mixture of styles and, in certain cases, trendy looks that did not age well. For some reason, I imagined a judge living in something very traditional, maybe a territorial style home with kiva fireplaces, or maybe a large ranch house with rich wood paneling and a wall of gorgeous native rock. The Blackman residence turned out to be neither.

Concrete slabs upended at angles, cantilevered rooflines, and a teak front door that stood a good twelve feet tall—it was either built as the latest style in 1960-something, or it was very new as the modern mid-century style began to trend back into fashion in very recent years. Didn't really matter to me, as it's not my taste, but I had to admit it was one of the larger and showier homes on this road. I cruised by slowly, looking for signs of action.

No movement at any of the large windows. The graveled drive and adjacent dirt area showed a set of tracks that appeared to have very recently backed out to the paved road. Looked like the judge had left for his golf game. Since my intentions were not altogether honorable, nor legal, I drove to the next corner and pulled off at a wide spot in the road.

I saw no one else around, no walkers or neighbors watering their yards. Of course, the reason most people lived up here among the boulders and sagebrush was so they could go with xeriscaping and not have to water a yard. I tucked my purse beneath the car seat, pulled my hair into a ponytail, tucked my phone into a pocket, and plugged in earbuds before setting off at a pace I hoped would make me look like an exercise nut.

With a quick glance around, I approached the Blackman's front door and pressed the doorbell. It's always good to be sure some maid doesn't pop up to answer it, and to verify that the tracks leading away from the house didn't belong to someone who'd slept over and the judge himself wasn't about to emerge from the shower. The chimes echoed with a hollow sound, and again when I rang a second time. Good.

On the off chance the man hadn't checked the door before he walked out through the connecting door to the garage, I tried the handle. Of course, I wasn't *that* lucky. Still, I could check all the possibilities. A skinny path of stepping stones led around the uphill side of the house and I followed them.

The back, west-facing side of the house revealed why the spot was so alluring. From the edge of a spacious patio, the mountainside dropped away to reveal the entire city laid out below, completely at my feet. No wonder Judge Blackman acted as if he owned the world—this view could make a person believe it.

I had to remind myself I wasn't here to enjoy the panorama at my feet. Taking a peek through the nearest window, I got the gist of the layout inside: kitchen with huge center island, long dining table at the far wall, and a massive great room with a sectional couch bigger than my backyard. It faced floor-to-ceiling windows and glass doors to the wide patio where I stood.

This, in itself, was another living area, with several furniture groupings, more dining space, and rock fire pit. Everything felt magazine-perfect and not a soul was moving, which relieved my mind about there being a maid or chef somewhere on the premises. I gave a tug at the frame of the kitchen window but it didn't move. None of the French doors budged for me. But a side window had been neglected. It stood open about two inches, and a perusal told me it led to the laundry room.

I found a short garden stake near a chamisa bush and used it to pry the screen from the window. Set that aside and raised the sash enough to boost myself through, making mental notes all the while about each of the small steps I would undo as I left, to make sure I'd covered my traces.

The room smelled of detergent and cat box. I wondered if the resident feline was the verbal, greeter type or if he/ she was one that would dash under the bed at the first sign of a stranger. Either way, it seemed smart to close the window. I don't have any qualms about helping myself to evidence or taking a person's ill-gotten gains; I just don't want harm to come to their pets.

The door opened into a short hall, which led to a longer one, which showed an impersonally decorated guest bedroom, a bath, and a study. Always a good place to begin.

Apparently, the modernist decorator had his way in here too. The desk was a sheet of plate glass on chrome legs with a sleek computer on top and a space-age chair that was undoubtedly the most ergonomic thing on the market. It certainly wasn't the most attractive. Built-in cabinets along one wall housed file drawers (I discovered) and a decent-sized safe, securely locked. Dammit. I riffled through the obvious places but found no sign of the little black object I'd seen him take from Quinto.

On the opposite side of the room was a leather couch, two side chairs, and a chrome and glass coffee table. The program from last night's gala lay on the table, along with the burgundy bow tie the judge had worn and a lone highball glass. It smelled of scotch. His tuxedo jacket was draped over the back of one of the chairs. It appeared the judge had come home alone.

I went through his pockets, but no black book. I could guess all day—the possibilities were endless. It could be locked in that sturdy safe across the room, he could have slept with it under his pillow, or he could have passed it off to someone else last night. It could be with him now, on the golf course. I could only operate in one place at a time, so it made sense to check the rest of the house.

The master bedroom seemed the logical place. I envisioned another safe in there, one carelessly left unlocked. The little door would be standing open and inside would be his wife's jewelry, a stack of spending money, and the black packet. In my mind's eye the little book would open to reveal wondrous secrets, including everything I needed to prove Rory McNab's innocence and put the slimeballs behind bars instead. I shook my head and the dream-bubble burst. A ruthless politician and an unfeeling predator in jail? Seriously? I reminded myself about truth, justice, and the American way. Who am I kidding—this *is* the American way.

Okay, so even if I couldn't singlehandedly leap tall buildings or put powerful men in prison, maybe I could figure out how to exonerate an innocent man and get him back home with his dying father before it was too late. I straightened the tuxedo coat and hung it back neatly over the chair, as I'd found it.

Passing through the huge living room, I saw double doors standing open at the other end. A flash of fuzzy gray and white zipped from the room beyond and disappeared behind the huge sectional sofa. Looked like kitty wasn't going to be the friendly sort. At a closer glance, I could see the corner of an elaborate bedspread hanging crookedly toward the floor. Obviously, an important man doesn't make his own bed.

At first glance, the master bedroom followed the same color scheme as the rest of the home, ebony flooring with pale gray area rugs. But the bed was a cozy cherry sleigh and a tall armoire of the same rich wood stood between two tall windows, which were draped with the same gray and burgundy print as the bedding. I stood a moment in the doorway, wondering where a safe might be. If concealed behind one of the Betty Sabo paintings, it was closed up tight. None of the beautiful landscapes was a tad out of place.

My guess was the armoire—it would be easy enough to conceal a small safe behind a wood panel and bolt the whole thing to the wall. I walked past the bed, eyeing the large piece of furniture, thinking most likely the double doors would open to reveal a set of drawers and compartments.

The room was dim enough that I didn't immediately notice the large object on the floor on the far side of the bed, but when my foot slipped in something gooey, I whirled to look down. That's when I realized the judge hadn't gone golfing, after all.

Oh, shit! My heart went into overdrive and there was a

buzzing in my ears. The hair on my arms tingled, and my brain froze. What the hell had happened here?

A person without clothing loses all dignity, especially one whose flabby gut and lack of muscle tone had been so neatly concealed by an impeccably cut designer tuxedo. I took in the sad sight at a glance, along with the blood that had saturated the gray rug under the body and pooled at its edge. He lay facedown, pasty-white buns toward the ceiling, arms and legs sprawled outward. I couldn't see a wound and I didn't want to.

I've worked on several murder cases, but the private investigator's role generally doesn't come into play until much later. The police handle the messy stuff. This was the first time I'd been in the room with a body so—I couldn't think of the right word—so fresh.

My first instinct was to get away—far, far away. I should get out of the house and call the police. If I stayed another second, I would probably throw up and mess up the crime scene. My shoe skidded again and I wiped it on the corner of the rug that wasn't already dirty, leaving a red smear. My every move was making it worse—I had to get out of here. I pulled off my shoes and ran in my stocking feet. I'd cleared the bedroom when the doorbell rang.

I felt my eyes go saucer-wide. No way was I going to answer it.

I spun and dashed into the living room, trying to get my bearings and remember the route to the laundry room and window I'd left unlocked.

A fist pounded on the door. "Police! Open up!"

Shit, shit, shit!

A glance at the huge windows along the back of the house and my gut went watery. Two cops stood out there, staring in, and they'd spotted me.

Chapter 24

There was no blending into the woodwork now. I took a deep breath. No matter how it looked, I was innocent—okay, almost innocent. I'd let myself into someone's house without an invitation, true. But the body in the bedroom—I had nothing to do with that. And once I explained it, the police would understand. A picture of innocent Rory McNab and his experience with the law flashed through my head, but I forced it away.

Turning toward the two cops at the back doors, I dropped my shoes and held up my hands. The male officer drew his pistol, while the female cocked her head and spoke into the microphone on her shoulder.

Two sharp raps sounded on the door behind me, and a voice shouted, "Keep your hands up, approach the front door slowly and unlock it. Then step back!"

I'm not always well behaved, but this time I did exactly as told. I backed away as the uniformed officer at the door came forward, gun in hand. Within seconds, the other two came in behind him.

"Are you alone in the house?" The voice was no-nonsense.

"Yeah, but—"

"Want to explain why you chose to visit through the side window?"

Not really. I could try the old forgot-my-key ploy, but it wasn't going to work this time. "How did you know—"

"A neighbor saw you. Not smart, lady."

"Her vehicle is parked at the corner," said the female officer who had stepped outside to talk to a woman who looked like the neighborhood busybody.

"Did you plan to carry the big-screen TV all that way?" said the one with attitude.

Meanwhile, the other one had patted me down and, learning I was unarmed, put away his weapon. While the woman officer went back outside with her notebook at hand, the other guy began poking his head in other rooms.

"I—*no!* Could I just say something?"

"Murphy! *Holy crap!*" The guy backed out of the master bedroom. "We gotta get Homicide out here." His face was a chalky, marshmallow hue when he stepped over and touched the other officer's sleeve.

"That's what I wanted to tell you ..."

"Turn around and put your hands behind your back. Slowly."

I felt cold metal on my wrists. This was about to get a whole lot worse.

* * *

Homicide Detective Kent Taylor must have been somewhere nearby. He arrived within ten minutes and a whole team showed up right behind him. Taylor and I have crossed paths quite a few times, and I thought a sort of friendship was beginning to form. Well, maybe it's more like respect for my brother. By the look on his face when he recognized me, admiration was definitely not the feeling.

"Charlie Parker. Why am I not surprised?"

"Kent—uh, Detective Taylor, this is not at all what it looks like."

Yellow tape had been strung across the road, around the Blackman property, and down the hill behind the house. A cluster of neighbors now gathered at the perimeter, craning their necks for a gander.

I heard the helicopter before I saw it, the bright yellow Bell 412 operated by Channel 7. *Oh god.*

"Could we …?" I tilted my head toward the news channel's ground crew who had just shown up in their vehicle with the satellite dish on top, all ready for live-at-the-scene coverage. Obviously, word had gotten out that something horrible had happened at the home of the prominent judge.

Taylor picked up on my concern about the media. "Yeah, not good. Walk casually in front of me and we'll go sit in my car."

As if any amount of casual attitude would conceal the fact that my hands were cuffed behind me. At least the detective's vehicle was inside the yellow tape and the crowd couldn't get to us. Walking out there in my socks was bad enough; at least he allowed me the dignity of sitting in the front passenger seat instead of having to duck my head and climb into the back. I could practically hear cameras snapping away.

"Could I at least call Ron?" I asked. "It would be awful for him to see this on TV before he has any warning."

"In a minute. First, I need you to tell me what happened."

I opened my mouth, trying to choose where to begin. "Last night at this theater fundraiser—"

"Charlie—twenty-five words or less. What happened this morning, here in this house?"

"I don't know."

"You still got more than twenty words left."

"I'd hoped to find an item that contains evidence in a case we're working. The judge was supposed to be playing golf so I thought I'd take a little look."

"That accounts for the screen being off the laundry room window?"

"It was loose, anyway."

He gave me a look. "They bagged your shoes. Looks like there's blood on them."

"Okay, so I went in the master bedroom to see if our missing item might be there. The curtains were drawn so it was kind of dim. I didn't see the body—"

I paused, trying to read the look on his face.

"Go on."

"I felt my shoe slip, for some reason. I looked down. He was on the floor on the far side of the bed, out of sight from the door. I knew I had to get out of the room so I could call the police, but then it turned out they were already here."

"Did you touch the body?"

"Ew—no! He's naked."

A flicker of a smile showed on Taylor's face, but he hid it right away. "What other rooms of the house did you visit?"

"The study, or home office, or whatever you'd call it."

"Anyplace else? When we dust the whole place for prints we'll only find yours in the laundry room, the master bedroom, and this study?"

"I don't think I even touched anything in the bedroom. No, wait—maybe on the way out, I might have touched the foot of the sleigh bed or the doorjamb … I don't remember."

A disturbing thought went through my mind. I probably shouldn't say anything more until I had a lawyer. But Taylor hadn't placed me under arrest or read my rights or anything. As far as I knew this was still informal questioning. So far.

"Those news people have the long lenses on their cameras," I said, faking a casual smile for their benefit. "I need to let either Ron or Drake know what's happening."

He gave a huge sigh. "Look, I tend to believe your story. You're a pain in my rear, Charlie Parker, but I've found you're normally truthful with me."

Oh, I am, I am. "Thank you."

"I'll need to talk to you again, once we've processed the scene. Don't leave town."

"You're letting me go?" This time my smile was completely genuine.

"For now. Like I said, don't leave town." He motioned for me to turn in my seat and he unlocked the cuffs. He handed back my cell phone and car keys. "Walk directly to your vehicle, drive away, and don't come anywhere near this house, ever again. That's just a friendly little bit of free legal advice."

He actually did smile this time, but I was so busy getting that car door open I didn't take the moment to savor it.

"I don't suppose I'm getting my shoes back."

The smile widened. "Not on a bet."

On that pleasant note, I scampered out. With the passenger door closed, I gave a little thumbs-up gesture to let the cameras know I was in good with the cops. Hey, nothing to see here, folks. I paused just long enough to take off my socks. I could at least pull off the illusion that it was a perfectly normal thing to walk barefoot down the road in October.

I did as directed—drove away and never looked back. Well, except in my rearview mirrors, making sure none of the media vehicles followed me. Although I hadn't found the evidence I'd hoped to get, for the moment, I was off the hook. The moment, unfortunately, would only last until the six o'clock news came on that night.

Chapter 25

The murder of Judge Aldo Blackman was the top story on all the local stations, and my phone began ringing at 6:05 when friends spotted me talking in the car with Kent Taylor. The old folks, who live for that nightly newscast, caught it first, and the first to call me was Elsa.

"We're all gathered in the living room here, after our early supper, and I saw you. Hon, what did you get yourself into?"

I started to explain but I could tell by the background sounds that she had a crowd around her. I pictured a bevy of oldsters, plus a few nurses and orderlies, giving Elsa the celebrity treatment once she piped up and said, "Oh, I know that girl." They come from a simpler time, when appearing on the evening news might have been a good thing.

"Everything's fine, Gram. I'll tell you all about it later."

"Yes, when I get home I'm having you over for tea and we'll catch up on everything."

"That sounds good. I love you." We were nowhere near ready to have the conversation about whether she would be released to come home and live alone again.

The second call was Ron, who simply said, "Monday at the office, we need to talk."

Since another call was already coming in, I merely agreed and took the other call. I assured Sally she would hear all about it at the office. My old friend Linda Casper was concerned, but once I reassured her that I was fine we fell into talking about old times, the spa vacation we'd once taken together, and renewed promises to be better about staying in touch. From that point on, I ignored the phone.

Drake was well rested after a good night's sleep. We puttered in the garden a little Sunday afternoon, getting things ready for a change in the weather. Afterward, we decided a complete getaway would be nice, so we flew up to the tiny cabin we'd bought on the eastern slope of the Sandias. It was near the city but far from civilization, if that makes sense. Off the grid, once we turn off our cell phones there's nothing much to do there but hike, watch the wildlife, or kick back with a book—exactly what I needed.

Right up to the moment we got back to the city late Monday evening.

Drake guided the helicopter to his usual spot in front of the hangar, and I turned on my phone to find a series of increasingly unfriendly messages from Detective Kent Taylor. Uh-oh. Well, how was I to know he would want to chat again so soon?

I was in the process of formulating a response that

wouldn't make me look like a completely irresponsible citizen when I spotted him striding toward us.

"You were under strict orders not to leave the city," Taylor said.

I know shock and guilt registered on my face. "We— we didn't really go anywhere."

"Really? Don't go with 'it was just a joy ride around town.' The dispatcher already told me you filed a flight plan yesterday afternoon, which said you were going up near Cerrillos. You blatantly disregarded my order, stayed away overnight, and ignored a number of attempts to reach you by phone."

Drake apologized and explained where we'd been, using his calm and rational voice that usually works with anyone, but Taylor was having none of it.

"Can we just get to the bottom line, Kent? Whatever you were calling to ask me, just ask it now." I felt my temper rising.

"I will. But we're doing it downtown."

"Am I a suspect now?"

"We have a lot of questions. Come with me."

That's when I spotted two vehicles outside the chain-link fence, one a black-and-white cruiser. Taylor took my arm and starting leading me in that direction. I shouted to Drake to call Ron and our lawyer. Shaking off the detective's grip, I promised to walk quietly beside him. Still, he put me in the back seat of the cruiser for the ride to the city center.

At the downtown main police station, Taylor disappeared and I was left with two uniformed officers who showed me to an interrogation room. I felt dirty, and it wasn't only because I hadn't used some of our precious, limited water at the cabin to have a shower this morning.

The room had the stale smell of a place with no windows, a place where fear and unsavory criminal types dwelled in equal measure. The table in the center of the room had the grime of a dozen unwashed hands, and I hated the mirrored wall across from the chair where they told me to sit.

Payback for being unavailable all day was waiting in this disgusting setting for twenty minutes until Kent Taylor showed up with a fresh, steaming cup of coffee in hand. "Oh—didn't they offer you anything?" was his response when my gaze lingered over it.

I wanted to snap back at him but something told me this wasn't the time. I put on a weary smile and tried to look cooperative, although I still had no clue what direction this meeting would take.

Taylor took his time shuffling through the pages of a ring-bound notebook. "You attended a theater fundraiser Friday night."

"True."

"Judge Aldo Blackman was also there."

"Along with several hundred other people."

"Tell me about the altercation between the two of you."

I had to stretch my mind to remember the brief exchange. "It wasn't exactly an *altercation*. The judge became somewhat flirtatious. I walked away."

"But you'd been tracking him all day. Sitting in his courtroom, following him at the golf course, then the gala."

When he said it that way, it did make me sound kind of stalker-like. Obviously, he had used the past few hours productively. If he knew that much about my movements, he'd talked with people I'd spoken to at the courthouse. I wondered if he'd also cornered Lisa Browning. "RJP has a new case and Judge Blackman is part of it."

"Oh? And what would that be?"

How little could I get away with telling? "An old court case. The defendant wants us to see if there's evidence that could reverse the verdict."

"Wouldn't this person's lawyer handle that?"

"Lawyers charge hundreds of dollars an hour and, other than digging through documents, they'd rather have a private investigator do the legwork."

"Fair enough." He flipped to a new page in the notebook, but I had a sense we weren't finished with that topic. "Saturday morning. Walk me through it again. Why were you at the judge's house?"

"As I said yesterday, I'd gone by to see if I could find this piece of evidence. It looked like a notebook or small leather portfolio. I hadn't planned to steal it or anything, just take a peek and see if there was anything related to our case."

This case that's years old. I could see the thought run through his mind.

"I rang the doorbell. The night before, I had overheard the judge say he was playing golf, but thought maybe his wife would be home and, frankly, hoped I could talk her into showing me this little notebook."

He tapped his pen on the notepad. "And when no one answered you just thought you'd get inside and help yourself."

"I walked around back. Mrs. Blackman might have been outside. She wasn't, so I circled the house and noticed the loose window screen."

"You do realize you've admitted to breaking and entering?"

"I didn't break anything—I just entered."

"Unlawfully."

Yeah, there *was* that. No way was I going to admit I've done it dozens of times. I sat quietly with my hands in my lap.

"And then you just *happened* into the room where a murdered man lay on the floor. Tell me about that part of it."

"Kent—Detective Taylor—it's just like I told you yesterday. I thought I might find the black notebook in the bedroom, I went in to check …" I tried to repeat verbatim what I'd said in his car Saturday morning. "I didn't have any weapon with me. Hell, I don't actually know how he died, except that it produced a lot of blood."

"Shot at close range, precisely in the heart. You own a gun, don't you? And Ron says you've gotten pretty good at the firing range."

"*Seriously?* I was searched, and I didn't have a gun with me. Did you find my gun at the scene?" Thank goodness mine had been in the safe at home that day. I have a carry permit and might very well have had it with me.

Taylor rubbed a hand across his few remaining strands of hair. "Okay, no. We did not find your gun at the scene."

"Has the medical investigator determined the time of death yet? Surely, it was awhile before I got there. And you do have the neighbor who reported seeing me go through the window, right? So you know I wasn't in the house more than ten or fifteen minutes."

He let my questions hang in the air. He didn't want to concede, I could tell, but he wasn't feeding me any information either.

"Some people who attended the same social fundraiser Friday night said the judge was flirting with you. You sure you didn't want to get back at him?"

"We've been over this and you know my answer. I think we're going in circles, but if you want me to keep going, I'll want a lawyer present."

That appeared to be the magic key to my release. The sun had been setting when we landed at the airport; it was now close to midnight. No wonder I felt exhausted and short of temper. I'd been brought downtown with only the clothes on my back—no purse, no phone—so I used one on a desk and called Drake. He sounded worried and said he was on the way.

Chapter 26

My happy homecoming was marked by tension until I had the chance to explain fully to Drake. As soon as he realized how close I had come to being railroaded, he had a whole new appreciation for what I was trying to do for the McNabs. We sat up talking and it was nearly three a.m. by the time we went to bed.

When I woke at eleven o'clock I had a momentary sense of panic. I couldn't remember sleeping this late, ever. I pulled on pajama bottoms with my tank top and straggled through the house. Drake had left me a note in his neat printing on the kitchen table:

Took Freckles with me to airport. Called Ron and said you were taking the day off (he knows about the police visit). Unplugged phone. Rest up! Love you!!

I sighed and reached for the coffee pot. Cold. The

idea of following his instructions and going back to bed sounded so appealing, I nearly did it. But the clock was ticking for Fergus McNab and I would never forgive myself if I was one day late in getting Rory back for him.

I went to the bedroom where I dumped yesterday's smelly clothing into the hamper and chose a fresh change for today. The shower felt hot and good, and my brain was much more coherent afterward. By the time I made a run through the drive-up at a fast food place and downed half the coffee and most of the ham and egg sandwich, I was ready to face the office.

Sally greeted me with a freckled face full of concern. Was I okay? What happened? All the usual.

"Come up to my office," I suggested. "I'll get Ron so I only have to say it all once."

So that's what we did. I went over the Saturday morning debacle that led to my conversation with the police in front of the judge's residence, my mistake in going up to the cabin with Drake for the night, and the fallout that sent me downtown to talk with Kent Taylor a second time. Sally gave me a hug and a lot of there-there stuff she probably uses with her kids when one gets a boo-boo.

Ron doesn't have quite the same gentle manner. Once Sally had gone back downstairs to her desk, he basically reiterated that most of my actions had been stupid— always a way to make a person feel better—and suggested we get back to work. I bristled for a moment but couldn't actually disagree with him. Plus, it felt better to take action than to sit around and dwell on my mistakes.

I decided to throw my brother a bone by asking his assistance. "So, what do you think our next move should be?" Not that I was finished checking out the people involved in the trial, even though that hadn't netted anything useful.

He'd been listening while I rattled off the names. "What about someone else in the prosecutor's office? Maybe now that Quinto has moved on to Santa Fe, someone else would talk to us."

At least he said *us*. It meant we weren't completely on the outs.

He scrolled through contacts on his phone. "Try Howard Ramsey." He read off a number. "He's a good guy, he's been there a while, and he owes me a favor."

"Will he remember the McNab case?"

"No idea. All you can do is ask. If nothing else, he might have the pull to get you a copy of the trial transcript quicker."

While we talked, I pulled out the photos from back in the day and showed them to Ron. "These are from the Damian Baca trial." I pointed out Damian, Rory McNab, and Rory's partner Christopher Brown, who were all walking together into the courthouse. "This other shot shows afterward, and there are a couple of people I don't recognize here."

Ron shrugged. "The guy with the scar … I don't know his name, but I've seen his face before. I'd be willing to bet he was somehow involved with Damian in the drug bit. He must be somebody farther up the line in the organization. My guess is he was there after the trial to be sure Damian didn't say the wrong things to the wrong people."

"That was my guess, too. Just wish I had a lead on him."

"Yeah, of course the real question is who was behind wanting to see Rory McNab take a fall."

No kidding, Sherlock. What did he think I'd been doing all along? "Okay, then, what about these photos from

Rory's trial—recognize anyone there? I've spoken with his defense attorney, Helen Bannerly. It was like talking to a closed door."

"Then she's hiding something," Ron said. "Why wouldn't a defense lawyer want to see her client exonerated, even if it was years later?"

"Any ideas on what she's hiding?"

"Something that goes way back but could still be damning today. Something that would interfere with her current career or mess up plans for her future."

"Such as …?"

"I don't know. That's why we ask."

"Helpful, Ron, real helpful." I felt my temper rising again. "Can you at least pitch in here, give some ideas, or suggest different tactics?"

He *finally* picked up on my frustration. "I'll talk to Howard Ramsey."

"Thank you. After all, it's you he owes the favor, not me." I shot him a terse smile. "I'll do some background research on Helen Bannerly and see what I can learn about her history."

"Hint—start with college. Before that, nobody gives a damn about what you did, but a lot of long-term relationships begin in a person's twenties."

My heart softened again. "Thanks, Ron. I appreciate your help." I shooed him out of my office and logged on my computer.

I'll admit I'm not into social media. I'd seen the devastating effects when a couple of teen girls in the neighborhood became caught up in following the opinions of others. But this was important and I decided to muddle around with it. I discovered Helen Bannerly everywhere.

Her Facebook page focused on happy times with a very handsome husband and two angelic blonde kids. Disneyland, Grand Canyon, four smiling selfie-faces with San Francisco as a backdrop. There were beaches, amusement rides, romantic dinners in bars. She had more than two hundred friends—I had no idea whether that was good or not—many of them were tagged as relatives. Her Twitter and Instagram accounts seemed to revolve around school sports; both daughters were starting team softball.

I'd heard LinkedIn was about business, so I headed over there where I was forced to create an account of my own. Getting caught up in the myriad scraps of information they wanted, I finally realized I didn't need to tell it all. I entered some made-up basics and then began searching for contacts. And there was Helen Bannerly.

She grew up in Albuquerque, attended Highland High School and UNM. While at UNM Law School she worked a couple of internships, one as a clerk for Judge Aldo Blackman.

Ah-ha.

Interesting—but what did it mean? I looked at the dates and it appeared her employment with Blackman had ended five years before Rory's trial. Helen had graduated with honors, passed the bar exam, and been snapped up by a prestigious firm here in town. A bunch of published articles followed, awards for civic contribution, promotion to senior partner. All of this before she represented Rory McNab.

Had she known Rory before she took his case? Maybe an old friendship—an old romance?—was the reason she'd represented him on the jury tampering charges. If she believed in his character, she might have been likely to take his case even without much favorable evidence. I mulled all of that around for a while, but something didn't quite connect.

For one thing, neither Rory nor Fergus had mentioned knowing Helen before the case. I'd almost had the impression that she was a name grabbed from the phone directory. But that didn't make sense either. Rory had been a young, hotshot lawyer. He knew people, had connections. He wouldn't have reached into thin air for the name of a lawyer to keep him out of prison. He would have chosen someone he trusted.

I thought of Herman Quinto, part of the same circle of acquaintances during those years. On a whim, I searched for his social media links. He was everywhere, yet his online presence felt contrived—created by a PR firm—unlike Bannerly's family-centric posts. One post on his candidacy site gave a phone number where constituents could set appointments. I called it. Why not go right to the source to ask about Rory's trial?

What I got for my efforts was a friendly-sounding voice that firmly told me Mr. Quinto's schedule was full. Telling the woman that a dying man's last wishes were involved did nothing to soften her response.

I went back to my online research but the pieces weren't quite coming together. I was lightly drumming my fingers on my keyboard when Ron's face appeared at my door.

"Got your transcript for you," he said. "Howard says you can pick it up at the courthouse anytime after four o'clock today."

"Wow—nice job."

He gave a strange little courtly bow and said he was heading out to do surveillance on another case. I glanced at the clock—it was already after three. I could kill another forty-five minutes and then head downtown to pick up the transcript.

As to Helen Bannerly, I thought about going back to her office, trying to learn more, and probably getting stonewalled again. Whatever she didn't tell me the last time, it was fairly certain she wouldn't just offer it up now.

But I did revisit her Facebook page and found a mutual friend, a girl I'd known from high school. She responded quickly to my friend request and I was in.

Following Cathy's conversations led me to Helen's timeline and I picked up on the fact that these two tended to share juicy tidbits about such weighty topics as losing ten pounds before the holidays. A couple of threads led toward personal doings—who all had showed up at the class reunion and how Nancy somebody sure had let herself go. It only took a few minutes of reading to figure out that Cathy was the instigator, most of the time, when it came to the snoopy bits.

My kind of gal. I started the conversation by responding to something she'd posted and added an 'OMG it's been forever!!!' to see what she would come back with.

It was easy enough to throw out tidbits that were generally known: everyone had loved the fries at Mac's Drive-In, and wasn't senior year when that haunted house movie came out. I couldn't actually remember doing any of those things *with* Cathy, but they seemed like innocuous little conversation starters. Half an hour flew by—I was beginning to see how people got hooked into spending their days in these chats—and I needed to get downtown. At least I had set the hook. Tomorrow I would try reeling her in.

Chapter 27

I hauled the trial transcript pages home. I had expected a huge document that would require a lot of skimming, but in fact the whole thing was about the thickness of a novel. It just didn't have any of the interesting bits. With no scenery or visual clues, it was like watching a movie with the screen turned to black or reading a book that was nothing but dialogue. Missing was the drama of the attorneys rolling their eyes at each other, the tears when witnesses became emotional, the boredom on the jurors' faces.

Drake brought a bake-at-home pizza and sat down to a football game on TV while I camped on the sofa beside him and launched into my evening's fascinating read. I thought of it as a script and fit Rory McNab, Herman Quinto, Helen Bannerly, and Judge Blackman into the roles. I searched out the names of each of the jurors I'd spoken to.

Billie Jones came across as nervous in the courtroom as she had when I spoke with her. She stated that a man approached her in the parking lot one morning and said Damian Baca was not guilty and she should vote that way. Quinto phrased his questions to get the maximum benefit for his case against Rory; when Helen Bannerly cross-examined Billie, she didn't even bother to ask for a description of the man or whether he expressly said he was speaking on behalf of Rory McNab. Quinto had successfully scored against her.

When Emelia Sanchez took the stand she said much the same things. Man in parking lot, a veiled threat about how she should vote. Neither attorney asked her to describe or identify the man—her recollection to me had embellished a little there—nor did anyone specifically ask her to rule out Rory McNab as the one who approached. The details she'd given me last week were nowhere in this court document, including her impressions about the relationship between the scar-faced man and Damian Baca.

Another witness reminded me that I had become sidetracked; I'd meant to get to this one and had not done so. Jack Karkakian stated that he owned a furniture store, Karkakian Imports. He began to elaborate a bit about his business when Quinto cut him short.

"Yes, there was a threat," Karkakian had said. "Not to me personally, but a man came in my store while I was on jury duty and scared my wife pretty bad."

"Tell us about that," Quinto urged.

"Well, it was a Tuesday so things were a little slow. He approached our employee who was dusting the lamps—"

"We really only need to know what was said to your wife."

"I'm getting to that. She was working on the bookkeeping in the back, and the employee pointed this man in the right direction. My wife said he just showed up in the doorway and stood there for a minute. When she asked if she could help him, he said, 'Yeah, deliver a message to your husband. Tell him he'd better not vote Damian Baca guilty'."

Surprisingly, the defense didn't object to the testimony as hearsay.

Quinto played up the fear factor. "That must have been very scary for your wife."

"It was. She couldn't concentrate on her work, and she almost got into a wreck on her way to pick up my little boy from school. They went home and locked themselves in, and by the time I got there for dinner that night she was still shaking."

Helen Bannerly asked the witness if the man had said anything else. Nothing about whether he mentioned Rory McNab. If I, with no legal experience, could think of objections, why hadn't Rory's lawyer pressed harder? It seemed obvious Helen Bannerly could have asked much more probing questions and drawn out information that would have helped Rory.

I set down the transcript, adding two things to my to-do list. Visit the Karkakians to see if I could jog their memories, and talk to Fergus again about bringing in a new lawyer to review the case. It seemed there might be grounds to have the verdict overturned.

Next morning our routine began early, as Drake was off to do a photo shoot near Santa Fe. I found myself with coffee at hand, browsing social media again and landing on my old acquaintance Cathy's Facebook page. She had responded to my last little comment with You still in ABQ? We should get together.

How convenient. Just when I was wondering how to initiate a conversation and pump her for more information, she dropped the opportunity right in my lap.

For sure. How great would be it be to have Mac's fries again! When's good?

Cathy must have received the ping immediately because within two minutes she'd come back with It's my day off so how about 3?

All right. I gave her a thumbs-up emoji and it was a date.

I closed the lid on my computer and turned away. In my head was a list of things I should try to accomplish, and there was not time to keep poking around and looking up old friends. A quick shower and I was off to the northeast heights to find Karkakian's furniture store. I toyed with the idea of calling ahead to be sure he would be there, but have found it's best to see a person's face at the moment I introduce my subject. They have less time to dwell on it and shift their story to what they think I want to hear.

The family business operated three stores around the city. Two sons had come of age since the founding of the little empire, and Pop had seen to it that each had a readymade career. Meanwhile, the original seemed to be the headquarters and my guess was the senior Karkakians would keep offices there.

The Hoffmantown neighborhood is an eclectic mishmash of the old and the new. Some businesses have been there since the 1950s; others came and went, including a corner full of chain outlets of the type found in every strip mall center in America. Cheap haircuts,

discount electronics, pet grooming, and a craft store filled
that area. I knew Karkakian's had been around long before
these guys showed up, so I made a right on Wyoming and
spotted it in the next block.

It was early enough in the day that the parking lot out
front held only three cars. A narrow alley ran beside the
building, and my guess was the employees parked behind. I
pulled in to the front lot, giving myself two spaces between
me and a little red Honda sedan.

Inside, a woman in her forties was whisking a feather
duster over some knickknacks on a bookcase. I chuckled,
remembering the court testimony where the store owner
said an employee was dusting when the stranger had come
into the store and confronted his wife. As a person who
barely keeps the dirt off one houseful of furniture, I
couldn't begin to imagine what it took to keep a place this
size looking fresh all the time.

I asked if the boss was in and the woman pointed me
toward the back. Behind a long sales counter, I could see a
door marked Office. A second employee responded to my
query by tapping at the door, opening it, and announcing,
"Some lady here to see you."

Jack Karkakian was shorter and rounder than I'd
expected. He used to do his own TV commercials and I
remembered a blustering, dark-haired man with an oily
smile and a lot of action with wide-spread hands and
excited intonation in his voice—have *we* got the deals for
you! He was grayer now and I caught only the faintest trace
of the wide smile when he greeted me.

"Can I help you? Did you already have a look around
the store?" He shot a look across the big showroom, ready
to chastise the employee for not having sold me something
yet.

"Actually, I'm not here about furniture. This is something only you can help with." Some stroke of genius at the last second told me to play up to the ego.

He preened a little. "My office?"

I followed him to the small room behind the counter, where two desks sat facing each other. One held neatly stacked invoices in the center. Around the edges were a stapler, page-a-day calendar, telephone, and a computer that was at least a decade out of date. The other desktop was a mass of paperwork—brochures and large poster board with clippings of furniture pictures pasted on. No doubt the art department at the newspaper would have to redo the whole thing, but I supposed the older man's tendency was to stick with a system that had worked well in the past.

"Don't mind all this," he said as he pulled a chair from a corner and set it near the messy desk. "It's ad layout day and I like to do it myself."

I tried for an encouraging smile. "I won't take much of your time. Here's my card. We're looking into the trial and conviction of Rory McNab, the lawyer in a case where you were a witness about ten years ago."

His forehead wrinkled in thought.

"You were a juror in a case against a Damian Baca, who was acquitted on drug trafficking charges. Rory McNab was his defense attorney, and later McNab was accused of jury tampering. I've read the transcript. You testified that someone had threatened you, through your wife …"

"Ah, now I remember. I remember it well. Poor Shirley was terrified. The guy had a scar on his face, and she said he was real rough-looking and scary. I had been at the courthouse for two days, and when I got to the store that second afternoon she wasn't here. My Shirley, she's always here. She and I—we're the backbone of this business. Well, my sons grew up in the business and they each have a store now, too. We're a close family." He pressed his fingers together to prove it. "Those boys have turned out to be excellent businessmen."

I could see this digressing fast. "So, back to the time of the trial, Mr. Karkakian—"

"Jack."

"Yes. Jack, did you ever find out who the man was, the one who made the threat?"

"I don't know his name, but I kept a keen watch out for him. If I'd caught him hanging around my store, watching my family … I'd have …"

"Did you ever spot him at all? During the rest of the trial or after?"

"I caught sight of him once. It was the day the jury came back with the verdict. He was outside the courthouse. He made eye contact and gave me a little nod. I knew it was him. He looked really satisfied with the way things turned out. And after the news reporters were done interviewing the lawyers and all, I saw this guy get in the same car as Damian Baca."

"Have you ever seen him again, after Damian's trial?"

He shook his head, then paused. "Wait. I did. He was at the back of the courtroom the day I had to go and testify—when they put that Damian's lawyer on trial."

Hmm. I took a moment to get the picture in my head. "Did the scarred man do or say anything that day?"

Jack shook his head. "Not that I saw."

"When you were asked about your vote on the Baca trial, none of the lawyers asked whether the man who threatened your wife said the message came from Rory McNab. So I'll ask it now—did he say or do anything to make her think McNab was the one who was pressing for the vote of innocent?"

A voice came from behind me. "I can answer that."

I turned to see an older woman who walked to the second desk and set her purse down.

"I'm the one he spoke to," said Shirley Karkakian. "He said 'deliver a message to your husband. Tell him he'd better not vote Damian Baca guilty' and that was it. He shook his finger at me and he had this ugly, scary look on his face. But those were his only words."

I could tell that even repeating the incident made Shirley a bit uneasy.

"I asked your husband this, and I'll ask you as well—have you ever seen this man again since the trial?"

She shook her head vehemently but her eyes still betrayed fear. She held the door for me, the implication clear that it was time for me to leave.

Chapter 28

The Jeep had become hot and stuffy inside, so I opened all the windows and let the breeze clear the air as I drove south on Wyoming. I was only ten minutes or so from Fergus's place and it seemed a good idea to check in with him again, although I wasn't sure what, specifically, we needed to cover. Mainly, I hoped if I went over what I'd read in the trial transcript something might jog his memory.

An extra car sat outside the trailer, one with Colorado plates. I parked in the limited space next to it and walked up to the door, where a woman in her early fifties met me. She had long brown hair with strands of gray, a youthful face with minimal makeup, and seemed fit in her jeans and bright purple V-necked shirt.

"Are you Charlie?" she asked. "I'm Christine." She opened the door and stepped aside while I entered, puzzled.

"Dad's in the bath," she said. "Would you like some coffee or a soda?"

Dad? "Yeah, sure. A Coke sounds great. Um, I have to admit surprise here. Fergus never mentioned a daughter."

A *chuff* escaped her. "I'm not terribly surprised about that. It's all about Rory and always has been."

Ooh. "I noticed you're from Colorado?" She'd stepped into the kitchen and I took a seat at the small bar which divided it from the living room.

"Yep." She bustled about the tiny space, opening cupboard doors until she located a glass. "I went to CSU right out of high school, met the right guy, married young. We've got two girls who—I can't believe it—are already in college. I never had any desire to come back to New Mexico. Of course, Mom was alive back then and they were still farming the place at Hatch. But I knew the minute Rory decided what he wanted to do with his life that the parents would tag along. Youngest child, only boy, spoiled completely rotten—it was in the cards by the time he was five or six."

Christine had poured a mug for herself from the old electric percolator on the countertop. She set my Coke and an ice-filled glass in front of me.

"I guess that explains a lot about the current effort to get Rory exonerated and back to Albuquerque before …" I glanced over my shoulder in the direction of the bathroom.

"We can talk. He takes forever with his morning routine, and he's hard of hearing anyway so say anything you want."

Okay then. "So, what's your take on this whole mess your brother found himself in?"

She leaned forward with her forearms on the counter.

"I have no opinion on whether Rory actually did what they said he did. It wouldn't surprise me. He really found his niche with the law and he loved winning at all costs. *But*, he also had his eye on bigger things—I know, because Dad sent me every damn news clipping about Rory's successes, especially his declaration to run for state Senate."

She pushed a few loose sugar granules into a little pile with her thumb. "I find it hard to believe he would risk that career and everything it would lead to just to get some punk drug dealer acquitted. Yes, a win in that case would have looked good—maybe—people don't always want to see druggies let off. You see what I mean—what would be the point?"

I did get it. And she was right. What *would* be the point?

"So, who would have threatened the jurors? And, even more, who wanted to see Rory convicted and sent to prison?" I was mostly musing but she answered.

"Believe it or not, considering I don't give two shakes about my brother, I've actually thought about it quite a bit over the years. My closest guess is the drug guy and his people were the ones behind the jury tampering—it only makes sense. And I think it's pretty much a no-brainer that the man who wanted Rory in prison was his rival, that Quinto guy." She shrugged. "Anyway, that's my take on it."

"Didn't Rory and Herman Quinto work in the local D.A.'s office at one time?" I asked. "Quinto on the prosecution side and Rory as a public defender."

"For a while. I don't remember exactly when Rory branched out and went in partnership with that other friend from law school."

"I wonder if the animosity from Quinto goes back that far, to their time in the same department but on opposite sides of the courtroom."

Another shrug.

I heard a small sound behind me. Christine looked up and her expression closed. I turned to see Fergus standing in the bedroom doorway, and I wondered how much he'd heard. He came into the living room, a quirky, almost humorous little smile on his face.

"So, Charlie, you took out that crooked judge for me, did you?"

"Hi Fergus." A glance back toward Christine told me Fergus had already told her about the judge's death. "I can see why you'd be happy to see some kind of vengeance on Judge Blackman, but sorry to say it wasn't me. He was dead when I got there."

A flicker of disappointment registered on the old man's face. Obviously, he would have loved to tell everyone that his private investigator handled the case decisively and to his liking.

"Fergus, my job is only to find out the facts. If we come up with evidence that gets Rory off the hook, we will do that. We won't be randomly killing off his enemies."

"I'm dying anyway—nothing's stopping *me*."

"Fergus …"

"See, the way I figure it is the judge is already gone. Good. Now there's that sonuvabitch Quinto. And if I have the chance, I think the lame-ass lady lawyer deserves it too."

"Dad! Don't be talking this way," Christine piped up.

"Hell, I may be old but I'm still pretty good with my damn shotgun. And I got nothin' to lose. What am I gonna live anyway, another month or two? Might as well make the world a better place."

Chapter 29

I froze in my seat until I heard Christine chuckle. "Come on, Dad, you haven't had your breakfast yet. I've got some new bananas for your cereal."

She parked Fergus at the table, still grumbling about the state of the world, and took me aside.

"While he's eating I'll unload the gun and hide all the ammo in the trunk of my car. He's all talk. How's he going to track down this guy anyway?"

"You're sure? We could—"

"I'm sure. Anything you do to contain him will only piss him off worse. We'll let him think he's got the choice."

The whole idea made me uneasy, but she was his daughter and apparently, for a while at least, was here in a caregiver capacity. I said goodbye to both and headed for my vehicle. I still had a fairly full day ahead of me.

Morning visiting hours at the rehab center were in full swing. I passed a little family group where the patient was obviously relating his rehabilitation progress in the 'torture chamber'—apparently the man didn't care for the exercises.

I found Elsa in the common room—what she had called the living room—chatting with two women of about her same vintage. All were dressed in soft, loose sweats and jackets. One of the ladies sported a bright pink headband around her white hair. Conversation screeched to a halt when I approached and caught Elsa's eye.

"Charlie! Hon, I'm so glad you're here." She patted the empty seat beside her on the plastic covered sofa.

The other two were ogling me frankly.

"She's the one, Norma," said pink-headband lady with a nudge at her friend's arm. "I told you that you slept through the news the other night. You missed the whole thing."

I think she believed she was whispering—she kept eyeing me sideways in quick little glances—but the other woman must have been hard of hearing. She made her friend repeat the information twice.

"Are you up for a walk?" I asked Elsa.

"You bet." I had to give her points for enthusiasm, which boded well for her eventual release.

She scooted to the edge of the sofa but needed a hand when getting to her feet. We took it slowly, nearly five minutes to traverse the length of the hall. She asked about my little adventure with the police, and I gave vague answers I wouldn't mind having repeated throughout the facility.

"I know you can't say much here," she said in a confidential whisper when we stood in a little alcove where a large window at the end of the hall gave a nice view of the mountains. "But don't forget, you're coming to my house for tea when I get home and you can tell me all about the case then."

I gave her a hug and said the only thing I could. "We'll do that."

For all her enthusiasm, I could tell she was tiring quickly, so I escorted her back through the common area and down another corridor to her room. By the time she settled in bed she was talking about having a little nap before lunch. I tucked her in and went in search of her doctor.

What I got was a physical therapist who'd been working with Elsa each day since her arrival.

"She's doing amazingly well, considering her age and the severity of the heart attack," the forty-something woman told me.

"She certainly has her old spunk. She's already planning a tea party for me when she gets home." We shared a little smile over that, but I needed to turn the conversation serious again. "Is that going to be possible? Her going home?"

"I noticed you walking along with her. I'm sure I don't need to tell you she's still pretty fragile and she tires easily when it comes to getting around. You know her home situation—can she handle it? Are there stairs or uneven surfaces? Is the bathroom close to her bedroom … those are the types of things we need to consider."

"It's a medium-sized house, all on one level. She has lived alone for more than twenty years and I'd guess she actually uses less than half the space. The guest bedrooms have been closed off for a long time, unless company comes, which is rare. So, living room, kitchen, bedroom and bath are her little world. Well, aside from her garden—

that's where she really comes to life."

"I'm afraid gardening will be out of the picture for a long while. At least with winter approaching maybe it won't be such a temptation."

I agreed. "So, you really think she may be able to live on her own again?"

"I didn't exactly say *that*. She'll need help. At the very least, someone to spend a few hours and take over the household chores. She shouldn't be cleaning house or making her bed. And the problem we see with many elderly is that she'll find cooking to be a chore so she'll stop doing that. She'll tell herself that she can live on peanut butter and crackers or some other little favorite snack, but she won't be getting a balanced diet or the nutrition she needs to stay strong. Feeling weaker, she'll tend to become sedentary, which is even worse. It will be best if she has someone to take little walks with, something non-strenuous but that would keep her active."

I digested the information, picturing the situation and wondering how we would work all this into our fairly crazy schedule. Drake and I were used to flying off to any place a job popped up, often on a moment's notice, and there were many times I worked at the RJP offices well into the night. I love my gram and I owe her so much but could see myself becoming resentful as I ticked away hours watching her become querulous at my demands that she eat. A family confab needed to happen soon.

Back in my Jeep, I called Ron and filled him in with what I'd just learned.

"How much of that would her Medicare cover?" he asked.

"Not much, but—" A vague memory tickled me. Years

ago, Gram had mentioned an insurance policy, something her late husband had bought for the two of them. "Let me check on something, Ron. I'll call you later."

I pictured him staring at the dead phone in his hand, wondering why I'd bothered to call him at all, if I already knew the answer. Fifteen minutes later I'd arrived home, let Freckles out of her crate, and made my way over to Elsa's with key in hand.

Her house had the slightly dusty smell of a place that had been empty for days. I made a mental note to have a cleaning service come on the day before Gram would get home. I refused to consider the alternative—that she might never return to this house. Meanwhile, I had just one question to answer. I stood in the kitchen, staring around, trying to remember where she kept important papers.

The answer, it turned out after twenty minutes of searching, was in a plastic box with a hinged lid, a thing about the dimensions of a file folder and six inches deep. I pulled it from the upper shelf of her closet and carried it to the bed, where I lifted the lid and riffled the contents. This was too much to read on an empty stomach, so I closed the box and carried it back home with me.

Sliced turkey and Swiss cheese from the deli, piled onto light rye bread, made a hearty sandwich, and after gobbling half of it I was set to deal with paperwork again. I pulled everything from the file box and set it on the kitchen table, looking through it while I nibbled potato chips and the rest of my sandwich.

Elsa's filing system was neat enough. At the top of the pile was a large brown clasp envelope, which I discovered contained old photos. Elsa and Mr. Higgins so young I wouldn't have recognized them except that I'd seen other pictures of this vintage around the house. This was an informal shot, taken on a picnic somewhere with tall pine trees surrounding them. A blanket on the ground and a wicker picnic basket. The two of them sat on the blanket, holding hands and smiling. I wondered who had been with them that day; obviously someone else took the picture unless they'd had a fairly sophisticated camera for the times. I wanted to look through the rest of the photos, but I was on a mission. I set the brown envelope aside and continued to rummage.

Farther down in the stack, I found her will—which I already knew about, as she'd given me a copy the last time she'd updated it—along with the insurance policies on her house and car. And, eventually, an envelope from the Life and Surety Insurance Company. From the postmark, it had been in here nearly forty years. I wondered if the firm was even still in business.

Inside, I found what I'd hoped for. Mr. Higgins had, indeed, purchased and prepaid for a nursing care policy, which appeared to be what's now called long term care. I scanned enough of the pages inside to see that it most likely would cover what we needed. Before I became too hopeful, though, I'd better find out if the Life and Surety Insurance Company still existed.

I was deep into an internet search when I realized the hours had escaped me and I was due to meet Cathy at Mac's in exactly eight minutes. Yikes.

Chapter 30

Mac's Drive-In had changed surprisingly little over the years. Back in the '50s people sat in their cars and all the boy/girl flirting hinged upon whether you could park within shouting distance of your intended match. At some point, a bunch of the parking spaces had been replaced by an addition to the building, and indoor dining at booths with chrome-legged tables and fake-leather tufted seating took over.

I barely remembered Cathy from school. We'd shared a class or two, and she was a couple of years ahead of me. She was in law school by the time I entered my CPA programs at the university. Luckily, in the past few days I'd been all over her Facebook and LinkedIn pages so I had a good idea of who I was looking for. The other clue was the woman waving madly at me from a corner booth at the front windows.

"I saw you as soon as you parked!" She'd slid out of the booth and we did one of those quick hugs that has begun to mean nothing, since everyone in the world will give you a hug these days.

I smiled big and made happy noises, while searching my memory banks for hints about any shared history. Truthfully, I didn't remember her well at all. A quick perusal of my old yearbook yesterday had showed her with long, dark hair that hung lankly past her shoulders, bangs that looked as if they been trimmed with garden shears, and a needy smile. The smile was the only feature she'd retained.

The dark hair had become a rich chestnut with golden highlights, cut in layers with the ends flipping up in a way that gave her whole face a lift. The too-heavy eyeglasses were gone—replaced by contacts, no doubt—and her makeup was light and natural.

"You look great," I said, as my excuse for staring. "Practicing law has agreed with you."

"Oh, actually, I hated the law. I'm a yoga instructor now. I have my own studio, and we're thinking of opening branches around the state."

"Wow." My one and only attempt at yoga classes hadn't gone well, and although I knew it would probably be good to give it another try, I hadn't worked up the enthusiasm for it yet. I dropped my purse onto the seat and slid into the left side of the booth. "So, do you even consume things like Cokes and fries anymore?"

She laughed, but the tiny hint of neediness showed in the smile. "Oh, sure. Now and then. Well, especially the fries here!"

"I ran across Helen Bannerly recently," I said, pretending to study the milkshake flavors on the menu. "She's done well in her law practice, although I was surprised to learn that she'd turned away from criminal law. I suppose it was that case about ten years ago …"

Cathy picked up the hint. "Helen Bannerly. God, we were so close for a while back then, following the fast track in law school, taking intern jobs."

A waitress interrupted to take our orders and I paused until she'd walked away.

"Helen clerked for Judge Blackman, didn't she? What a shocker about him, huh."

"I am not surprised. The man was so … so blatant. It only makes sense that somebody eventually came after him."

"What do you mean—blatant?" I had a feeling I knew.

"His moves on the women, of course. I mean, some of them went for it willingly, I guess. Helen was one. But, I tell you, he'd chase anything in a skirt."

"Wait a minute—Helen? He and Helen?"

"Oh yeah. They had a thing going for a while. She broke it off when she met Travis. She'd been working so hard at the career track, but she really wanted a family. She and Travis wanted kids. She thought Blackman was out of her life." Cathy stopped talking when our food arrived, and we each savored a few of the piping hot fries right away.

"Okay, you said she *thought* the judge was out of her life. He wasn't?"

"He came back, pushed her. She told me he even threatened to tell her new husband about their affair if she didn't continue to see him."

"That sounds really convoluted."

"It's Blackman. He sees—saw—what he wanted and didn't take no for an answer. Helen was scared of what he might do. She knew the clock was ticking on her chances to have kids and she couldn't afford to have Travis leave her."

"Did all this happen right before she left criminal law? Was Blackman the reason she didn't want to be in the courtroom anymore?"

"Now that you mention it, yeah, I guess so. We were both having our own crises with lawyering. I'd burned out early on, the long hours as an associate in a dumpy firm, and my heart wasn't in it to get out there and make a name for myself, not the way Helen did. She and I would get together for a drink after work now and then, commiserate. That's when she told me about the judge."

A hidden affair and wanting to keep her marriage together. If others knew about this, it would certainly explain why Helen didn't try too hard to get Rory McNab acquitted. She had probably received the same threats the jurors did, only in her case she had something real and important to lose. Still, Helen wasn't the only one.

"But you say Blackman was like that with a lot of women. I'm surprised he wasn't more concerned that his wife would leave him."

"According to Helen, Phoebe Blackman is quite content with her life. She's got all the money she needs, travels everywhere, does her own thing. As long as she appears at his side sometimes at society functions and doesn't make a fuss over his behavior, she has whatever she wants." Cathy dipped the last of her fries in ketchup.

The conversation turned to present-day subjects, where I got the complete rundown on Cathy's family members and her thriving business. She barely asked about my work or husband, and that was fine. I could tell from the hour we spent together that we weren't going to take up as old chums or anything. We split the check and made vague promises that we should do this again sometime.

All the way home I considered Helen Bannerly and her

situation. Coerced into an affair as a young law clerk intern, probably wined and dined by an older man who never intended to leave his wife and offered no real future. She finds a man who can offer the future she wants, and she's coming up on the deadline to have kids. It shouldn't be any surprise that she wouldn't risk it all. It was a simple thing, not to try very hard to get Rory McNab off the hook.

I thought back to the one conversation I'd had with her. She was cool and collected and sure of herself—now. But she'd taken steps to get away from the parts of her life which had become uncomfortable. Then I remembered the way her manner had changed when she mentioned Herman Quinto. Could he have been the person behind the threats? I would try again for an appointment to talk to him.

Chapter 31

"Charlie, I need your help!" The voice held desperation and I struggled for a moment to recognize it. I seldom pick up a call from an unknown number but I'd been distracted as I pulled into my driveway and walked toward the front door. "Dad's taken the gun. I should have known he'd pull something. I'm *so* sorry."

Christine McNab.

"He's after Herman Quinto. He left me a note."

"Christine, slow down. Take a breath. How do you know this?"

"He brought up the subject of Quinto and said there was a big rally this evening at Tiguex Park. He was getting more irate by the minute and he went to get his shotgun. When he checked and saw the ammo was gone, he got furious with me."

"So, you didn't give in and give back the shells did you?"

"Oh no. After a couple minutes of ranting he went to his room and quieted down. I figured he'd got the whole thing out of his system so I went to take my shower. When I came out, he and the gun were gone, and he'd left a note that just said 'Don't think you can fool me, missy. I have more ammo than you'll ever know.' Charlie, I'm worried."

"You think he's gone down to the park?" I could picture the setting, a large wooded park at the edge of the Old Town area. I didn't think a shotgun would have enough range for Fergus to try anything sniper-style from a tall building, and surely the senator would have major security to see that no one carrying a weapon could get into the crowd of supporters.

But still—what if—

"Does your father have more than one gun?" *Please say you found them all and took* all *the ammo.*

"Um … um, I can't remember. When I was a kid he used to go deer hunting."

Great. That would require something more powerful than the shotgun I'd seen.

"You'd better go on the assumption that he's got something else and took it along, Christine. Have you called the police?"

"No. I'm scared to. You know how those things go when you hear the news stories. They'll go all SWAT team at him, and he'll be killed before he even gets the chance to surrender."

I felt a rock drop to the pit of my stomach. It was probably true. And even though Fergus was about to die anyway, this would be a horrible way for him to go. Not to mention the additional taint on the family name, a family that didn't deserve it.

"Charlie, can you meet me there? We could find him before the police do, and I'm sure we can talk him out of this crazy plan."

Ugh—it was the last suggestion I wanted to hear.

I took a deep breath and got a picture of the park in my head. "Okay, let's meet at the west edge of the duck pond. The stage where they hold events is at the northeast part of the park, but we'll have to get there and check it out to see how close we can get."

I spun back toward the Jeep and climbed in. I must admit I haven't attended a political rally since my college days and I've got no idea how those things work now. Security concerns are way beyond what they used to be, and for all I knew only people with tickets and some kind of pre-screening would get within a mile of the senator.

Starting the car, I gave myself a reality check. This was a New Mexico state senator who hadn't yet won a seat to Congress. How important was he, really? On the other hand, I told myself, when it came to his publicly staged events and the image he wanted to project, he would be as important as he wanted to be.

Parking near Old Town can be a challenge, but today the area near the park posed special challenges. I found myself thinking ahead to how we would get Fergus out of there, an unsteady old man toting his gun, wanting to make a quick exit. Every street skirting the park had been cordoned off; cops were directing traffic in one-way patterns that don't normally exist. I had no choice but to follow along. The parking lot for park visitors was jammed full and an orange-vested attendant shook his head at any car with a turn signal on, waving us onward.

Street parking seemed iffy—only the occasional too-small space showed up. I finally just swung into a garage I'd used before. It was full to the fourth level, where I finally snagged a spot, locked up, and ran to the elevator. While I waited, I scoped out the view from this angle.

Trees obscured the park details, but I could hear music and the sounds of a crowd being prepped for excitement. The duck pond stood somewhat in the open, and I spotted a bright purple shirt on a woman—Christine.

The elevator dinged and the door slid open, but something else had caught my eye. A small man in a red plaid shirt was walking purposefully along the perimeter of the park, heading in the direction of the stage at the south end. At his side, a long, thin object hung down parallel to his right leg.

Anyone standing in the park would probably not notice the gun; he did a good job of keeping it low. I watched helplessly. At a full run it would take me at least three minutes to get to him. Christine was closer, but she didn't know it. I grabbed my phone from my back pocket and hit the button to redial her number.

The elevator beckoned, but I knew I would lose my vantage point the minute I got to ground level. I stared at Fergus as the phone rang.

"Charlie?"

"Yeah. I'm in the parking garage about a half block from you and I've spotted your dad. He's got the gun. He's walking the pathway along the east end of the park, heading south. Looks like he's going toward the stage area. There are a couple of motor homes behind the stage backdrop. I'd bet that's where Quinto and his entourage are."

"Okay. I'm heading that way," she said. "They're warming up the crowd and it sounds like they'll be introducing the candidate really soon. Hurry!"

Some other people had stepped into the elevator and the door closed behind them. I dashed for the stairs and took them three at a time, practically bouncing off the handrail as I used it for balance. At the street, I had to dodge between cars and heard a squeal of brakes when I dashed across. I got stern looks from people who thought I was trying to cut in front of the admissions line, but I tore past them and followed the side street toward the last place I'd seen Fergus.

The motorhomes stood ahead, more than a block away. I had to stop for a minute to scan the crowd. A glimpse of a red shirt sent me racing ahead. I stuck to the side street where I could run; most of the people were milling away from it and heading toward the center of the park. I lost the red shirt for a moment but kept going toward the motorhomes.

A second later, I saw the red again. The man had stopped, facing toward the stage. It wasn't Fergus.

Shit!

"Charlie!" I heard my name, a faint high note in the general noise of the crowd. Christine's hand was waving back and forth above the heads in front of me.

I sidestepped and slipped between bodies until I reached her. "Did you see him?" I panted.

"Only for a second."

"He has to be somewhere right around here." I scanned the area where the motorhomes sat. The door to one of them opened and a man in a dark suit stepped out. It wasn't Quinto, but he couldn't be far behind.

On stage, someone was getting to the real rah-rah part of his speech, and I sensed they were gearing up for the star of the show.

"Let's split up and circle these two vehicles," I suggested. "If you can get close enough to grab, go for the gun instead of your dad. We need to get it out of his hands."

"Agreed." She turned right and I went left, turning my head in all directions.

I didn't know if Fergus would try to place himself beside the candidate's motorhome or if he would be watching from a short distance away. I hoped he didn't plan to take aim at the stage itself; the perimeter of it was crawling with security, most of whom were probably off-duty cops. They wouldn't mess around with him, even if he was an old man.

I rounded the corner of the larger of the two vehicles, a silver-gray thing that looked like a Greyhound bus, and there was Fergus, facing me. He was holding a rifle at his side and the black barrel nearly blended with his dark blue jeans.

"Fergus, it's Charlie. Don't do anything crazy here." I had my hands out to my sides, fingers spread. "You need to set the gun down on the ground."

And then what? I hadn't got quite far enough in my thinking to figure out what we would do next.

Startled, he hadn't expected to see me here.

I took advantage and moved in quickly, sweeping by and reaching for the rifle. Luckily, his finger wasn't on the trigger—his old hunter safety rules at least told him that much—and I got a good grip between the stock and the trigger guard. Surprised by the move, his grip didn't hold, and I quickly put ten feet between us.

"Okay, Fergus, we're going to figure out how to get out of here and take you home—"

Christine came running up at that moment. "Dad,

what have you—?"

Unfortunately, two uniformed cops were right behind her. Before I could blink they'd drawn their service pistols on me. I laid the rifle on the ground and froze.

Chapter 32

This isn't what it looks like." It was the first lame statement out of my mouth and the second time I'd uttered it in recent days. I could tell by the looks the two cops gave that they'd heard it a million times.

The gun lay on the ground with no one in reaching distance, so at least they kept their heads and didn't shout for all of us to hit the dirt or something equally dramatic.

Christine spoke first. "She disarmed him," she said, pointing at Fergus. She gave the quick explanation of who everyone was and what we were doing here. "Dad came here out of a stupid, misguided approach to a family problem, not because of a political statement or a wish to harm a lot of people."

The older of the two officers had already sent the other one to cuff Fergus. I said nothing and kept my hands visible.

Christine kept babbling, telling them her father was unwell and how they really didn't need to charge him with anything, no crime had been committed, and so on until the officer told her to save the story until we all got downtown and they could sort it out. He'd picked up the rifle, using a handkerchief to handle it. I supposed there were no evidence bags quite this big in his back pockets.

The younger officer looked toward me, itching to take out another set of cuffs.

I took a respectful stance and lowered my hands. "Charlie Parker, RJP Investigations. We're helping Mr. McNab look into a family matter involving his son. I'm sure he didn't mean to—"

"Hell," Fergus said, "the only thing I really did mean to do was to take that worthless Herman Quinto off the face of this planet."

Not the right thing to say. The older cop took charge again. "Mr. McNab, you're under arrest for the attempted murder of Herman Quinto. You have the right to remain silent …"

Christine sent me a helpless look as the officer went through the spiel.

"We'll need you ladies to come downtown and make statements," he told us. "Tucker, take them in your cruiser. I've got the suspect with me."

Giving assurances that we wouldn't cause any trouble, Christine and I were allowed to walk to the police car without being cuffed or manhandled. I dreaded there being more video of me on the evening news accompanied by police, but no reporters mobbed us. From the other side of the large backdrop came Quinto's voice as he greeted the crowd and they cheered raucously. Any media attention was surely directed to the stage at this moment.

Ahead, I saw Fergus turn to look toward the noise, a glare of resentment on his face. We'd foiled his plan and he wasn't happy.

* * *

The sun had set in spectacular orange and pink over the west mesa by the time we reached the police station. We were led to separate interrogation rooms, and I didn't see Fergus at all. I took a seat—I'd swear it was the same grimy table in the same dull room where I'd been only a few days ago—and waited to see what would happen next. They had my fingerprints on the gun, and I'd been the one holding it when the officers spotted us, so I couldn't be at all sure I wasn't in big trouble.

My fears were somewhat assuaged when Kent Taylor came into the room and his first words were, "Charlie Parker, three times in one week. We've got to stop meeting like this." It was the way one corner of his mouth tilted upward that reassured me.

"Well, it's definitely some kind of record for us." I shifted in my seat. He didn't take a chair, just perched one hip on the edge of the metal table. "What's happening with Fergus?"

"Not much. The man could benefit by having a lawyer here. He's blabbing all over the place how he planned to kill Herman Quinto."

Ouch. I wished I'd thought to shout advice out to Fergus before he was taken out of my sight. "He was advised of his rights at the park, but he's not a guy to listen to common sense, I'm discovering."

"This is all related to that old case where his son was convicted?"

"The old man is dying. He has cancer and they say it won't be long, maybe a couple of months. He just wants to see his son exonerated and back at home before he goes."

"Touching." Taylor raised one palm in a conciliatory gesture. "I'm not being sarcastic. I feel for the guy. I feel for the family. But we can't just turn loose every criminal whose family has a sad story. Rory McNab was tried and convicted, and he made it worse by escaping and remaining a fugitive for almost ten years."

"I know." I had hoped to find the evidence to overturn that conviction but the clues weren't coming together for me yet, and time was running out for Fergus.

"You're not charged with anything, Charlie. You can go any time."

"What about Fergus? Surely you're not going to put the city to the expense of a murder trial when the defendant probably won't live long enough to sit through the whole ordeal."

Taylor gave a 'we'll see' kind of shrug.

"Where's Christine, the daughter? I should talk to her, see if they want me to stay on the case."

The detective beckoned for me to follow, and I tagged along to the next interrogation room along the hall. Christine sat at an identical table in a room just like the one where I'd been. Taylor let me in.

"Charlie!" She stood up and hugged me. "I can't believe this is happening."

With a pointed glance toward the mirrored wall opposite, I said, "We'll talk later. I'm going to check some things at my office. Call me as soon as you learn what they'll do about your dad. Get him an attorney. This is serious."

"I, uh … okay. I don't know any in Albuquerque. Can you recommend someone?"

The ones I'd encountered recently weren't exactly tops on my list, especially for criminal defense, but I finally pulled a name out of my hat—a guy who'd helped a friend a few years ago. I gave Christine the name and she said she would look him up and call right away.

"Fergus will be arraigned in the morning and the attorney needs to be there. Don't wait on this."

She assured me and said she would call me later, if that was okay. Feeling as righteous as a person can who's failed her client (but at least I did the right thing in the eyes of the law this time), I left the police station and got a ride back to the garage where I'd left my Jeep.

I had lied. The intention was pure, to go right back to work for Fergus and Rory, but suddenly I couldn't face a night at the office. It had been *way* too long a day and my brain was numb.

Fergus was a guest of the city jail for the night and Christine was doing all she could to get legal representation for him. I had done my duty, for now, and would be much fresher to consider the options tomorrow. Right now, all I wanted was my husband and my dog and a hot meal, in that order.

Chapter 33

I attended the arraignment at ten o'clock the next morning. On his attorney's advice, Fergus kept his mouth shut except to utter the words "not guilty" at the appropriate time. The attorney made the very logical argument that his client was in no shape to leave the city, and was under doctor's orders to move into a nursing home because of his ongoing need for medical care. The judge, a stern-looking woman with short black hair, banged her gavel and ordered it so. Trial would begin January fifteenth.

Christine and I looked at each other. It was the judge's kindly way of letting Fergus go away to die in peace.

The old man sputtered in protest about the nursing home. "I'm perfectly fine to go home. That lady judge, she don't know nothin' about me."

"Whatever you say, Dad. Let's get in the car."

A chilly wind funneled between the buildings, raising goosebumps on my arms despite my jacket. Knowing about the doctor's orders ahead of time, Christine had called me early this morning to ask my help in getting Fergus settled. She had brought basic clothing and his medications from his trailer; a packed bag was in the back seat of her car. I would follow along to raise the voice of authority if the father refused to listen to the daughter.

By the time we arrived at Mountainview Elder Care, some of the steam had gone out of Fergus. His night in detention had to have been rough on him. Dark, puffy circles under his eyes and a gaunt look to his jawline gave it away. One burst of stubbornness appeared when Christine opened the passenger side car door and he refused to get out. I stepped over.

"Fergus, come on. It's getting colder out here, and they've got a really comfy bed in here for you. Rest up for a while and then there will be some lunch."

"I want my own bed and my own pajamas."

Christine had reached in the back seat and she held up the suitcase. "Got your PJs right here."

I had my hand on his elbow and gave a lift upward. The bones jutted through his shirt and jacket. At least he didn't resist.

"Okay, let's get inside and see about that lunch." I made sure he had his feet under him, but I wasn't about to let go of my grip. The old guy still had a gleam in his eye that told me he was thinking of making a dash for it.

We'd no sooner gone through the front double doors than a woman in a brightly flowered pullover top and coordinating pants came forward with a beaming smile.

"Mr. McNab! We are *so* happy you're here." She gave a

flirty wink and showed some dimples. "The ladies will be *so* eager to meet you. There aren't many men here and the women *love* to dote on you guys."

He made a grumpy sound but I noticed his eyes had quickly scanned the foyer.

"We're going to take a little tour. I'm Bunny, by the way." She took his arm. "Your daughters can sign the papers and meet us in room 114."

Bunny and Fergus headed into a large room, very reminiscent of the common area at the rehab facility where Gram was. This whole nursing home scene began to trigger the same feelings I'd had about taking her there after her hospital stay.

Christine told me Fergus's doctors had arranged everything. She handed the suitcase to me while she read and signed a few forms, then we headed down a hallway where we located Room 114 on the right.

"Let's just put his things out where he'll see them," she suggested. "Maybe he'll see this as a *fait accompli* if it appears he's already moved in."

Shades of a few days ago, when I'd set Gram's toothbrush and combs in a different bathroom with the same look. With two of us unpacking, it took less than five minutes. She had set Fergus's favorite picture of himself and Rory on the nightstand.

"Well, I should leave you and your dad alone," I said.

"Can you hang around a little while? We need to talk about getting Rory back here before it's too late. You and your husband are the only ones who know where he is."

"Your dad won't tell you?"

"Not on a bet. I tried." Her voice dropped to a whisper as we heard Bunny's voice approaching. "I'll spend a minute here. Meet me in the lobby."

Since my job was to reunite father and son before it was too late, I couldn't very well refuse. I kept myself occupied by listening to the residents beg to go home. All I could do was to hope with everything in me that Gram would do well enough to stay in her own home with a caretaker or visiting nurse. When tears threatened to overtake me, I stepped out to the front porch and let the wind mask the sad emotions.

Christine joined me about five minutes later. "Sorry. He's confused, doesn't understand why he can't be home alone."

"If we can get Rory to return, do you think the doctor would allow Fergus to leave here?"

She shook her head. "He really needs medical care. The last forty-eight hours were rough. I think he used the last of his spunkiness ration with that stunt at the park. I wish he'd just stayed home and kept his opinions about Herman Quinto to himself." She rummaged in her purse and came up with her keys, and we started toward the parking lot. "I can stay in Albuquerque today, but by tomorrow I need to be on the road for Denver. My boss is squawking—loud."

"Okay, so you need to reach Rory."

"He's somewhere in Maine? Honestly, yesterday was the first I'd heard of that."

"Yeah. Apparently he and your dad have stayed in touch."

"How do I find him? And how on earth will he get back here?"

"There are cell phones in a kitchen drawer at Fergus's place. The last I knew, the red one was active. Apparently he and Rory get untraceable ones and just buy minutes for them. My guess is Rory's number is the only one programmed into it. Give that a try. If you reach him, there's a flight out of Portland that got me back here. It's one very long day of flying with a couple of connections, but I imagine Rory will find a way to do it. Those two are close."

She nodded. "Yeah, they are. Dad would bust his ass to be with Rory—I just hope my self-centered brother will do the same for our father."

I didn't know what to say to that. "Let me know. I can meet with him, take him to Fergus since you're leaving."

"Thanks for everything, Charlie. I'll be back. I'm sorry to say, it will probably be fairly soon."

"Yeah." We hugged out there in the parking lot, and I headed to the office where my plan was a little hazy.

With the hoopla surrounding Judge Blackman's death, the surprise of meeting Christine, and Fergus's rather ill-conceived plan to take out Herman Quinto, I'd lost track of where I was in the investigation to find exonerating evidence for Rory. I could always go back to the trial transcript and look for more clues. I picked up fast food and planned to eat at my desk while filling Ron in on the latest.

But Ron was out for the rest of the day, Sally informed me, so I used the few remaining minutes before she was due to go home to ask what was being said on the news about the judge and the election.

""The judge's funeral is day after tomorrow," she said. "They've been talking about the tragedy of his death, but a friend at the daycare center told me his wife was in Clarice's Boutique yesterday buying a whole new wardrobe of resort wear. Quinto is running way ahead in the polls. I guess he was a big hit at the rally in the park."

"Nothing about an attempt on Quinto's life?"

She shook her shaggy blonde head. "Not a thing."

Poor Fergus. Not even a mention of what he'd thought would be a blaze of glory. Well, I didn't plan on being the one to break *that* news to him.

My phone rang as I was walking up the stairs and I glanced at the screen. Christine, already.

"Rory's coming home tomorrow," she said. "I still have to leave, so I won't see him, but I gave him your number. I hope that was okay."

"Sure. I need to talk to him. So the cell phone in Fergus's kitchen worked to reach him?"

"Yeah. You want Rory's number?"

I took down the number, although it wouldn't surprise me a bit if Rory changed phones again before coming to New Mexico. I had a feeling he would still be doing all he could to keep a low profile.

Chapter 34

Ron always tells me a big part of investigative work involves sitting quietly and thinking, putting together the evidence he has gathered. I used that as my justification for sitting at my desk for the next two hours, doing nothing at all. Well, I can't really say *nothing*. I paid some bills and got my invoicing up to date, while my mind ran through the various witness interviews—too many—and the list of suspects I'd discovered—too few.

I had a strong feeling the judge's death was related in some way to his philandering, but I couldn't put together a scenario that felt right. If the wife was packing for a cruise, I could see her on the suspect list, but how her activities related to Rory's conviction for jury tampering was completely beyond me.

Quinto was still a key player I hadn't spoken to, but

when I phoned his office again for an appointment, all I received for the effort was another rude brush-off. I tamped down my increasing frustration.

By four o'clock, I decided an evening without any reference to this case might be the thing to clear my head and show me a fresh angle. I called Drake and asked him out for a movie date and we met at the theater.

We lingered in bed the next morning the way we used to do, happy and satiated until well after nine. A shower together, breakfast out at our favorite place for Eggs Benedict, and it was approaching noon before I showed up at the office. Sally teased me and Ron got a knowing look on his face. I ignored them both and my ringing phone saved me from making excuses.

"Is this Charlie Parker?" asked an unfamiliar male voice.

"Speaking."

"Christine said I should call you when I got to town."

"Rory?"

"Let's say it's Rudy."

I calculated the flight time and couldn't imagine how he'd arrived so early in the day. "Okay … Rudy. You're here now? Where are you staying?"

"We'll get to that later. I'm going to visit my dad now."

"Do you want to come by my office afterward? I can give you directions. I'll get you caught up on the investigation as it stands right now."

"Maybe." A sound like a hand rubbing over whiskers. "I'll call. I'm staying invisible, you know."

"Okay, I get that. So, yeah. Call me." I hung up wondering if I would actually ever hear from him, or whether the one perfunctory call was only because his sister had insisted.

Well, Fergus was my client so it didn't really matter what Rory thought. On the other hand, Rory was the one person who probably knew what was going on ten years ago. He'd certainly been frightened enough to believe he had to get out of state. I needed to talk to him more in-depth than these one-word sentences over the phone.

I arrived at Mountainview Elder Care fifteen minutes later. All the cars in the parking lot had New Mexico plates but I made a slow pass through to see if any carried obvious signs of being rentals. There was one with a tiny sticker from Budget on the back bumper. Fergus's room didn't face the parking lot so I doubted Rory would get a warning of my arrival. I parked near the rental car and went inside.

Lucky me, I was greeted by Bunny at the front door.

"Hi again. I came to visit with Fergus McNab for a little while," I said.

She fell in step beside me. "Popular man today," she said with a perky lilt to her voice. "I'm glad. The poor man …" Her voice dropped a notch. "It's hard to watch them fade this quickly, even when … you know … the outcome is certain."

I nodded. Room 114 came up right away. "Well, thanks, Bunny. I'll just …" I gave a vague wave toward the door.

Bunny was right. Fergus was visibly dwindling, even in the past twenty-four hours. He lay in the bed, his skin gray against the white sheets, his thin arms and bony hands resting on top of the covers. Except for the two bright spots on his cheeks, I would have thought he was unconscious. His eyelids fluttered open when he realized I was there. I looked around the room.

"Didn't your son come by?" I asked.

A crooked smile twisted the old man's face. "Okay, Rory, come on out," he said.

The closet door opened and a younger, fitter, dark-haired version of Fergus stepped out.

"Rory, I'm Charlie." I extended a hand and after a moment he shook it.

"Sorry. I heard voices in the hall. Have to be cautious."

"Sure. I understand." Although I didn't. Surely he didn't believe everyone in Albuquerque would still recognize him, especially since he'd lost close to forty pounds and was much more muscular and trim than his younger self. "So, did you have a good flight? You made great time."

"I took one leg of it last night, into another city, then did the second half this morning."

The caution again. He was much more soft spoken than I'd expected, in fact, a gentler manner all around. I saw nothing of the brash young attorney who had appeared in the photos I'd been studying recently. It might have been the effect of what Gram would call 'being taken down a peg' or it could be that time and living alone in the woods had changed and mellowed him.

"I would really like the chance to talk about what your dad hired us for. I know you are leery of strangers and all that."

Fergus waved a hand back and forth, as if to say 'Hey you, I'm still here.' Rory turned to him.

"Trust her, kid. She's a pain in the butt—stopped me from ridding the world of Herman Quinto—but she's honest and she's trying to make things right so you can come back to stay."

I laughed at his description. He wasn't at all the first person to call me a pain. The mood lightened.

Rory looked at me. "I'm staying with Dad for a few hours, but I'll call you later."

I thanked him, wished Fergus well and squeezed his hand before I left. Less than two hours later, I got the call.

"He's sleeping a lot," Rory said. "I didn't figure there was much point in sitting there. I need to settle in but I don't think I dare go stay at his place. I'm still not trusting that Quinto wouldn't go to some lengths to put me away."

"He's running on a law-and-order ticket, so yeah. This would be the time to impress the voters by bringing in a fugitive."

"I don't feel like I know the city very well any more. So much has changed. I was thinking of one of those little motels on Central."

"Um … they can be pretty unsavory. Lots of gang activity in those neighborhoods these days." I gave him the name of a weekly inn on Menaul, the kind of place mostly used by businessmen who wanted a little studio where they could reheat a meal and stay in when restaurant food got tiresome.

"Why don't you check in and get settled, then you can come down to my office, or—"

"I'll call again. Give me an hour."

It felt frustrating, getting the brush-off every time I tried to suggest a plan, but I understood his reluctance to trust. Not to mention ten years of hiding out—he'd developed survival instincts beyond anything I'd ever had to deal with myself.

I went home, fed Freckles, and snacked on some sliced ham and a few chunks of cheese. I had no idea how long a meeting Rory would tolerate. I might get to ask two questions before he flitted away again, or I might have the chance for a real discussion of his case. I was considering which would be the most important of the topics to get out of the way first when he called back.

"Right up the street from the motel is a bar. Meet me there in twenty minutes." He hung up so quickly I couldn't be certain he'd heard my response.

Drake came home and I told him the situation. "This guy is jumpier than a cat at the dog pound, but I really need to meet with him." I gave him the name of the bar and told him I would call or get a text to him when I got there and again when I left.

"Are you that worried, hon? I can follow you and sit outside ..."

"Probably better if you don't. I tell you, he's used to being on the run and any hint that he's being watched would probably send him rushing back off to Maine. It would break Fergus's heart to lose touch with his son again so quickly. I'll be fine. It's not like the place I'm going is a dive."

"I'm going to send you a text each hour. If all is okay, just send me a smiley face back."

I laughed at his cute idea of clandestine tricks but agreed to the plan. I had to admit it felt good to have someone watching my back.

Assuring Drake the bar wasn't a dive might have been a little generous. It turned out to be a hole-in-the-wall place, but I could see why Rory chose it. It had the right amount of noise and seemed to be filled with blue-collar neighborhood locals. The atmosphere was dark and smoky with a laughing crowd at the one pool table in the far corner, while seats at the long bar were occupied by people in chambray shirts and ball caps who were sharing stories and glancing at the TV mounted above the bar. A jukebox played country music and quite a few of the patrons got up and danced. I spotted Rory in a small booth at the back where the lighting was dimmest.

"I didn't know what to order for you," he said. He had a sweaty mug of Michelob in front of him.

"One of those is fine," I said. I don't actually love beer so it's a safe drink to nurse along for however many hours I sat there. "Thanks for agreeing to meet me."

He shrugged. "I was shocked to hear from Chrissy. I had no idea Dad was going downhill so fast. Back at my place, he was popping a lot of pain killers but the way he broke the news about the cancer made me think he had a couple years still. I didn't think a whole lot about the pills. I guess the night in jail really tore him up—they've got him hooked to a morphine pump now. That means it's getting close, I guess."

We went silent while the waitress set my beer down in front of me. I handed her some cash and told her to keep the change.

"I'm glad you could come. It means a lot to him. No problems with ticketing or flying? Sorry, probably none of my business but I assume you don't want to use your own name."

"No. Yeah, I've got a Maine driver's license under another name. As much as I live off the grid, there are still times … well, there are raised eyebrows if a person can't show at least one type of identification. It's weird because the cabin where I live—well, it had been abandoned with all the furniture and everything. In a drawer were important papers, including birth certificates for, I guess, the couple who once lived there. I borrowed his. Had to add five years to my age, but it worked for my purposes."

"Wow. You know, I've never given it much thought. You know, what it would take to disappear."

"It's not as easy as you would think in this day and

time. ID is just one thing, but credit cards are traceable, fingerprints, DNA. I know I'm cautious beyond belief." He held up the beer mug. "Prints can be taken from a can or bottle a whole lot easier than the handle of one of these. I wear gloves in the rental car and hotel room. I know it's not foolproof but—"

He paused and swallowed hard. I could tell the routine must be exhausting. I couldn't imagine keeping it up for so many years.

"I've missed New Mexico. The winters in Maine are … well, you can imagine. And the bugs and things out in the woods. I was raised in a small town, but this is beyond."

"How do you live? I mean, what kind of food …"

"Fishing in the lake, growing a few simple vegetables. Over the winter I stay in and I've actually developed a little skill with a paintbrush and canvas. At least that's what the lady in Grandy says, the one who owns the bookstore. She sells a few of my pieces during the summer tourist season, and it's enough to keep me in books and staple food supplies."

"Must get lonely out there."

He stared at his mug for a moment. "You know, I'm not sure what kind of life I'd want now. Mostly, I missed Dad. We were close, always. He helped me get away, you know."

"I'd heard."

"Well. This isn't what you came to talk about."

"I'd hoped you might have some information that might help your case. Fergus blames Quinto, your lawyer, and the judge, seemingly in equal proportions. But I've had a devil of a time coming up with anything concrete, anything that would help us reopen the case or get the verdict thrown out."

His eyes had gone to the TV screen across the room where, even with the sound muted, I could tell the news story was about Judge Blackman's funeral. I'd forgotten it was today.

"Do you think he was involved in either the jury tampering or rigging the case against you?" I asked with a nod toward the screen.

Rory's jaw tensed, a muscle twitching beside his ear.

"Most of what I've learned about the judge—some of it by firsthand experience—is what a womanizer he was. I found someone who knew he had an affair with your attorney, Helen Bannerly. Supposedly, it was old news way before your case came along, but I'm not so sure."

"Don't be sure of anything concerning old man Blackman. He was a predator of the worst kind, and not just with women."

Chapter 35

I think my jaw dropped. Rory continued to aim a dark stare toward the screen until the Blackman funeral news coverage was finished. Had he been one of Blackman's victims? If the judge went after males and females alike, it certainly threw a new twist into the picture.

When Rory turned his attention back to me and I asked, he simply said, "Look around. You'll find others. I learned that when I got into the Damian Baca case."

Mention of the original case brought something else to mind. "There was a man with a scar on his lip. I saw him in a couple of the photos right after the trial. Who is he?"

Something shifted very subtly. He shrugged and drained the last of his beer. "Just some guy. He knew Damian—maybe a cousin or something. You know those families—they have a million cousins."

Before I could figure out whether that was a racial slur or what, Rory had slid to the end of the booth. "Look, I gotta go. Been a long day."

With that, he stood and walked away.

My phone pinged with a text from Drake. I answered: Looks like we're done. I'm heading home.

I abandoned the half of my beer that sat in the glass. Told you, I'm a cheap date. The conversation ran through my mind during the drive home. I had hoped Rory would jump on my news about Blackman's affair with Helen Bannerly, that the old legal-eagle in him would light up and say it would be enough to present as evidence to overturn his conviction. And maybe, just maybe, he would be the tiniest bit grateful for the work I'd put into trying to save his ass.

So, okay, that wasn't happening—at least not yet. But Fergus wanted answers and it was his money covering our fee, so whether Rory cared or not, I would do my best for the old man.

I fell asleep with the conversations running through my mind—everything Rory had said since he arrived in town—and the scenes replayed in my dreams all night as well. I jolted awake at 4:57 a.m., realizing I'd seen the man with the scar recently.

He was the dark-suited man emerging from Quinto's motorhome at the rally. I'd been so focused on the suits— then on Fergus—I hadn't processed that bit of detail. If he was related to Damian Baca, as Rory had told me, what was he doing as part of Quinto's entourage now at election time? I still didn't know the man's name, but I did know Baca's and I knew where he worked.

A quick call to the casino and I learned Damian would report for work at five p.m. Visits to the two elders in my

life took up much of the day (Elsa raring to get home,
Fergus visibly fading and hooked to IV lines now). I didn't
see Rory at the nursing home and Fergus was unclear as to
his son's whereabouts. He seemed unclear about a lot of
things now, and I wondered what was in those IVs.

At four o'clock I headed across town. Traffic could be
a bear, and I wanted to allow plenty of time to be waiting
when Damian showed up for work. I hoped he was the
type to arrive early and we'd get the chance to talk; if he
was one who rushed into the building four seconds before
his shift started, I might have to sprint alongside from the
car to the building just to insert a question or two.

At 4:40 I arrived at the casino property and cruised
around until I found the crowded employee parking lot.
Strategically, I wanted to be near the walkway where
everyone had to enter the building. It would be ideal to
park facing the lot so I could watch cars come and go, and
could get a long look at Damian before he noticed me. It
didn't quite work out that way. The lot was jammed, and
the only suitable spot was on the western edge. I backed
into the slot and scanned the activity.

Hotel maids were outbound, finished for the day. Guys
with grass stains on their pant legs had to be landscape
maintenance—they, too, were leaving. As cars pulled away,
others arrived, most likely the evening casino workers.
They were dressed, made up, and coiffed to face the public
and be charming because their tips depended on it.

At five minutes before the hour I spotted him walking
briskly toward the walkway. I hadn't noticed which car
he got out of—darn it—but there was no doubt it was
Damian. I jumped out of my Jeep and race-walked toward
him.

"Damian!" I called out when I got within shouting distance.

He paused, puzzled, and it was enough time for me to catch up.

"Damian, hi, I'm Charlie Parker."

"My bills are all caught up and I don't owe any child support," he said. He was studying my face. "You were here before—I'd say a week or so ago."

"Wow, great memory."

"It's my job to know who's doing what at my casino floor. You played a slot for a long time, never won much, kept eyeing the crowd at the craps table. Now you're catching up to me out here—what do you want?"

"Sounds like I need to offer you a job. Your observation skills are way better than mine." I handed him my card.

He actually looked at it. "Private investigator, huh. May I ask what this is about?"

"Do you remember Rory McNab?"

"Of course. He did a damn fine job of getting me out of a jam." Damian pocketed my card and rubbed at a spot just above his nose. "He also knocked some sense into me."

"What do you mean, 'knocked some sense'?"

"Took me aside after the not-guilty verdict and pushed me up against the wall in one of the conference rooms. Told me he knew for a fact I was guilty and that if I didn't change my ways real soon, I'd be right back in court and eventually I'd be in prison. He told me what it would be like for a guy like me. I might think I was tough stuff, but thrown in there, I'd find out what tough really was."

"You must have listened." I tilted my head toward the upscale casino building.

"Not at first. I puffed myself up and basically told him

to get screwed. I could run my own life. But later … well, his words came back to me. I'm grateful to him for what he said that day. Most lawyers would have collected their money and blown me off. Not Rory McNab."

"Did the two of you stay in touch?"

"After he went on trial, himself, well …" He wasn't telling me everything, but the implication was clear. Suddenly, he probably hadn't been so sure about Rory's lecture on honesty. He'd started walking toward the building again and I trailed along.

"One more question. There was a guy in the photos after the trial, a man with a scar on his upper lip. Someone said he was a cousin of yours?"

"Lots of guys have scars. Could be anybody." Damian picked up the pace. "I'm gonna be late. Sorry."

Damian Baca had a great memory for faces. Why wouldn't he be able to recall the man on the courthouse steps on what was a pivotal day in his life? He might have turned his life around, and he might be polite and convincing. But he was lying about something, and I felt sure the lie involved the man with the scar. I could understand a guy covering up for a relative. The question was, why? I had no evidence the unnamed man had done anything wrong. So, what would Damian be covering up?

Chapter 36

Rush hour traffic crept along, which gave me plenty of time to think about the case on the way home. I had a feeling I was getting sidetracked, mired in little details, when I should be looking back at the major players, the people who had been involved from the beginning. Besides Rory, there were Judge Blackman, Herman Quinto, and Helen Bannerly.

I knew about Blackman and Bannerly's affair. I suspected Quinto had been aware of it at the time. From something Helen's friend Cathy had told me, I wouldn't rule out the possibility of blackmail. But if that was the case, who was the blackmailer and who the blackmailee? And what about Damian Baca—he'd been a minor player at the time, but he could have known something and been willing to cash in on it, or willing to be someone else's errand boy.

It was like dumping a jigsaw puzzle on the table and trying to assemble it without benefit of knowing what the finished picture was supposed to look like. Any of them could have been damaged by certain information: Helen Bannerly's marriage was at stake; the judge's marriage, not to mention his position on the bench, especially if it came out that he had an equal fondness for young males as for young females; and Herman Quinto's big political aspirations would have either been dashed, or enhanced, but was he willing to take that chance?

"You're very quiet this evening," Drake said.

He had made chicken parmesan and was tossing a salad when I walked in. I spread butter and garlic on bread and toasted it—my great contribution to the meal—and we ate at the kitchen table.

"Sorry, I guess I'm living inside my head at the moment."

"The case?"

"Mostly. And Fergus. It's sad and scary to see how fast he's fading. It's almost as if his big wish to see Rory has been granted so now he can just relax and die."

He gave me a sympathetic look as he squeezed my hand. "If I can do anything to help …"

"Yeah, I know. Thanks. You're the best."

"I know." His grin lightened the moment. I tossed a wadded paper napkin at him and it landed in the sticky marinara sauce on his plate.

We spent the evening in front of the TV, Drake immersed in a football game, Freckles stretched out on the couch between us, while I tried to transfer my runaway thoughts to paper. I knew I'd never sleep if my brain stayed in overdrive as it had been for the past few hours. It's amazing how many hours of good sleep I've recovered after picking up a notepad. All the names, all the connections that I knew of—I penned everything, although in no particular order. It was still an unassembled puzzle but I was beginning to see connections.

Somewhere around nine, Ron called.

"You do realize that we need some arrangement in place for Elsa when they send her home." He loves to start a conversation with a veiled demand, and for some reason these always come at the moment I think I'm calm enough to sleep.

"I've been thinking about it, but there hasn't exactly been a spare moment. Can we get on it tomorrow at the office?"

"I have a deposition."

"Okay then, *I'll* get on it tomorrow at the office." It was enough to shut him up, and I added more notes to my paper.

I was beginning to understand the whole 'sandwich generation' thing. At least I didn't have children, other than Freckles, to fret over. Ron did. Career and husband, for me, had to be juggled with my obligations next door, and I told myself I could manage to put career on hold for a while if need be. Ron didn't have that luxury. These benevolent thoughts kept me from wanting to strangle him.

I spent an edgy night. At one point, Drake groaned when I rolled over and pinned his arm under me. He had a job later this morning so I opted for a blanket on the couch so he could get some rest. By five a.m. I gave up the pretense of sleep, brewed some coffee, and sat down with

Elsa's insurance policy and the internet.

The name of the issuing company didn't sound familiar to me because it had been acquired by another before I was old enough to care about the word insurance. A merger and a takeover had happened in the intervening years, and it was awhile before I came upon a site for the present-day mega entity known as Omix Life and Health.

The website was long on glowing promises of a secure future and photos of gray-haired people riding bikes, surfing, and standing on mountaintops—short on any mention of what really happens by the time someone needs the use of their insurance funds. A glance at the clock told me it had taken nearly three hours to get this far in my search.

Somewhere during this time, Drake had risen, showered, gobbled down some cereal, and planted a kiss on my head before departing. I barely registered the news when he told me who the client was and where they would be flying; luckily, he'd written it down and stuck the note to the front of my phone.

By noon I'd found an actual person at Omix Life to talk to and ascertained that, yes, Elsa's policy was still in effect and would cover the cost of a caregiver at home. My next task was to find one. Long story short, I spent two days talking with candidates on the phone, followed by two more days with Ron interviewing the ones who made the first cut. By the end of the week, we were both in love with Dottie Flowers.

Make that three of us. On a visit to the rehab center, Dottie had wooed Gram with her natural friendliness and caring attitude. The large black woman had enough age to empathize with the elderly, enough physical strength to deal with their needs, a pillowy bosom for comforting.

Plus, her credentials as a dietician and physical therapist gave me a lot of confidence. On the first meeting when we introduced her to Gram, the two of them were talking garden-speak within fifteen minutes, discussing what the calendulas—whatever they are—needed to bed them down for the winter. By spring, I could see these two setting tomato plants and laughing over the apple blossoms.

I drove home after their meeting, noticing all the little signs of the changing season, and realized today was Halloween. I made the effort to stop and pick up a bag of candy, but as it turned out we only had visits from fewer than a dozen little princesses and goblins. At one time, this had been my favorite night of the year when, as a kid, I loved to load up on all the goodies. Now, as our neighborhood has aged, the occasion seems merely a blip on the calendar.

Gram's house stood dark still, but that night I slept well for the first time in a week.

The next morning we got the call. Fergus McNab had passed away quietly in his sleep.

Chapter 37

During the same call, Christine said she would fly to Albuquerque this afternoon. I asked about her extended family; they would drive down in a day or two. Neither her husband nor her children had ever met Fergus. The rift between father and daughter had run deep but she would be here to pay her respects and to see Rory. I got the feeling there was not a lot of sisterly love lost on him.

I offered to pick her up at the airport but she insisted she would need a rental car to get around town anyway. She planned to go directly to the funeral home and then check into her hotel and have a long bath and a quiet evening.

"Will Rory meet with you?" I asked.

"I don't know and I don't care." Her voice sounded tired and the day had only begun. "I'm sure I'll find out when I get there."

"Christine …?"

"I know. I'm sorry I don't sound more sympathetic to my brother, but if he hadn't drained all Dad's finances, the medical care could have come quicker and been more effective."

"I'm sorry." It was all I could say.

I called the few people who should know about Fergus—Betty Wilkerson and Ron. The neighbor gave the usual condolences; Ron told me to do whatever I needed for Rory and Christine. Since our client—technically, Fergus—was now dead, I wasn't sure of our standing. Would Rory want me to continue gathering evidence or would he prefer to simply disappear again?

My cell rang just as I was ending the land-line call with Ron. Unknown number. I debated, but picked it up.

"Charlie, it's Rory. You heard about Dad?"

"Yeah, Christine called. I'm sorry."

He didn't say anything and I wondered if he was crying. But his voice sounded firm when he said, "Turn on the TV, Channel 4. There's a story about the judge."

"Blackman?" I trotted to the living room and picked up the remote.

"Yeah. Look, I don't want to stay on the line. I'm gonna go by the funeral home later if you want to come by."

"I will if you'd like me to." Across the bottom of the screen ran a banner on which I caught the words 'sexual harassment' and 'Aldo Blackman.'

"I'd like to meet with you," he said. "There's more you should know. I'll be there at eleven."

I agreed but the connection was already gone. I turned up the television volume.

"… more women. Seven in the past week." The too-pretty news anchor had a solemn look on her pouty lips.

"Yes, it will be interesting to see how this breaking story plays out," said her male counterpart. "Meanwhile, Rachel Givens is at the Blackman home with this, just in."

On camera, an anchor look-alike with long black hair and perfect makeup nodded her head in response to the voice coming into her ear. After a moment she responded to her cue. "Yes, Jake, that's right. We're here at the home of Judge Aldo Blackman, the man who was brutally murdered a little over a week ago and is now being named as a sexual predator by an increasing number of women."

I could see the familiar angles of the modern concrete house in the background. A black limo sat at the edge of the road in front of the massive structure. It appeared someone had cordoned off the street so the reporters couldn't insert themselves in the yard.

"Our attempts to reach members of the household have met with silence." The reporter tried to make it sound as if this was not a complete invasion of the widow's privacy.

Someone behind the camera shouted and the girl reporter turned toward the home. The limo driver, a black-suited man, had stepped out of the car and walked around to the back seat passenger door. The camera operator performed a shaky zoom-in. All it really showed was a lone figure, clad in yellow, dashing for the open car door. The driver quickly closed it, then walked to the home's front door and accepted two large suitcases from someone inside. He hefted the two bags into the trunk of the limo, got into his seat, and pulled away, being none too careful about the tape across the road or the news vehicles gathered at the other end.

"Jake, it appears that Mrs. Blackman is taking a trip

somewhere," reported Rachel, who apparently couldn't actually come up with anything intelligent to say.

The anchors in the newsroom seemed a little flummoxed. Obviously, they had allocated a bit more camera time to their girl in the field. Although she delivered a surprise for the camera, there was nothing quotable or conclusive about the report. The two at the desk made up a couple of impromptu comments then cut to a commercial.

Interesting. I half imagined the media vans crowding behind the limo and following it in caravan to the airport where, no doubt, the judge's wife would catch a plane for one of the coasts or a major hub city. Her destination wouldn't tell them a thing and I doubted the airline personnel would reveal that she was taking off for somewhere tropical. I felt a wave of smug superiority, knowing I had semi-insider information from Sally's spy friend at Clarice's Boutique.

I wondered what the wife was thinking. Her life had probably been stressful, knowing her husband had cheated. Now that it was coming out how many more women there were, and the fact that many of them were unwilling partners, she had to be feeling humiliated and freaked out by the media limelight.

On the other hand, her departure would have been rather clandestine before this morning's news. She'd purchased a tropical wardrobe last week, before the judge was killed. A thought hit me. What if his own wife was the killer? Could she have prepared the whole thing—maybe to include an anonymous tip about his predator instincts— well in advance?

The thought stopped me in my tracks. Had I been looking in the wrong direction all along?

Chapter 38

Eleven o'clock came quickly. I'd managed to stay busy all morning and with one ear tuned to the TV in case they interrupted with some version of a 'breaking story' pertaining to either the harassment victims, the Blackman murder, or Mrs. B's escape right under their noses. Nothing yet.

Rory's rented white sedan sat at the far back corner of the Teller Mortuary parking lot. I took a spot nearer to the door and went inside, where I was directed to a small, private room.

"They're getting him ready. I thought maybe this dark wood for the casket." He looked at me with red-rimmed eyes.

"Did your father express any preferences?"

"No, and I'm embarrassed to say—" His voice cracked

and he turned his back and took a deep breath before he faced me again. "I'm embarrassed to say that I never asked. I guess I thought when he came to my cabin a few weeks ago that he had a lot more time. And then when Chrissy told me to get back here …"

He sighed. "I should have come sooner. Actually, I should have stuck it out and stayed, done my time. At least we would have had visits, Dad and me. I might be getting out soon anyway, and it wouldn't have taken such a toll on him."

"Whose idea was the escape plan? Did your father come up with it?"

"No, don't blame him. We both thought about it. He wanted to help and he loved being a part of it. I should have vetoed the plan and faced the music."

"But your dad … he said he thought your life was in danger. The charges against you, the trial and verdict that would have imprisoned you … he honestly believed it would amount to a life sentence and that it was all set up."

"Tell me," he said, "what was Dad's take on it? Who did he blame?"

"Surely he told you."

"Of course. But I'd be interested to know whether he had another theory, something he didn't want to share with me."

"He thought it was Quinto's way of taking you out of the running, politically. If that's the case, it worked."

Rory nodded thoughtfully. "Yeah, it's pretty much what I thought too."

"I'm still trying to figure out Damian Baca's role. Why was it so important to get him off those drug charges? Was it enough to bring down a promising young lawyer like yourself?"

Something in his face closed. "There *was* no role. Damian. He had no part in it."

"But—"

The door opened just then, admitting a woman dressed in a gray suit with a light blue blouse. She had pale hair, impossible to tell whether it was blonde or white, and was carrying a leather portfolio case, the kind with a tablet on one side and room for other paperwork on the other. Behind her came Christine.

She stiffened when she saw her brother. I sensed a similar reaction from him, even though I'd turned toward the others and didn't actually see him.

"Rory." She advanced a few more steps into the room.

"Chrissy." His use of the diminutive warmed her and they met in an awkward embrace for less than two seconds before they pulled apart again.

"I came directly from the airport," she explained. "We need to get the arrangements made."

From her purse she pulled a few sheets of paper, folded in half.

I turned to face Rory again. "I'll wait outside. I can take you both to lunch, if you'd like."

No one jumped on the lunch invite, but I went outside anyway and staked out a spot to wait near Rory's vehicle. I figured he was the more likely to disappear.

An hour passed. Luckily, the lovely weather had hung around and it wasn't unpleasant in my Jeep with the windows down. When the two emerged, the chill between them was gone but I couldn't exactly discern a lot of warmth either.

Christine came directly to my window and leaned over to speak. "I'm going to pass on lunch. I was up half the night so I need to get a room somewhere. And I want to go by Dad's place and make plans to get his stuff taken care of. The memorial service will be day after tomorrow. Come if you can—please."

I nodded. "Of course. Thanks for inviting me."

I got out of my car before she'd driven away, wanting to catch Rory. He was behind the wheel of the white sedan.

"You doing okay?" I asked.

"Peachy. Cremation."

I'm sure my face registered puzzlement.

"Dad wanted cremation and he never told me. I never asked. Chrissy knew all about it. She had some of his handwritten papers with instructions."

"She must have discussed it with him when she was in town last week."

"Anyway, that part of it went smoothly. I guess she told you there's a little memorial on Wednesday, and his ashes will be buried next to Mom. A few old Hatch friends who live here now will probably be the only ones around. I think Chrissy's husband and kids are going to drive down. I don't know them and they don't know me so I'll stay out of the way."

"That seems sad." I couldn't help it, it just popped out.

"Well, it's more about self preservation. Technically, there's still a warrant out for my arrest, and this time the prison sentence wouldn't be a lenient one. I'd better look at getting out of the state again. At least I had my chance to see Dad and spend a little time with him."

"Are you leaving right away then? I … well, I'd hoped we could talk some more. I feel I still owe it to your father to work on clearing your name."

He gave a weary smile. "Yeah, I guess he still wanted that. Among those papers was information about an insurance policy and a note in Dad's handwriting saying the money was to cover an investigation into my case and obtaining my release."

"He had told me that, but you know it's not really necessary. Beyond a few hundred in expenses so far ..."

"We'll go with his wishes. Stay on the case."

"Okay, then I need you to help with more information." I glanced around the mortuary parking lot. "Can we talk about this somewhere else? I'm still good for that lunch."

"I don't trust restaurants, especially with Judge Blackman's story all over the news right now. How about if I follow you to your office?"

"Sounds good."

Twenty minutes later, we pulled down the long driveway beside the Victorian and parked behind the office, an arrangement that seemed to put Rory at ease. I realized how much of his life he'd spent being wary of his surroundings. It must be driving him crazy to be in a city where he might be recognized, to show up in places where there seemed to be eyes everywhere.

It was like leading an abused puppy indoors for the first time in its life. His eyes darted to every corner of every room. He actually took a step back when he spotted Sally at her desk. I skipped any formal introduction—she knew exactly who he was—and just said we'd be upstairs in my office.

He poked his head into Ron's empty office and into the bathroom, reassuring himself. In my office, he stood back from the front bay window and scanned the street. It's a neighborhood of old houses, some are still residences; the places like ours which have been converted to businesses aren't the type that draw a lot of traffic. Life goes on very quietly.

"At the risk of sounding like a mother hen, I was serious about lunch," I told him. "You're looking even thinner than when you got to town. Besides, how often can you get a pizza at that cabin in the woods?"

He uttered the closest thing to a chuckle I'd heard from him yet, and I took it for a yes. I picked up the phone and placed the order, then told Sally over the intercom to buzz me when it arrived.

Swiveling my desk chair to face the room, I waved Rory toward the loveseat near the bookcase.

"Okay, I need your help," I said. "I feel as if most of the pieces are here, but I'm missing something. I've got Damian Baca, Herman Quinto and you from the first trial—the one where Baca was acquitted. Then I've got you, Helen Bannerly, and Judge Blackman from the second trial. Do you see how the common denominator here is *you*?"

He tilted his head.

"Tell me what I'm missing."

His gaze went to somewhere in the middle of the room but he didn't answer.

"Are we really looking at three completely separate things? Damian's acquittal, your conviction, Blackman's death—are they *actually* unrelated?" The moment I said it, I knew better. From the start, the Baca trial and Rory's subsequent charges were inextricably linked.

He gave me a look. "The speculation wasn't far off. Quinto and I wanted the same state Senate seat. Yes, one of us could have moved to a different part of the state, represented a different district. We might have both been elected. But both of us had business interests and roots here in Albuquerque."

"Was it all about politics? Did either of you really perceive the other as a threat to your careers?"

"Quinto and the judge go way back—Blackman went

through a lot of young law clerks on their way up the ladder. It just turned out in Herman's case that they added golf and the same social set of friends to the mix."

Something sparked a memory. "You knew about the judge and his young law clerks. Helen Bannerly was one, and she experienced something ..."

"Blackman's predator nature? The intimidation and overt moves were—"

"Were you one of those, Rory? One of the judge's conquests? Last time we talked, you said his attentions were not limited only to women."

"It would have killed my dad if—" He stopped, realizing.

I felt a wave of sympathy and gave him a full minute of silence. A new thought came to me—the morning news and pictures of Mrs. Blackman getting into that limo.

"Rory, do you think the judge was still doing it, still using his power against the new interns and clerks?"

"I ... I have no way of knowing that."

"But it wouldn't be out of character, would it?" I took a breath. "Do you think it's possible that his wife finally had enough—that she'd found out about one more woman or, more shameful for her, one more young man—and maybe she snapped? That she's the one who killed him?"

He shook his head. "No, you're on the wrong track. Well, I've been away for a while and haven't watched the players, but everything I knew about her, Mrs. B was very much a victim. She coped by drinking a lot and by living her own life. She would take these trips, be gone for weeks."

"To avoid knowing what was going on?"

"Well, she always seemed to disappear about the time Blackman took up with a new little honey."

I remembered the judge at the gala with his much-younger companion. Perhaps that's exactly what the wife was doing now, taking a long trip so she could avoid the unpleasantness at home. I thought of the scene in their bedroom, the judge lying naked and dead on the floor, the massive amount of blood, the otherwise perfect house with its magnificent view of the city. What a shame that Phoebe Blackman couldn't have the perfection part of her life, without the sordidness. Rory could be right about her being a victim—but sometimes victims snap.

Our pizza arrived just then and I went downstairs to get it. Rory was at the window when I came back up, staring down at the departing delivery car.

We put slices on the flimsy paper plates that had come with it, using the corners of my desk as a table. We could have gone downstairs to the kitchen to eat, but I didn't want to break Rory's concentration on what we'd been talking about.

"Tell me about Helen Bannerly," I said after we'd each wolfed down one slice. "As your defense lawyer, did she offer any advice when you went to trial? Any apologies afterward?"

He stared upward for a few seconds. "Advice at the time of my trial … 'trust me and trust the process' she said … and there was the old 'everything will turn out okay.' Is that what you meant?"

"Pretty weak, huh."

"Afterward, let's see. I was standing there in shock when the verdict came in. Of course, I'd been surprised and impatient when she didn't ask more direct questions of the witnesses. She rested the defense case much too soon and didn't take any of my suggestions seriously. We argued about it. So, afterward, yeah, let's just say I was surprised and yet not surprised. The judge announced the verdict, tapped his gavel down and said I would be sentenced in thirty days' time. Helen turned to me and whispered a simple 'I'm sorry' and then she packed up her briefcase and walked out."

He'd abandoned his plate and tossed a wadded napkin on top of it. "I got swarmed by family—Mom was in tears and Dad was practically shaking with anger. And what did I do? I turned around to comfort them."

"And then later?"

"Oh, I made appointments with Helen to discuss appeals and trying for a mistrial and all the usual. We met maybe once or twice before she admitted she was in over her head and she'd rather I found a different attorney to handle the appeals. I couldn't exactly disagree with that, could I? I considered taking over, filing the appeals myself."

"But?"

"In the eyes of the court, that sort of thing looks like a classic whiny move—I'm smarter than my attorney so I'll take over. It rarely helps and usually hurts the defendant's case."

I thought of the other things I'd learned about Helen Bannerly, what her friend Cathy had told me about the blackmail.

"Did you ever have reason to believe Helen skimped on your defense because she felt threatened in some way?"

He gave it some thought. "Not at the time, no. Frankly, I felt as if I were living in some kind of bubble of unreality. The whole thing, from the moment I received the summons and was told I was accused of jury tampering—all of it was crazy. Helen came highly recommended as a defense attorney. I'd only known her marginally, but she had a good reputation. But I've thought about all of this for years now.

When you say 'threatened' yeah. Thinking back on it, there was something going on with her."

He had left his chair and was pacing the room during this last bit.

"I need to get going," he said, heading toward the door. He was halfway down the stairs before I got out of my chair, and I was still fumbling for what to ask next.

By the time I reached Sally's desk, Rory was out the back door. Interview over.

"Everything okay?" she asked. I could see she was in the process of shutting down her computer and clearing her desk. It was the end of her half-day.

"Yeah. Want some pizza to take home for your kids?" I didn't really wait for an answer but went back upstairs, kept one more slice for myself, and closed the box on the rest.

She gave a grateful smile—one dinner plan done—and left by the back door. I found some ice and poured a Coke in the kitchen, aware of her car backing out and pulling down the long driveway.

When I walked back into the foyer, a man in a suit was standing inside the door. He opened his jacket and flashed a badge.

"U.S. Marshal, ma'am. We have some questions."

Chapter 39

My heart did a couple of loud thumps.

"You've been in contact with a Rory McNab." It wasn't a question.

"Apparently you already know that."

"We received a tip. What was the nature of your conversation?" He moved into our conference room and waved me toward a chair, taking over my space, although his manner wasn't confrontational or belligerent.

"His father passed away this week. Rory and his sister are in town for the memorial service." It wasn't a lie at all.

"But you've been asking about McNab for a while now. So his visit was not a surprise." Again, not a question.

"Agent … sorry, I didn't get your name."

"Wickett." He placed a business card on the table between us.

Daniel Wickett. U.S. Marshal. Albuquerque District Headquarters office.

"Agent Wickett, I'm unclear what you're here for. You know Rory McNab was here just now. I met with him this morning at the funeral home and offered pizza for lunch. If you wanted to speak with him you could have come in and confronted him. If you want to know where he's staying, you could have followed him."

"We did. Another car."

"And so … what is it you think I could tell you?"

He gave an impatient eye-roll, the first emotion I'd seen. "How did you know Rory McNab would be at the funeral home this morning? How is it you are involved with the family?"

"Simple enough. Rory's father, Fergus McNab, knew he was dying. He wanted to see his son before it was too late."

"And you facilitated that?"

"Not much. They had been in touch. Fergus also wanted his son exonerated for a crime he says Rory didn't commit. He wanted our firm to look into it and see what evidence might exist."

"This would be about his conviction for jury tampering?"

"Yes. Actually, I'm surprised something like that would reach the federal level, especially since it's been ten years and seemed like a minor incident at the time."

I half expected him to go all Tommy Lee Jones on me and inform me with a serious expression that there *are* no minor incidents, but he didn't.

"It goes deeper." He made the cryptic statement, apparently hoping I would feed him some additional information.

I didn't bite. "In what way?"

"New Mexico politics has a shady reputation."

And the sky is blue. "So, this is political. And you think, what? That it goes back to the rivalry between Herman Quinto and Rory McNab ten years ago? You said you were looking for Rory based on a tip. Let me guess. The tip came from the Quinto campaign."

"I'm here to request your assistance," he said. "We don't know who to trust in Santa Fe."

I chuckled. "*No one* knows who to trust there. Most of them don't trust each other. It's not that different from Washington. I can't tell you anything about politics. I stay as far away from all that as I can. I only go into the voting booth because it's a citizen's duty—frankly, everything else about it gives me the creeps."

"I was hoping you'd say that."

I think my jaw dropped.

"You're not under anyone's influence. We know that about you."

"Okay, now that really *is* creepy. You're not reassuring me."

Wickett sat back in his chair and unbuttoned his jacket. "Kent Taylor at APD Homicide is looking into the murder of Judge Aldo Blackman. He's the one who suggested we chat."

This time I *know* my jaw dropped. Kent Taylor actually trusted me to talk to federal agents? "APD somehow thinks the judge's death is politically motivated? But at the federal level?"

"I can't tell you a lot. You have no security clearances, no standing with our department. You're a peripheral witness at best."

Gee, thanks for *that*. "What do you want from me?" I finally asked.

"You seem to be the only person Rory McNab trusts. We'd like for you to act as intermediary—meet with him, report to us."

Spy and pass information. I squirmed in my chair. "And you think this will help build trust with Rory? He's skittish as a cat. If he has the faintest idea you're talking to me, he'll stop telling me anything. How is that going to help?"

He didn't answer but pulled a photo from inside his jacket. When he placed it on the table in front of me I saw it was the man with the scar.

"Who is this?" I asked.

"His name is Jorge Balderas."

I studied the picture to be sure. "He's Damian Baca's cousin—or is he?"

"They're related."

"Closely?"

"They are first cousins, but there's bad blood between their fathers so the two families aren't tight."

"But Damian and this Jorge—they're close?"

He took a moment with his answer. "As kids, yeah. Before Damian got caught on drug charges, twelve years ago, they were together a lot."

"I saw him in photos after Damian's trial, the one where Rory McNab defended him. What happened to him after that?"

"He's around."

I waited to see if he would tell me Jorge now worked for Herman Quinto. He didn't. Either I knew something the feds didn't know, which seemed unlikely, or he was holding back information to see what I would reveal. I hate these little cat-and-mouse games.

"Damian Baca claims to have cleaned up his act and gotten completely away from the drug trade," I said. "Is that true?"

A half-nod. "Seems to be."

"So what about this cousin? Is he done with drugs, too, or still involved?"

"We believe he's still in it up to his neck," Wickett said. "He's higher up in the cartel than before, so it's harder to catch him with the goods in hand. But the connections still exist."

"And, what? You think Rory McNab is also involved?" It could go a long way toward explaining how a guy lives for ten years with no income. His story about selling paintings at the local bookstore had seemed pretty weak to me.

"Rory McNab and Damian Baca are still in touch. We know that from Baca's side of things. Apparently, McNab goes through burner phones faster than the characters on *Blacklist.*"

He said some more, but I never heard much past 'Rory and Damian are still in touch.' My thoughts took off, racing back over our conversations.

Wickett's phone pinged with a message. He took one glance at it and was in motion, pushing back from the table and standing. Apparently the message didn't get me off the hook; he said something about my calling him as soon as I learned anything new, assurances that he would contact me again … it went by in a bit of a blur until he was out the door. I locked up behind him and stood there a moment before meandering back upstairs to the slice of cold pizza I'd left behind.

The food held no appeal. I drummed my fingers on the desktop until the sound began to drive me nuts. Had

Kent Taylor actually told the feds to contact me? I dialed his number with a little trepidation—I had once been a suspect myself.

"Charlie, do you have anything new to share with me?" Taylor said. Not his usual greeting, which was normally somewhere between tepid and grumpy.

"Well, no, not exactly. I was wondering how the investigation is going." I thought of the numerous rumors I'd heard about Blackman and his proclivities, but wasn't sure anything I knew would actually qualify as evidence.

"It's going. That's all I can say."

"Because …?" Apparently, he wasn't going to bring up the Marshal's name, so I wouldn't either.

"Because that's all I can say."

The man can be so frustrating to talk to. Kind of like when my mother's answer to *Why?* was "because I said so." I hated that. A kid wants more info. And this kid wanted more info, but I wasn't getting it, and Taylor's tone made it clear I wouldn't be able to pester him into talking.

Chapter 40

Questions pummeled me—of course, now that Marshal Wickett had left and I couldn't ask them.

Jorge Balderas, the man with the scar, the great unknown of my case until now. The feds said he was still heavily involved in selling drugs; I knew he was associated with Herman Quinto in some way, either as part of his campaign entourage or … or what? His stepping out of Quinto's motorhome the other evening could have meant many things.

Were they social pals? I doubted it.

Was Quinto a customer? Entirely possible, but I doubted they'd be seen so publicly together if that was the case. The Important Ones don't meet with drug dealers—they have their 'people' for that.

Did Balderas work for the senator's campaign? On the

face of it, that's what it had appeared.

Surely, the feds would know this if they were spying on all the players in this little game. But maybe their focus was all going toward Damian Baca and Rory McNab. Still, he'd shown me the photo of Balderas. If not for Wickett's statement about corruption in New Mexico politics, I could well imagine him and his agency turning a blind eye toward Quinto's campaign activities.

I wrapped the cold pizza in a napkin, started to toss it in my waste basket, realized it would stink up the whole room by tomorrow, pushed it away.

How had an effort to put a dying father and fugitive son together turned into this? It made my head hurt. I spent a couple minutes in a self-indulgent, pity-party, *why me* funk before deciding the whole thing wouldn't go away just because I wanted it to. Now I had to make the effort to get the answers.

The feds wanted intel on Herman Quinto; APD had a murder to solve; I desperately wanted out of the middle. I began by writing down what I knew, listing the players.

Phoebe Blackman – beleaguered wife, socially humiliated, putting on a brave face

Helen Bannerly – affair with the judge, blackmailed because of it? pressured into letting down her client?

Damian Baca – says he's cleaned up his act, seems to be true (his job), maybe not true (officials can be bribed—duh!)

Jorge Balderas – other than what Marshal Wickett just said the man is like a ghost to me, Damian's cousin, still dealing drugs, working for Quinto's campaign (maybe)

Rory – still in touch with Damian Baca, WTH!!— what else is he not telling me?

I formulated a list of questions and went over them several times. With Rory, especially, questioning him would be like approaching a wild critter in the woods—the slightest misstep or hint of aggression on my part would send him running. Which was exactly why the feds had approached me rather than trying to haul him in. They didn't give a crap about his jury tampering conviction. They wanted him available—to point the finger at Quinto, to help break up some major drug ring ... or take down major politicos or ... whatever it was.

I shoved my notepad aside and paced the floor. Why didn't they just follow Rory until they caught up with him, take him to whatever brightly lit room they take people, and question him until he caved? Keeping him out of prison was their bargaining chip, and it seemed it would be a pretty effective one.

The answer hit me as soon as I faced the bay window and saw the street below. Rory remained elusive and they'd had no luck catching him. Rory would talk to me. I was the bait.

It was a disturbing feeling.

But it made perfect sense. Catching me with the element of surprise on his side, Marshal Wickett got me all set up with the scenario, but he could have called it off at any moment. Then came the text message and he bolted. Something had happened—the vehicle that had tailed Rory away from here had lost him—or maybe not.

Rory had developed excellent evasion skills and he must have spotted the car right away. In this quiet neighborhood, it would have been easy-peasy. I gathered my list of suspects and headed out.

Crawling along in traffic on Central, I nearly shut off the top-of-the-hour news on the radio, until I caught Fergus McNab's name. I turned it up.

"... was the father of Rory McNab, the lawyer arrested ten years ago on jury tampering charges. The elaborate escape, seemingly planned by father and son, was headline news at the time but no new leads have been found." The solemn voice reading the story switched abruptly to a perky female who informed me that traffic was 'slow-and-go' on the major downtown arterial streets. Yeah, I kind of already knew that.

I arrived home to find the McNab story at the top of the news on TV as well. In a segment that went well beyond the usual length of a local-interest piece, they had resurrected Fergus's arrest more than a week ago and made much of the fact that he'd been after Congressional hopeful Herman Quinto. A not-subtle reference to Quinto's being the frontrunner in the race let me know this particular station leaned heavily toward the senator's political party.

The video showed Fergus being walked into the police station, every bit of his age and physical frailty evident. Then they flashed back to rehashing the story of Rory's conviction, with footage from the day of his verdict when he and Helen Bannerly had stood on the courthouse steps. Helen seemed harried, under pressure. Her answers were terse and not upbeat.

Rory stood by, slickly groomed, pudgy in what had been his comfortable role as an up-and-comer in local politics. I couldn't help but notice the difference from the lean outdoorsman he'd become now.

He stepped toward the camera, edging Helen aside and put in his own two cents: "This is not over. I am not guilty of these charges, and will be working tirelessly to uncover the truth and prove my innocence."

The news anchor, sitting elegantly at her desk, turned to her co-host. "Of course, we all know that, within a short time, Rory McNab vanished, a fugitive from the law. Informed sources at the time suggested Fergus McNab most likely helped his son in his disappearance."

"That's right, Patty. And now, we may never know the truth."

I felt my blood pressure rising at the waste of time. Other than tarnishing an old man's reputation, what had that story actually accomplished? I switched to another channel.

This one was even worse. They'd apparently already talked about Fergus's arrest and now his death. A news team stood outside Fergus's trailer, catching the moment live as the reporter tapped on the door and Christine answered. The reporter gave some faux sympathetic comments about how this must be a difficult time for the family, then thrust the microphone in Christine's face for a response to the question, "How are you feeling right now?"

I saw Christine stand a little taller and take a deep breath. "I'm *feeling* as though my family's privacy has been invaded in the worst way. Leave. Now."

She closed the door, leaving the questioner on the front step without much else to say. The in-studio newscaster quickly butted in with some inane closing remark and they skipped to another story. Served them right, as their misguided attempt at live coverage flopped, big-time. I felt a little rush of triumph on Christine's behalf. Her response had been dignified.

Unfortunately, the overall impression on camera was that this had been an ill, old man living in a dumpy trailer park, perhaps driven to desperation in his final days, all because he couldn't let go of the idea that his son had been wrongly accused.

Chapter 41

I couldn't let go of the idea that this sudden bout of news coverage didn't just *happen*. There are too many murders, rapes, and horrific accidents vying for a news department's time, and the death of one old man in a nursing home didn't normally *begin* to compete. So, who had tipped them off? For that matter, who had alerted the Federal Marshals' office to dig into all this?

It hit me that the answer had to be Herman Quinto. If not Quinto himself, someone in his campaign or someone sympathetic in law enforcement. No one, other than the police and the family, had known of Fergus's intentions with the gun that night. The arrest was done quietly, the arraignment ... Wait—the arraignment. Someone in the courtroom?

The possibilities whirled in my head. Someone learned

that Fergus had set out to get Quinto; they must have told the candidate or his security detail. Who else would benefit by spreading this whole story via the media? We were getting into the final days before the election, the time when all publicity is good publicity, as long as it puts the candidate in a sympathetic light. Portraying Fergus as a nutcase or desperate old man against the polished I-love-the-people politician—it had to be campaign tactical brilliance.

I would bet money that the evening news tonight would have Quinto on camera making sympathetic noises about this poor old man. It would become the perfect way of leading in to the many ways he would campaign for better care for the mentally ill and stricter restrictions on gun ownership and tighter laws on housing conditions in trailer parks. Was there ever a politician who didn't figure out a way to cover all the angles—tell the people what they wanted to hear?

Drake came in just then and said the three little words every woman loves to hear. "What's for dinner?"

I had been standing in front of the fridge for several minutes. I suppose it was a logical question, but I must have given him a blank look. He came up behind and wrapped his arms around me, his body warm against my back.

"I'll tell you what," he said. "You take Freckles for a walk. I'll come up with food."

I love this guy.

So does Freckles. She saw me put on a coat and pick up her leash, and she went completely wriggly. She was bounding out the front door before Drake even had a chance to wash his hands.

The streetlights were coming on and I was glad I'd opted for the jacket. This is the time of year when we have gorgeously warm days, but the temperature plummets by twenty degrees about five minutes after the sun goes down. The dog and I made a quick sprint down to the park, two blocks away, where I let her off the leash long enough to race around until her energy flagged. Meanwhile, I kept mulling all the info pertaining to the McNabs and the people I wanted to talk to.

By the time we arrived home there was a fantastic gingery smell coming from the kitchen and Drake was dishing up plates of stir-fry. The guy is a whiz in the kitchen. I tell you, I would have looked at the few veggies in the fridge and wondered what on earth to do with them. He'd chopped and stirred them into this fantastic medley.

I asked about his day. Routine, he said, just flying some A-list actor from the airport up to his ranch outside Santa Fe. He asked about mine, and seemed much more impressed by the visit from the Federal Marshals' office than by the actor who'd talked nonstop about himself for two hours. I laughed. Better to listen to someone's ego than to be quizzed by a government agent, I thought. But we let it go at that.

I woke up in the morning with an itch to wrap up this case. Fergus's memorial would be this afternoon; no doubt Rory would disappear soon after. As I lay in bed savoring the last few minutes of warmth before I had to get up, I allowed myself the luxury fantasy of just letting it all go. Let Fergus be put to rest. Let Rory vanish into the woods. Let Herman Quinto win the election and learn for himself that a state senator from New Mexico would be a minnow in the ocean of Washington, DC.

But that wasn't fulfilling my promise to Fergus—that I would try my best to find the evidence to exonerate Rory, to allow him to move back to his home state or at least to use his real name and walk the streets freely.

* * *

Helen Bannerly wasn't happy to see me. I'd made the appointment in Elsa Higgins's name and she'd blocked out a whole hour, so she couldn't very well dodge me or invent another pressing engagement. At first, she pretended she didn't remember me or my previous visit, and I let her go along with that through the introduction and getting-settled part.

"It's been bothering you, hasn't it?" I asked. "Knowing you could have done more to prove Rory McNab didn't do what they said, and you didn't ask the right questions."

She squirmed in her chair, gave some attention to a flaky cuticle.

"Something more was going on behind the scenes."

A cool pose, her lips in a straight line, chin high, but her eyes gave it away.

"Helen, who was blackmailing you? I know about you and the judge, and I know you would have done anything to keep it quiet."

When her lower lip quivered, I knew I had her.

"Helen? A man's family was separated by this. His father gave up the last ten years of his life without being able to see his son."

A fat tear pooled in the corner of her eye.

"There were pictures," she whispered. She cleared her throat. "I didn't know the man."

"The blackmailer?"

"Yes. He had photos—pictures of Aldo and me. Nothing, um, you know, pornographic or anything. But there were shots of us in a quiet restaurant, holding hands across the table, heads close together. If my husband had seen them, there was no innocent explanation."

"How could he prove those weren't taken years earlier? Wouldn't that have been the logical thing to say if he confronted you?"

She shook her head. "I wore my hair longer then. In the photos it was cut in the style I've worn ever since. The truly damning thing, though, was that one of the pictures clearly showed my wrist and I'm wearing a bracelet Charles gave me."

"So it was proof, but how did it relate to the case you were defending at the time?"

"I asked the man what he wanted from me, in exchange for the photos. It surprised me when he didn't ask for money. He said Rory McNab needed to go to prison for his crimes." She dabbed the tear away before it could roll down her face and spoil her makeup. "We were due in court in two days. I didn't think there was much in the way of a case against Rory ... I just didn't know what to do."

"So you did nothing?"

"I presented the evidence I'd come up with. I didn't hold back any vital information, if that's what you're thinking. There just wasn't much. It was a flimsy case, all based on my having to prove a negative. How do you prove someone *didn't* do something? I honestly thought the prosecution would have maybe a few facts proving he did do it, and all I could do was create reasonable doubt for the jury to believe he might not have."

"Herman Quinto prosecuted both cases, didn't he? The one against Damian Baca and the one against Rory? Do you think that was coincidental or political?"

"Coincidence? No, I don't think there's any way. Quinto pulled strings to get the case against Rory McNab. As far as it being political, seriously? Is the Pope Catholic?

Of course it was political. It was no secret that both Rory and Herman planned to make a run for the one open state Senate seat from this district." She had leaned back in her chair but sat forward now, her index finger jabbing the blotter on her desk. "I've thought about this for years. Quinto didn't really need to win that case—all he had to do was smear Rory's reputation."

"Which he could have done through the media, right? Just the fact that a political candidate was on trial for dishonesty would have sealed his political aspirations and made Quinto's victory a sure thing."

"Most likely, but in politics you can never be sure. Also, the timing had to be just right. Too early, and someone else would have jumped into the race. But by making sure the arrest and trial happened after the filing deadline, Quinto had it made. Convicted, Rory would have been automatically out and Quinto would run unopposed. Innocent, Rory's future could have gone either way. Voters could have chosen to be sympathetic, or they could have turned on him."

"I need to ask just one thing: Did you withhold any evidence that clearly would have gotten Rory acquitted?"

"No. I wouldn't have done that. I couldn't have lived with myself. My marriage was important and I went to great lengths to protect it, but not at the expense of a man going to prison."

The mention of the reason behind the blackmail brought another aspect to mind. "Why did you go back to seeing Aldo Blackman? I understand about being young, an intern in his office, all that. But once you were away from him, married to someone else … why risk it?"

"Have you ever had the attention of a powerful man,

Charlie? Has someone with charisma and money *and* power shined the light of his attentions on you?" She didn't wait for an answer. "It's unbelievably compelling. You feel like a helpless little shaving of metal in the presence of a magnet. The night the pictures were taken was the first time I'd seen Aldo in three years, but the charm and romance were all there. I agreed to meet in the restaurant, and it was fully my intention to tell him I was happy and didn't want to see him again. But he said all the right words, reached for my hand, leaned over to whisper in my ear. That had to be the moment the photos were taken, by someone at another table who was very discreet about it."

"You were set up. Do you hear what you're saying, how you're describing this? Everything was perfectly in place!"

Her face drained of color. "What—you think Aldo *knew*? That he could have been involved in the blackmail too?"

"He and Herman Quinto are—were—great buddies. Why else would Blackman call you, out of the blue, after several years? He was going to help his friend politically."

"He … he could have done that in the courtroom."

"And he did. But having you in the chain … they didn't know what evidence you might present in court so this was extra insurance. Risky though. You could have blown them both out of the water by revealing this."

She made a scoffing sound. "It wouldn't have hurt Aldo. He already had the reputation. You don't get it, Charlie. A male cheat is perceived as a stud. A female cheat is called a slut, and I don't care how modern we think we've become, that's still how it plays out. In this case, it would have played out publicly. He would have made some 'I never had sex with that woman' statement, and I would have lost everything."

I felt a little silly, having made the suggestion. She was absolutely right.

Chapter 42

Unless I planned to show up at a funeral in jeans, I needed to get home and change clothes. A quick rummage through my closet brought out a dark green skirt and blouse. Other than one pair of slacks and a cocktail dress, I don't own a whole lot of black. I figured Fergus wouldn't have cared.

The mortuary had set aside a small chapel for the service, but with only a dozen people, an urn of ashes, dolorous music, and three sprays of flowers (one from Drake and me), it had a pitiful feel to it. Christine's husband officiated, saying some nice words and reading a few Bible passages. There were some tears, but mostly the older friends said things about Fergus being out of pain now, about his finally getting to be with his wife in heaven, and how sad it was that Rory couldn't have been here. I listened and wondered if that last bit was for the benefit of the two strangers no one else seemed to know, the ones I would have pegged as law enforcement any day.

Christine had told me the service would be followed by a small family gathering at the cemetery where her father's ashes would be buried next to her mother, his beloved Mary Ann. As soon as her husband had run out of things to say, she stood up and included everyone in the invitation. I had already planned to follow along discreetly and check it out from a distance, hoping Rory would show up at some point.

Of course, the cops were probably thinking the very same thing. A lone reporter with a cameraman stood near the sidewalk where the mourners had to pass. The sight of them made my temper flare and I stalked right up to the female who appeared to be about nineteen.

"Seriously? You guys can't give this family some privacy to grieve? Get out of here. There's no story, so leave them alone."

Almost to my amazement, she didn't answer back with some smart remark about freedom of the press; she actually looked appropriately embarrassed. She turned to the camera guy, who shrugged, and they picked up their gear and headed toward a small blue car with the local TV station's logo on the side. I gave myself a little smile of approval—it was the first time I could recall playing the age-and-maturity card and having it actually work.

I crossed the parking lot, heading for my Jeep and caught Christine's eye. She gave me a quick thumbs-up. Indicating that I would follow her family, I joined the small procession behind the black limo with her husband, daughters, and two grandchildren. Four of the older couples came along in their own vehicles. I wasn't happy to see a dark sedan from the back corner of the parking lot follow us—the inevitable law enforcement contingent— or the two-person news crew who apparently didn't know what 'leave them alone' meant after all.

Last weekend had eaten up the remainder of our Indian summer weather. Today had turned blustery, and although the sun was shining, the wind had a bite to it. Albuquerque's cemeteries aren't of the variety with rolling hills, green lawns, and towering old trees like you see in the movies. We have a couple of those, but most are doing the best they can with a desert landscape, and many are downright pathetic little squares of dirt filled with white crosses and artificial flowers.

Fergus's wife must have had a say in the choice of final resting place because their double plot sat in one of the grassy places called 'perpetual care.' I didn't know if the term was meant to make the survivors think their loved ones were receiving special treatment, or if it simply meant there was a grounds crew who mowed the grass regularly. We arrived at one of hundreds of look-alike plots with flat, in-ground markers and a smaller-than-normal hole to contain the urn of ashes. I gave a quick look around, in what I hoped was a casual way, but didn't spot Rory. Still, I had a feeling he would be somewhere nearby.

The nice thing about the graveside portion of the service is that it's missing the heavy, sad music. For some reason that's the part that always gets to me. I walked across the grass, noticing the two men in the sedan (definitely law enforcement) had rolled to a stop fifty feet back and weren't leaving their vehicle. If Rory was near, I hoped he'd spotted them.

Again, Christine's husband said some final words. He

seemed good at it—I wondered, but had never asked, if he was a clergyman in real life. The old friends lined up to shake hands with the family members, seeming not quite comfortable with what they would perceive as the newfangled idea of hugging everyone you met.

I held back, wanting a word with Christine before I left. If nothing else, it seemed we should keep in touch over Rory's situation, especially if I was able to find the magic key to exonerating him. On a pretense of reading the inscription on Mary Ann McNab's grave marker, I scanned the area again. The dark gray car was still there. Otherwise, I saw two groundskeepers in navy dungarees— one holding a grass trimmer but keeping it quiet out of respect, the other carrying a shovel and rake toward a small shed about a hundred yards away. A lone man knelt beside a grave across the narrow access road. He'd removed his cap and placed a small bouquet on the grave, and his white hair revealed him to be much older than Rory.

"He'll be at our hotel in a half hour," Christine said in my ear, startling me. "Rory. I think I've convinced him to join us later at Furr's Cafeteria for a meal. We have to head back to Denver early in the morning. Come along, if you'd like."

"You don't mind? I really need to talk to him, especially if he's leaving town soon."

"I assume he will. In fact, I'm not a hundred percent sure he'll show up this afternoon. But it's worth a try. We can give you two some time alone." She spoke softly, keeping an eye on her two grandkids, who seemed to be itching to run and cavort on the grass.

They had chosen a hotel in the Old Town area, so it was a quick stop for me to run home, change clothes, and swap cars. If the agents monitoring us followed the family to their meeting spot, they would be watching for me to show up in my funeral garb and driving my Jeep.

When I arrived at the side parking lot, it was in Elsa's twenty-year-old boat of a Buick. I'd swapped skirt and blouse for skinny jeans and a fleece jacket, and my hair was now up in a ponytail with a ball cap pulled low on the forehead and a pair of huge round sunglasses I'd unearthed from a dresser drawer. A backpack over one shoulder contained a loose pair of pants that could easily go over the jeans, and the fleece could swap out for a shiny purple windbreaker. Hair and lipstick would require only a few seconds to change. Not that I'm paranoid about the government or anything, but the persistence of these guys was beginning to irritate me.

A strident *pssstt* caught my attention as I walked through the hotel lobby and I ducked into the gift shop to find Rory paging through a magazine from the rack. I gave my attention over to a display of elegant shawls.

"Don't bother with Chrissy's room. Those guys have the elevators and hallways covered," he said in a low voice which even the nosy-looking clerk couldn't hear. "Meet me at the Lowe's on 12th, the paint aisle, and we'll go from there."

He set the magazine down, slid out the shop's side door and disappeared down a little corridor that seemed to lead only to the restrooms. So, okay, change of plans. I bought a pack of spearmint gum, feeling somehow guilty. Stupid, I know.

Out in the Buick, I looked carefully over the entire parking lot for the white sedan Rory had been driving but there was no sign of it. I headed for Lowe's. I'd looked at paint chips for nearly ten minutes before Rory appeared at my side with the startling stealth of a tiger in the wild.

"Will you quit scaring me like that?" I demanded, hissing the words out through my teeth.

He pointed to a sunny yellow sample. "I like that one."

Really? I gave him a look.

"Is this where you want to talk?" I asked.

"Nah. I passed a little park on the way here."

I noticed his red jacket had changed to blue—reversible, no doubt. And here I'd been thinking my own disguises were pretty crafty. We walked out of the home center with a few paint samples in hand, ostensibly a couple going home to decide what color to paint the kitchen. I headed for the Buick and caught Rory eyeing it.

"I like it," he said as he approached the passenger side. "Let's go."

Tired of the drama with this whole setup, I broached my uppermost concern as soon as we'd pulled out of the parking lot.

"You and Damian Baca stayed in touch after his trial, didn't you? In fact, you two were friends all along."

He seemed a little surprised but didn't say anything.

"Was that the real reason you went to great lengths to get him acquitted on the drug charges? Was the jury-tampering real?" So tight was my grip on the too-large steering wheel that my knuckles stood out.

"No."

I pulled to the curb on a small residential street. "What about the blackmail of Helen Bannerly? Did you know about that?"

"Helen?"

I turned off the engine. "Come on. Damian had to be

behind it. His cousin, Jorge Balderas, had the photos. He's the one who ordered Helen to skimp on your defense."

Rory's face had gone a peculiar shade of pale green. "You didn't know …"

I could see his mental wheels turning.

"Damian wouldn't—" He couldn't quite formulate a sentence.

"You know that for a fact? Really, Rory. Who stood to gain and who stood to lose?"

He turned in his seat and met my gaze full-on. "You're on the wrong track with this. My arrest and conviction was orchestrated by Quinto and Blackman. No one else. The two of them are the only ones who wanted me in prison, and they'd planned a way to be sure I would be sent out of state."

He seemed so certain that I wavered. "You've been in touch with Damian all along, haven't you?"

A momentary flicker in his eye told me I was right. Now, I only needed to figure out what it meant. I had scratched the surface of the truth, at last, but this whole thing went even deeper.

Chapter 43

It all goes back to Herman Quinto and Judge Blackman. I repeated the thought in my head long past the time I delivered Rory back to the parking lot, where this time he got into a red minivan. He had probably changed motels, too, and I wouldn't be surprised if there was a new cell phone in his pocket. Actually, I reminded myself that I shouldn't be shocked if he was on an eastbound plane by this evening.

Rory's parting words to me in the parking lot had been, "I want you to stick with your investigation. Check your bank balance—you'll see a decent retainer in there."

It might have just been talk—after all, I'd already told him I owed it to Fergus to continue—but when I got to a stopping place and looked at the RJP Investigations account, sure enough, there was a new deposit for ten thousand dollars.

That fairly well clinched it; I had to keep working on this. Blackman was dead. Damian seemed in a safe place, with a prestigious job and no recent stains on his record. That left Herman Quinto as the other of the major players, and one Rory had specifically named.

With a mere three days left before the election, the senator was campaigning almost non-stop, so it was a simple matter to go to his website and find out the time and place of his next appearance. Tonight there was an open-mic political forum. I noted the time and planned to get there an hour early.

On the off chance that his last cell number was still valid, I called Rory.

"I need more information," I told him. "You told me your arrest and conviction was all planned by Herman Quinto and Judge Blackman. How? I'm going to confront him and I may only get the chance to make one or two points. What should I ask?"

The line remained quiet for several long moments, although I could hear him breathing, could almost hear him thinking.

"Whew—there's so much."

"Does he know who murdered the judge? That would be big."

"Yeah, it would. Back then, Damian had photos and delivered them to Quinto, blackmail photos against the judge. Damian told me Quinto bought them as insurance, to be sure any case of his that went to Blackman's court would get swayed in his direction. I imagine that would have been nearly *any* case because the judge could manage to hear what he wanted and pawn the other cases off to other judges."

"Including the case against you."

"Right."

"Did Damian keep copies of the pictures, plan to use them himself, maybe leak them to the press?"

"I … no, I doubt it."

Doubt. Not certainty.

"Is there any chance I could get hold of those photos? I don't think Damian quite trusts me yet, but if you were to tell him …"

"I'll make a call."

Ten minutes later, I had arrived at my office when my phone rang, showing an unfamiliar number. I remained in the car to take it.

"Charlie, it's Rory. Sorry, no photos."

"They're gone?"

"Forget the photos."

I wanted to pin him down as to whether they were destroyed or never did exist, but what was the point? He'd clicked off the call almost immediately. So I would go to the Quinto rally armed only with my wits and my anger over not being able to talk to him privately. Scary thought.

The upper windows of the Victorian were dark. Both Sally and Ron were gone now, and I honestly couldn't think of anything pressing for me here. Deciding to switch vehicles again before tonight's political rally, I backed the Buick out and headed for home. An uneasy, edgy feeling crept over me as I drove. Was I being a complete fool to confront such a dangerous man?

On the other hand, was Quinto truly a threat to me? Like many politicians, he was probably all talk. Other than the machinations done behind the scenes to pave the way for his career I had no evidence at all that he was capable of violence. All this self-talk was designed to convince myself I should go to the rally rather than holing up at home and staying out of it.

I brought Elsa's car to rest in her driveway. Having served the combined purposes of chasing around town in a different vehicle and giving Elsa's car a little exercise, I would be glad to be back in my own wheels now.

Drake was fixing himself a sandwich in the kitchen and offered me one, but I declined. My stomach still felt in a twist. I invited him to attend Quinto's rally with me, at which he laughed, vigorously shook his head, and told me he would rather watch reruns of *Friends* than go to anything political. Truthfully, so would I.

While he settled in front of a NASCAR race rerun on TV, I went to the bedroom and surveyed my attire in the mirror. Jeans and sweater seemed okay. I took off the ponytail band and shook out my hair, giving it a brushing for good measure and touching up my lip gloss. My pistol was now in the glove compartment of the Jeep, and that's where it would stay.

The rally was to begin at seven p.m. and I had a twenty-minute drive to get to the venue. Allowing time to park and get into the building, it was none too early to leave home now. I emptied my purse of all sharp objects, such as nail file and the tiny pen knife that comes in handy for a jillion tasks, along with the hand sanitizer gel that always gets me stopped in airports. Surely, my wallet, keys, small spiral notebook, and two ballpoint pens would pass inspection.

Everything went as planned. Once past building security, I accepted a glass of the complimentary champagne, more to boost my courage than anything else. Most of the people were milling about in the lobby, hoping to catch the candidate on a casual walk-through and shake his hand before he began speaking. I set my half-full plastic flute aside and decided to check out the seating arrangement.

Two aisles led from the lobby into the auditorium. While the seats in the center section looked to be the most prestigious, I noticed microphones set up on stands at the foot of each side aisle. This was where people wanting to ask a question would queue up for the privilege. I walked straight down the sloping walkway to one of them and took an aisle seat that ought to place me near the head of the line when the time came. Yes, people would have to step in front of me to take the inner seats on that row. No, I did not care. I had tried several times to talk with the senator privately—now he would meet me on my terms.

I'd hardly settled into my seat when angry voices over the speaker system caught my attention. Glancing around, I didn't spot the cause—a few dozen people had taken seats and most were chatting among themselves. With the second outburst, nearly everyone froze.

"Sir, your microphone is hot."

"Shit! Whose fault is that? Get the stupid little twat over here!" It was the familiar voice of Herman Quinto.

The curtained backdrop fluttered, there was a thud, and a moment later a young woman in a white shirt and navy blue skirt stumbled onto the stage through the split in the draperies. Her face flamed clear to the roots of her blonde hair. One shoe had a broken heel and she limped offstage without looking toward the audience. My heart went out to her.

The male voices no longer came over the audio system, but someone backstage was receiving an ass-chewing that was not exactly being kept secret. Clearly, they had no idea the auditorium was filling rapidly. The intern must have said something because, as if a switch went off, the voices stopped.

I seethed inside. Being on the receiving end of such a

tirade hadn't happened to me since college, but watching another poor girl humiliated was enough to bring my anger-meter into the red zone. As the seats filled and the lights dimmed, I thought about Quinto and the harm he had caused, for years now.

When I saw an aide walk up to the microphone in the aisle near me, I knew the Q&A period would soon begin. I got out of my seat and walked right up to the man, positioning myself first in line.

The master of ceremonies went into an overly long introduction, glossing the candidate to a high shine and telling us nothing new at all. Then Quinto stepped to the podium and flashed his public smile over the crowd. He went on a bit too long but, at last, he announced he would take questions.

The helper at the other aisle went first, holding the mike for a gentleman who led with a soft question about social services, which played right into Quinto's talking points about how he would always stand ready to serve the people of our great state. *Right.*

When the applause had died down, my turn came. My stomach did a small flutter when the man beside me whispered, "Go ahead." Was I playing with fire? Maybe. I did it anyway.

"Senator, you had quite a stellar record as a prosecutor before taking the Senate seat—could it be your blackmail attempt against another attorney was an embarrassment, a reason to come up with evidence to put away your competition, to send Rory McNab to prison, maybe even to murder a judge?"

The phrase 'you could hear a pin drop' is no exaggeration, I discovered. Faces all over the room turned toward me. Quinto's expression went dark and for a moment

I thought he might burst a blood vessel or something. The man holding the microphone for me gasped, just as the emcee stepped forward and said, "We are not here to listen to slander—next question please!"

I sensed a rush of movement behind me and a hand with an iron grip took my elbow. For the first few steps, I felt many eyes on me but attention soon turned back to the speaker at the other microphone. By the time we exited the auditorium, Quinto had brushed off my outburst with a joke and proceeded to utter some more platitudes that the people wanted to hear.

The lobby was eerily empty now, with only trays of used champagne flutes and wadded cocktail napkins to show for the lively hubbub earlier. I shook my arm to loosen the grip on me, but my captor wasn't quite so easy to get rid of. Two more men joined—one on my left, the other behind—and they walked me all the way to the outer doors. One pushed the glass door open and the others stood firm in their resolve that I would not reenter.

Fine by me. I'd learned two important things. Herman Quinto had a mean enough temper to humiliate an underling, and he certainly reacted strongly when accused of breaking the law. The man was a bundle of raw anger.

I shook off the feeling of the man's hand on my arm, soothed my ruffled feathers a little, and headed for my Jeep. Since my arrival the parking lot had filled completely and I traversed three rows of parked cars before knowing for sure I was in the right section. Edging between two cars as I headed for mine, I fished around in my shoulder bag for my keys. At the moment when I wasn't looking up, someone stepped into my path in the darkness.

It was the gun aimed exactly at my gut that caught my attention. My first thought was of my own weapon locked away in the glovebox, out of reach. Every hair on my arms bristled.

"Keep away from Senator Quinto," came the low growl. "It's someone else, somebody you know, who wanted the judge dead. The next time you come anywhere near Mr. Quinto, this will go a whole lot worse."

I couldn't breathe. I've been face-to-face with killers before, but this felt claustrophobic—the dark section of the lot, being wedged between the cars, and his 9mm Glock only inches beyond my grasp. I froze in place and willed my brain to come up with a plan. The man glanced around and there was a fraction of a second when the light from one of the parking lot lamps hit his face. It was the man with the scar—Jorge Balderas.

He saw my recognition and in the blink of an eye he slipped away and disappeared in the dark.

Chapter 44

I dashed to my Jeep, locked myself inside, and started the engine. Where had he gone? I cruised the length of two rows of parked cars, looking for a sign of Balderas, realizing the foolishness of actually finding him. That Glock had been real, and he had the advantage of knowing my exact position. He could stand up and shoot through my windshield before I ever spotted him.

The moment I neared the exit, I took it and headed for a major street where the traffic lights were not so widely spaced. By the time I saw a string of fast food places, I realized my hands were shaking. My confrontational attitude to Quinto, being roughly escorted to the door, and the warning from Balderas—it all teamed up to frazzle me. I pulled into the entrance of a Taco Bell.

My stomach was much too knotted to consider food,

and caffeine didn't seem like the thing to calm my trembling hands. I backed into a parking space, took a couple of deep breaths, and watched the movement of traffic. With no idea what Jorge Balderas would be driving, every little aberration in the flow put me on edge until I began to talk myself down from it.

Okay, I had willingly gone to the rally and had (stupidly) challenged the senator. So, yeah, I had practically asked to be thrown out. I needed to get over that and make smarter choices in the future. The parking lot face-off was another thing. It was as if Balderas had been waiting for me.

I tried to think back, to remember faces in the crowd at the rally. Quinto's staffers were all over the place, and Jorge must have been among them. He wasn't my escort out of the building, but he could have been following along. He might have been standing outside, able to see the two who dragged me to the door, and maybe he circled around as I approached my vehicle. He worked for Quinto so why would he warn me, why not get rid of me?

With everyone inside, I could have been beaten or killed in the parking lot and it would have been explained away by police as a mugging. Those things happen. No, Balderas didn't want to kill me or he would have done it. Did that mean Quinto didn't want me dead?

What was it he'd said as he faced me with the gun? He said it's someone I know who was behind the judge's death. *Someone I know ... who?* My immediate thought went to Damian Baca, Jorge's cousin. Now the question was, why? Damian had narrowly avoided the wrath of the court, so why would he hold a grudge all these years and take the chance on killing Judge Blackman? It just didn't make sense.

Helen Bannerly. Now there was someone with a stronger motive. Maybe all my questions had stirred up old hurts, old grievances. She might have confronted the judge, wanting to be sure she'd gotten all the photos and destroyed them, or maybe she simply wanted him to hear her. When we aren't feeling heard, when that person who wronged us doesn't even realize what they've done … it's a powerful temptation to speak out. Helen seemed a more logical suspect than Damian.

Twenty minutes passed, by the digits on my clock. My hands had quit shaking, my antennae had retreated. In the post-adrenaline low, fatigue hit me like a truck, and all I wanted was to go home. Tonight's scenario replayed in my head. Suddenly, I had a strong suspicion who had killed Judge Blackman—and there was nothing I could do about it.

Chapter 45

My phone rang before daylight. I rolled toward my nightstand to see who it could be. Only a very few people are exempt from the restriction of ringing my phone before seven a.m.—Drake, Ron, and soon Dottie Flowers. Drake was asleep beside me. But this was Ron.

"What?" I grumbled.

"Turn on the TV. You'll want to see what's going on." He hung up.

I rolled out of bed, instantly alert as I shoved my arms into the sleeves of my robe. It was 5:12 in the morning. As far as I knew, only one of our local stations had initiated an 'early riser' show. I went into the kitchen and switched on the small set there.

Kent Taylor's familiar face came on. Overly bright light shone off his face, giving him a deer-in-the-headlights look, as well as a really unflattering expanse of high forehead.

"… suspect was, unfortunately, shot by our officers after he opened fire on the detachment tasked with arresting him."

"On what charges was he being arrested?"

"Based on DNA clues found at the scene of Judge Aldo Blackman's murder, we determined Mr. Balderas was involved. He was being arrested on suspicion of committing that murder, although of course there would have been extensive questioning, followed by the due process of the law."

The camera panned out slightly and I caught sight of Daniel Wickett, the federal marshal who had come to my office. So, apparently, this was a joint operation of some kind. The reporter asked another question, which I missed by being distracted, but Taylor dismissed it and turned away. Another camera caught a scene with a black body bag on a gurney being wheeled to the back of the medical investigator's van.

Jorge Balderas—the man with the scar on his lip.

Saliva rushed into my mouth as I realized this man had confronted me less than twelve hours earlier, warning me and pointing a gun at my gut. I swallowed hard. The reality of having been in the killer's sights—it hit me hard.

The reporter recapped: "So, once again, in the early morning hours police attempted to arrest their lead suspect in the death of Judge Aldo Blackman two weeks ago. During the course of that confrontation, the alleged suspect opened fire and was killed by officers at the scene here near Central and Rio Grande Boulevard."

Less than six blocks from my home.

The news anchorman at the studio took over. "Shocking news, indeed, Pippa, perhaps all the more so because Mr.

Balderas was a key campaign worker for congressional candidate Herman Quinto. We still have no word on what possible motive could have driven this man to murder a judge."

His co-anchor piped up. "Breaking news is coming in that there are already protests by both civil rights leaders and watchdog groups who are claiming police brutality against the Hispanic victim. Mr. Quinto is expected to make a statement in time for our noon newscast, and we will be on the scene to cover that."

Both wore somber expressions and *tsked* appropriately at all the right places. I didn't envy Detective Taylor in the coming weeks. This thing was going to go both political and racial before it was all over, and he was stuck in the middle.

I probably knew more than I should, and the realization prickled at me. Rory's history with the judge, his friendship with Damian that had continued through the years, Damian's relationship to Jorge Balderas. I debated going to the police, but what would I say? Rory, when asked about the photo of Jorge, had dodged the question about knowing him. For all I knew, they were not acquainted.

Impatient about waiting for the coffee maker, I stirred instant coffee into a cup of microwaved hot water.

Rory's words came back to me. *"You're on the wrong track with this ... Quinto and Blackman together orchestrated my conviction ..."* Were the police on the right track, or was Rory correct? I wondered where he was right now. After the funeral, he'd indicated he might stay closer to New Mexico. With Blackman dead and Quinto probably headed to Washington, DC, he was becoming more comfortable here. I wondered if he felt the same as of this morning.

Christine phoned as I was eyeing a package of English muffins. I recognized her number and picked up.

"There's an Albuquerque story that's made the national news," she said immediately. "I think they're talking about that judge who ruled in Rory's case."

"Yes. That's the one. Do you know where Rory is right now?"

"I … not for sure."

"Christine, what's going on? He's mixed up in this, isn't he?"

"Charlie, can you promise some kind of investigator-client privilege?"

"It doesn't really work that way. But the more I know, the more I can help him. What has he told you?"

I heard a ragged sigh over the line. "I haven't slept since we got back to Denver. In Albuquerque, Rory and I talked—really talked—for the first time in years. I told him how I'd always felt, about what a spoiled kid he was, how Dad forgave him anything and everything. He actually acknowledged it and said he felt sorry about it. We mended a lot of old hurts. That part of the conversation was good."

A moist sniff, and she cleared her throat. "He told me other things, too. About the judge, about working near him as a young law student. The judge made advances … actually threatened both men and women who wouldn't go along with him. He says there were photos and recordings—" Her voice broke. "I couldn't believe it, Charlie. He was abused by this man. Others were too."

"I know."

"You do?"

"One of the women was Helen Bannerly, Rory's defense attorney. She was so mortified and scared by it that she went into a whole different branch of the law, one where she would never have to appear in a courtroom."

"My god, the damage the man did! No wonder ..."

"No wonder what?"

A long silence went by before she spoke again. "Charlie, there's more. Rory basically confessed to me when we were together."

"Confessed? To—?" My mouth went dry. Surely I hadn't heard correctly.

"Almost—well, not exactly—oh, god, I don't know for sure. He has this friend, a guy named Damian. My brother told me that he'd said to Damian that he wished someone would do away with the judge. A few days later, it happened."

"Are you sure? Everybody reaches a point where they wish some tormentor would be gone."

"But the way he said it, Charlie. I think he meant for Damian to act on it. That's solicitation of murder or ... I don't know the terms ... I just hear them on TV."

My mind reeled. Had Rory actually *paid* Damian? If so, it was definitely murder for hire. "Did he say anything about money—giving money to anyone?" I sank onto a chair at the table. I'd been so wrong in my conclusions this time.

"No—of course not. He was just furious that the judge had gotten away with making sexual advances and holding it over young lawyers that their compliance, or not, would determine the outcome of their cases."

Wow. The entire legal system turned on its ear because of one man who couldn't control his urges. I turned my back on my coffee and food. My stomach wasn't going to be able to handle anything for a while.

Chapter 46

I was sitting in the same chair at the kitchen table when my phone sent me a reminder notice; at first I couldn't remember what I had wanted to be reminded of. The message said **Dottie** at 11.

It was Gram's big homecoming day. I couldn't believe I'd spaced it out. Dottie Flowers was coming early and we would go through the house so I could make sure she could easily find things. She would stay in my old bedroom where, with her door open at night, she would hear if Gram called out for assistance.

She drove a cute little boxy purple car and tooted the horn as she pulled into the driveway. I'd stepped out our front door at that moment and she gave a huge smile and wave as she brought the car to a stop and spotted Freckles bounding toward her.

The clenching feeling in my gut eased. Dottie was a wonderful breath of normalcy after the past surreal twenty-four hours.

"Hey, Miss Charlie. You're just in time to help me carry my stuff inside." She said as she opened the back door on her vehicle. "Hey, little Freckle-honey. Dottie brought you some yummies. Just wait 'til I unpack."

Out came two large suitcases, a big folded quilt ("Gotta have this—my gramma made it"), a bowling bag ("in case Miss Elsa want to knock down some pins with me on my day off"), and a box filled with picture frames ("the grandbabies in California"). She piled the quilt and cardboard box in my arms and I held out a hand for the bowling bag. She picked up the two suitcases by herself, and managed a fancy hip-bump method of closing the door.

My eyes must have grown round because she laughed. "In this job, I gotta be what you'd call multi-talented."

We headed for the front door. Dottie had come over once before, long enough for a quick overview of the housing arrangement, and she remembered everything we had discussed at the time. She walked into the living room, set down the blue suitcase and carried the other toward the kitchen.

"This bag got my cookbooks and a couple kitchen tools I like. Wasn't sure if Miss Elsa has a juicer so I brought my own." She left the brown suitcase near the kitchen door. "She gonna love my carrot-blueberry juice. There's enough healthy stuff in it to get her runnin' around the back yard."

"Good for you. She'll love that."

I set her personal things on the bed in her room and came back for the blue suitcase, but she had beat me to it and hefted the huge thing up on a chair. Once she'd set the bag down, she reached into a pocket, told Freckles to sit (which the pup actually did), and handed out two treats.

"We'll leave you to get settled," I told her, "unless you want some help?"

"Oh, I can put my own stuff away any old time. We ought to make a shopping list. Miss Elsa could be a mite hungry when she gets home. They never feed you anything satisfying in those places."

We went into the kitchen, where a quick inventory showed well-stocked cupboards but a sparse fridge. "I cleared all this out when she went in the hospital. Sour milk and mushy lettuce wouldn't have made for a nice homecoming," I told her.

"Ew, you got that right." She was jotting notes on a little notebook she'd pulled from her pocket. "I'll just run to the store and get us some things. Was it three o'clock your brother s'posed to bring her here?"

"That's right. When I talked with her yesterday she said she wanted Drake and me to come over this evening to watch the election returns with her. Do you think she'll be up to it?"

"Well, let's give it a try. If she's too tired, she'll prob'ly just doze off in her chair." Dottie was gathering her purse and keys. "I'm planning a nice warm soup for dinner and y'all welcome to come."

"If you're sure it's not too much trouble to cook for three more. She's always been interested in the elections, so I bet she'll sit up." It was a midterm year, so I didn't expect things to get terribly exciting, but I was interested to see how it turned out in the Congressional race. Quinto had been ahead in the early polls so I doubted there would be any real surprise there. The thought made me feel a heavy sadness.

We parted, and Freckles and I ran a few errands ourselves, then settled back at home. An hour later, I saw Ron's car pull into Elsa's driveway next door. Gram at home! I instantly felt better.

Freckles and I raced out our front door at the same time Dottie came from Elsa's. We all ended up beside the car door Ron was opening for our sweet patient. Dottie gave Freckles a stern look and put her hand in her pocket. The dog immediately sat and received a little treat. I needed to take lessons from this lady.

Ron and Dottie offered elbows for Gram to use as they walked her up the two steps to her porch. I carried the tote bag I'd packed with a few essentials, what seemed like ages ago. It was overflowing now with cards and little packages, and I was happy other people had gone to visit her while I'd been so distracted these past few weeks.

By five o'clock, Dottie's chicken noodle soup began to send a fantastic scent throughout the house. Even Elsa, who had settled into her favorite chair for a little nap, perked up and eagerly joined all of us, where she reigned at the head of the dining table. I felt a huge flow of relief to see her here, glowing again and happy her little brood was together.

Drake and I cleared the table and did the dishes while Dottie tended to Gram and Ron organized seating around the old TV set in the living room. Election night coverage had begun hours ago with national stories. It didn't take long to realize that all the predictions about Herman Quinto's victory were coming true. He was to be our next U.S. Congressman. My heart was somewhat heavy, but I felt certain Washington and the political machine would welcome him with open arms.

Chapter 47

Never make promises to a dying man, unless you love him deeply. You just end up feeling negligent and once he's gone you can't even sit down with him and explain why you couldn't fulfill the promise.

I thought of Fergus all morning, of a father's blind love for his son and how he tried every possible avenue to clear Rory's name. The old man had been willing to die violently, to go down in a blaze of glory, as he called it, to get rid of the man he perceived as guilty—how wrong he'd been about Quinto. The man was no saint; he'd been friends with a real villain. But in prosecuting Rory McNab, it seemed he'd simply been doing his job. And now, it looked as if Rory wasn't so innocent after all.

I felt that my obligation to Fergus had come to an end. I would not be able to prove Rory innocent, after all. Even if the jury tampering case were to magically go away, a murder charge would be far worse. Murder of a district judge—surely there was a death sentence attached to that.

On the other hand, what's the obligation to seek justice when the so-called victim of the murder was a heinous person to begin with? Would society have prosecuted and hanged someone who'd managed to kill Hitler?

When my phone rang just before noon and showed "Unknown Caller" on the screen, I had a feeling. I took the call and heard Rory's voice.

"Charlie, can we talk?"

"Where are you?"

"Meet me at the Isleta exit off I-25. Fifteen minutes."

"It'll take me twenty to get there."

"Don't alert the police. Please. At least not until you hear me out."

Out of curiosity, I agreed to the meeting. Twenty-one minutes later I exited the interstate and looked around for my client. He'd switched vehicles again—this time to a black SUV parked at the edge of a bare dirt half-acre of space. He signaled from the driver's window and I pulled alongside, driver-to-driver so we could talk without getting out of our vehicles.

He looked older than his forty-nine years, older than just a few days ago, with bags under his eyes and hard lines etched on each side of his mouth.

"Chrissy called me," he said. "She told me about talking to you yesterday."

I nodded. "I suppose you've seen the news, about Jorge Balderas."

"Yeah. I really didn't think it would go that way. I never asked anyone to get rid of the judge."

"How *did* you think it would go?"

He stared straight ahead and let out a long, pent-up

breath. "Damian had a recording, Judge Blackman saying he would get me off, free me of the jury tampering charges, in exchange for the blackmail photos."

"Helen assumed it was someone within the judge's sphere who snapped the photos, that *he* was the one behind keeping her silent because he wanted to keep seeing her."

"Different photos. These were more graphic and showed Blackman with young men—and I mean *young*— as well as women. Law school students and interns, all so eager to please and ready to advance their careers. We were such a pitiful bunch."

"Wow. The man had no scruples at all, did he?"

"Not on that subject. Predators seldom do."

"But, if you had this proof, why didn't you come forward with it back then? Why let everything go so far now?"

"By the time I saw the photos and knew they existed, I'd already been convicted of jury tampering. I was mentally in a fog, awaiting sentence, and it was Blackman who would have determined my fate. The sentence would have been a long one, and I would have been sent out of state so I had no contact with anyone in New Mexico. I know this—it happened to someone else, and that guy committed suicide in a California prison a few months after he went."

"How does Damian fit into all this?"

"Initially, he was just a client of mine. He was young and had got mixed up with the Mexican cartel. His mother was such a good woman and he came from a basically strong family. Mrs. Baca pleaded with me to work hard to get her son acquitted, swore he'd learned his lesson and would stay clean if he got another chance. I believed her. The whole family was so thrilled when Damian got off, they welcomed me like another son and we've all remained friends. They were shocked at the whole jury-tampering case. Damian, in particular, vowed to help me if he could. That's when he got the recordings of Blackman saying he would let me off."

"I was curious about that. If a jury found you guilty, how was the judge going to get you out of it?"

"There are situations where a judge can override a jury verdict. It's uncommon. More often, the judge can go hard or easy during the sentencing phase, and that's what Blackman was holding over me."

"Okay, that was then—this is now." I felt my anger rising again. "You told your sister you wanted the judge dead. Did Damian kill him?"

"No, Charlie. It really was Jorge. I don't know what was said ... Damian won't give me any specifics. I assume he told Jorge what I'd said. Whether Jorge took it as a request, a command, a job ... I have no idea."

"They'll trace your connection to Damian and, because they're cousins, to Jorge. Can anyone prove you uttered that statement—about the judge dying? Would Damian have recorded you saying it?"

He shook his head. "No. I don't believe he would."

Believing something and knowing it, however, can be two different things. I had been convinced Quinto was the authority behind Jorge Balderas and his actions. I still wasn't certain.

A sad look came over his face. "I'm not sure where I'll go. Eventually, maybe Colorado. I'd like to be closer to Chrissy, get to know her daughters better, and her grandkids, before they're all grown up. But there's something I definitely plan to do first."

He held up a packet of photographs. "The judge's crimes can't be used to convict him of anything now, obviously, but I have a friend who writes a blog about predators. He posts warnings of the signs which kids, young people, and parents should look for. He names people, especially the powerful or wealthy who've gotten away with it. He tells the stories so other innocents can avoid them and law enforcement can watch for them."

Perhaps something good would come from Rory's actions, after all. "Why not just come forward, here and now? Bring these to light, yourself."

"I still have that conviction hanging over my head. And being a fugitive from justice for so many years, the law could come down hard on me, before I have a chance to accomplish anything." For the first time, he smiled a crooked little smile. "But we're working on it. Damian and I are putting together all the evidence we can muster. And I talked to Helen Bannerly. She apologized for the way things went back then. She wants to reopen my case and get me absolved. Quinto was the one who sent Balderas to intimidate the jurors. He had plans all along to discredit me and put me in prison—we know this but we need proof."

I wondered whether anything they could come up with would be enough to derail Quinto's political career now that he'd graduated to Washington.

Rory seemed to have read my thoughts. "One day we may have sufficient evidence, but until then I need to keep a low profile."

"So, you'll go back to Maine?"

"Not saying that. I have to keep my options open. I need to be able to vanish again." He stuck a hand out his window, reached across the space between us, and took my hand. "Thank you, Charlie."

"Did your dad know about the abuse—near the end?"

Rory withdrew his hand and gave the tiniest shake of

his head. It was some consolation to me, knowing the old man had never learned the worst of the secrets.

The first time, it had been Fergus's idea to help his son disappear. He'd told me as much. Now, Rory was in charge and I had no doubt he could do anything he was determined to do. At my slightest hint of stepping forward to tell what had happened, he'd already said he would evaporate. I had no doubt of this.

We parted, and as I drove away I pondered all that had happened. We'd spent the last half-hour only a couple of freeway exits away from the airport. Rory could get a last-minute ticket to anywhere and be on a plane, almost by the time I reached home. It wasn't the first time a client of mine had a dodgy story, and it certainly wasn't the first time a politician had sidestepped responsibility for his actions, I thought as I headed westbound toward a lowering sun.

Justice. It's a concept everyone wants to believe in, and here in America we like to think we have a good system for it. But I'm learning that things are not always black and white. There are gray areas everywhere, and how can any of us ever *really* know the truth?

I felt hopeful that eventually Rory, with Damian's support and Helen Bannerly's help, would be cleared of the allegations that had ruined his career. Perhaps Herman Quinto's dirty tricks would come to light in the process and come back to take him down politically.

I wondered where Rory would be in the next twenty-four hours, where he would be in a year, and how many discarded cell phones there were at the bottom of that lake in Maine.

Thank you for taking the time to read *Escapes Can Be Murder*. If you enjoyed it, please consider telling your friends or posting a short review. Word of mouth is an author's best friend and is much appreciated.

Thank you,

Connie

**Sign up for Connie Shelton's free mystery newsletter at connieshelton.com
and receive advance information about new books, along with a chance at prizes, discounts and other mystery news!**

**Contact by email: connie@connieshelton.com
Follow Connie Shelton on Twitter, Pinterest and Facebook**

Books by Connie Shelton
THE CHARLIE PARKER MYSTERY SERIES
Deadly Gamble
Vacations Can Be Murder
Partnerships Can Be Murder
Small Towns Can Be Murder
Memories Can Be Murder
Honeymoons Can Be Murder
Reunions Can Be Murder
Competition Can Be Murder
Balloons Can Be Murder
Obsessions Can Be Murder
Gossip Can Be Murder
Stardom Can Be Murder
Phantoms Can Be Murder
Buried Secrets Can Be Murder
Legends Can Be Murder
Weddings Can Be Murder
Alibis Can Be Murder
Escapes Can Be Murder
Holidays Can Be Murder - a Christmas novella

THE SAMANTHA SWEET SERIES

Sweet Masterpiece   *Sweets Begorra*
Sweet's Sweets   *Sweet Payback*
Sweet Holidays   *Sweet Somethings*
Sweet Hearts   *Sweets Forgotten*
Bitter Sweet   *Spooky Sweet*
Sweets Galore   *Sticky Sweet*

Spellbound Sweets - a Halloween novella
The Woodcarver's Secret

THE HEIST LADIES SERIES
Diamonds Aren't Forever
The Trophy Wife Exchange
Movie Mogul Mama

CHILDREN'S BOOKS
Daisy and Maisie and the Great Lizard Hunt
Daisy and Maisie and the Lost Kitten

Connie Shelton is the *USA Today* bestselling author of more than 30 novels and three non-fiction books. She taught writing for six years, and was a contributor to *Chicken Soup for the Writer's Soul*. She lives in northern New Mexico with her husband and two dogs.

Lightning Source UK Ltd.
Milton Keynes UK
UKHW010933231119
354069UK00001B/19/P